APRIL SEDUCTION

MERRY FARMER

APRIL SEDUCTION

Copyright ©2018 by Merry Farmer

Cover design by Erin Dameron-Hill (the miracle-worker)

ASIN: B07H6P8CQD

Paperback ISBN: 9781790211630

Click here for a complete list of other works by Merry Farmer.

If you'd like to be the first to learn about when the next books in the series come out and more, please sign up for my newsletter here:
http://eepurl.com/RQ-KX

❀ Created with Vellum

CHAPTER 1

*K*atya Marlowe, the Countess of Stanhope, was excessively proud of three things in her life: that she had raised three children to be intelligent, useful adults—or rather, soon-to-be adult in the case of her youngest daughter, Natalia—that she understood and had as much influence in the politics of the nation as most men, and that, on the cusp of turning forty-one, she still had the figure and complexion of a woman half her age.

All three points of pride were on display as she sat in the Strangers' Gallery overlooking the House of Commons Chamber as debate wrapped up for the day. She leaned slightly over the edge of the balcony—enough so that the men below would be able to see she was paying damn close attention—and so that they could see the way her new gown highlighted her impressive bosom—her older daughter, Bianca, on one side and Natalia on the other.

"I move that this session be adjourned," Sir Henry Brand called on the floor below.

The usual flurry of agreement that followed an adjournment motion rose up from the men, the motion was moved, and the chamber burst into disgruntled noise as the members of Commons rose from their seats.

"But it's only half nine," Bianca complained. "Usually sessions like this run past midnight."

"And they didn't bring up the rights of women once," Natalia added as she stood and stretched in a thoroughly unladylike way. She was only just sixteen, after all, and couldn't be expected to behave with decorum all the time.

Katya rose with far more grace. She stared at the men milling around in the chamber and caught the eye of her friend Alexander Croydon. One sharp lift of her eyebrow and Alex sighed and shrugged. Katya tried to keep her irritation from showing on her face. Alex was trying, truly he was. But there were forces in Parliament—both in Commons and Lords—that were intent on keeping the issue of increased rights for women from being raised.

"He's going to see that the bill they've all been working on is brought up for proper debate soon," Marigold Croydon, Alex's wife, who had been sitting with them, told Katya as they made their way to the end of the row. Marigold and her friend, Lady Lavinia Pearson, had missed few parliamentary sessions since they'd all arrived in London in January for the post-Christmas opening of parliament.

"Armand says they're no closer to bringing it up in Lords," Lavinia added with a sigh, pressing a hand to her stomach. She hadn't said anything to the rest of them yet, but Katya was willing to bet Armand would have an heir by the end of the year.

"It's because of the Irish Question," Natalia said, full of youthful enthusiasm and the same sort of pride in her intelligence that Katya had felt when she was her age. "Irish Home Rule is all anyone wants to talk about these days."

"I'm not saying Ireland isn't important," Bianca said with the same sort of confidence that accompanied youth, "but I do wish they'd hurry up and give us the rights we deserve."

The corner of Katya's mouth twitched with equal parts humor and pride at the interest and intelligence her daughters showed. Robert, their father and the long-dead former Earl of Stanhope, would have been appalled. Which, of course, only made Katya prouder.

"Oh, no. Papa appears to be in high dudgeon again," Cecelia Campbell said, a note of dread in her voice. She followed at the back of Katya's group and usually took everything in without making a sound. The fact that she felt the need to point out that her father was there and unhappy didn't bode well at all.

Katya stepped to the side, letting the others pass by her as she turned to seek out Malcolm Campbell. He stood talking to his closest friend, Lord Peter deVere, at the other end of the Strangers' Gallery, where women were forbidden to sit. Her heart thumped harder against her ribs at the sight of his glowering frown. Malcolm looked tired. The lines on his face seemed more pronounced, even at a distance. He was frustrated, which made her heart ache all the more for him.

As if sensing her stare, he glanced away from Peter and met her eyes. It didn't matter how long they'd known each other, how frequently their paths crossed, or how heated those crossings were. In an instant, it was as though electricity had filled the room. Every nerve in her body responded to him. Her breath caught in her throat. Butterflies filled her stomach, and a smoldering fire infused her core.

"I suppose we're going to get an earful once we get down

to the hall," Marigold said with a combination of dread and humor.

Katya shook herself out of her visceral reaction, grinning at Malcolm and arching one brow at him in challenge. The man needed something to distract him from the grinding disappointment of not effecting instant change or else he'd drive himself mad. He took the bait, narrowing his eyes at her with a look that could melt iron. Eyes still locked on hers, he said something to Peter. Peter glanced in her direction, then said something to Malcolm that looked like an admonishment.

"Are you coming?" Marigold asked from the exit door at the top of the gallery.

"I will be soon," Katya murmured, too quiet to be heard. She schooled her expression to cool indifference, then picked up her skirts and made her way to Marigold's side. "I don't know which is worse, men who constantly get their way or men who are constantly denied something they want."

Marigold laughed, the sound echoing in the narrow, stone stairway as they descended. "They're both equally insufferable," she said. "I'll probably be up half the night listening to Alex rant about the way Mr. Beach kept interrupting him when he tried to steer the conversation to women."

"Beach is an ass," Katya said as they rounded the corner and stepped out into St. Stephen's Hall. "Always has been, always will be."

"He's not the only one," Marigold said with a grin before excusing herself to cross the hall to wait for Alex.

Katya marched ahead to where Lavinia, Cecelia, Bianca, and Natalia were waiting farther down the hall. They made a pretty picture. Lavinia was newly married, but the other three were arguably some of the most eligible women in

London, though Bianca and Natalia wouldn't be on the market for another year or two, thank heavens. Cecelia, on the other hand, was to be presented at court with that year's crop of debutantes in just a week's time. Several gentlemen who passed the group on their way out seemed to know it as well and took a long, second look. Katya smiled. Her son, Rupert, the current Earl of Stanhope at the ripe age of twenty, had been in love with Cecelia for more than a year— he hadn't yet admitted it to Katya, but some things were obvious to a mother's eye—but he would have to step lively if he wanted to win Cece's attentions.

Not that she was eager for her son to become involved with Malcolm's daughter. What a ridiculous tangle that would be.

"Perhaps if they phrased the issue in terms of Irish women deserving their rights, then Mr. Croydon's bill could be brought up for debate sooner," Bianca was in the middle of saying as Katya joined them.

"Irish women deserve rights too," Natalia agreed with a nod.

Katya did her best to hide her smile as her heart swelled with maternal affection. Her daughters were beautiful fools, but so were all people, women and men, before they reached thirty at least. Heaven only knew the kind of foolishness she'd gotten into when she was her girls' ages.

"Men will always find a way to push women to the fringes, especially in politics, unless we stand up for ourselves and demand the changes we want to see," she said.

"You're quite right, Lady Stanhope," Lavinia agreed.

Katya's smile widened. Lavinia had become a dear friend in the last year, and as such, especially considering her new rank as Vicountess Helm, she had a right to address Katya by name, but she still hadn't dared to do it.

"She's only half right, as usual," Malcolm growled as he and Peter approached them from the gallery stairs.

Katya snapped straighter, turning to him with fire in her eyes. "I beg your pardon?"

Malcolm swaggered his way up to her side, striking what she was sure he thought was a fierce pose. "Men and women have to fight together if women are going to get their due in this world."

Katya's eyes widened, and she turned to him, feeling her heat rising in more ways than one. "And how much have men accomplished on our behalf thus far?" she demanded.

"Plenty." Malcolm shrugged. "You're allowed to watch parliamentary proceedings, aren't you?"

"Watch, yes," Katya said, her jaw and words tight. "But can we participate?"

"Through your husbands, yes, of course," Malcolm said, then threw in a deliberate pause. "Oh. That is, if you have a husband, Lady Stanhope." An impish spark filled his eyes.

Katya crossed her arms, glaring at him. "It's amusing how you make a point completely opposite of the one you intend to make every time you open your mouth, Lord Malcolm."

"And is my point wrong?" he continued to goad her. "Can you have any real, lasting effect on the policies of this government without a husband?"

"Well then, I shall just have to find myself one," she replied, the excitement of the skirmish invigorating her.

Malcolm burst into a grin that was both self-satisfied and painfully hopeful, but Katya looked right past him to a tall, awkward gentleman who walked through the hall with uncertain steps, looking lost.

"Sir Christopher," Katya called to him, stepping away from Malcolm.

Malcolm's grin vanished, replaced by a dark scowl.

Sir Christopher blinked and glanced over his shoulder as

though there were another, worthier Sir Christopher behind him whom Katya intended to address. His eyes grew wide when he realized she was talking to him. "Lady Stanhope," he said in awe.

"Sir Christopher, I haven't had a chance to congratulate you on your election yet." Katya strode to up to him, hips swaying and figure presented to perfection. All intended to poke Malcolm in his pride, of course. She took Christopher's arm and turned him toward her group. "I don't believe you've met my daughters or Lady Cecelia Campbell yet." She deliberately didn't refer to Cece as Malcolm's daughter.

"Um, why, no, I don't believe I have." Christopher put on a smile as Katya presented him to the younger women. His smile made him look like even more of a dolt than his look of confusion, especially when he made awkward, hesitant bows to each of the younger ladies. It was an unfortunate product of the way the man was constructed that he looked like a buffoon most of the time. Katya had been paying close attention to his voting record, his speeches, and the articles he wrote for political journals, though. Sir Christopher Dowland was far more intelligent than anyone gave him credit for.

"Malcolm, you've met Sir Christopher, haven't you?" Katya asked in a purr, sending Malcolm a teasing look. She continued to hold Christopher's arm as she did.

Malcolm scowled, a flush rising to his face. "I believe we met once," he said, his voice hoarse, holding out his hand. It was a clever gambit. Christopher was forced to relinquish Katya's arm in order to shake Malcolm's hand. "We met a few years ago, at Penrose House," Malcolm went on. He paused, then added, "I was sorry to hear of your father's death."

"Thank you," Christopher replied with a grave nod.

"How unfortunate that you should inherit the barony just as you are elected to Parliament," Katya added, sending a knowing look to her daughters. She never would have dreamed she'd be one of the scheming mother types, intent on finding a wealthy, titled husband for her girls—and truly, she didn't want them to be shackled in marriage at a tender age, as she had been—but it wasn't too soon to learn how to spot a catch when he was standing in front of you.

"Thank you, Lady Stanhope. It's been a bit of a whirlwind, but I have a competent land steward at Penrose, my father's affairs were all in order, and things are about as settled as could be expected," Christopher replied. His smile suddenly turned into a frown that made him look like a baby goat lost in the middle of a field. "Good Lord, that's not the right thing to say around ladies. Do forgive me. I never know how to address the fairer sex." He stopped, his face turning bright red.

Bianca and Natalia were having as hard a time not laughing as Katya was, but Cece was far more gracious. "Are you planning to attend the Spencer's ball next week?" she asked with a kind and open smile—something she had most certainly inherited from her late mother and not Malcolm.

"I was thinking of it, yes," Christopher replied, relaxing a bit. "It's where all the new debutantes will be after their presentation at court, right?" As soon as the question was out of his mouth, he blushed furiously. "Bollocks, that's not the right thing to say either."

"Neither is 'bollocks,'" Bianca muttered to Natalia. The two girls burst into giggles.

"Never you mind, Sir Christopher," Katya said, taking the man's arm once more when Malcolm started to gloat at Christopher's awkwardness. "It is where the newly-presented young ladies will be after their audience with the queen. But if you need practice, there are many, fine women with more experience who will be on hand to guide you through the hazards of a society ball." She shot a wicked look at Malcolm as she made her thinly-veiled offer.

Sure enough, Malcolm was livid. It served him right for trying to tweak her earlier. Granted, she didn't have a shred of interest in seducing Christopher, but Malcolm didn't know that, and what he didn't know kept him on his toes.

"Oh." Christopher blinked at Katya as though he'd slowly caught her meaning. His face turned bright red. "I say. Um... that is...interesting."

"Don't mind Mama," Bianca said with a laugh. "Baiting men is her favorite sport. She doesn't mean anything by it."

Katya's brow shot up. She was too shocked by the cleverness of her daughter's reply to be angry with her at the jab. Bianca wasn't even out yet—they'd made the decision to have her wait until the following year for her presentation, even though she was on the verge of turning eighteen, so that she could gain a bit more refinement—and she was a firecracker. The very idea made Katya beam with pride.

"I'll save a dance for you," Katya said to Christopher instead. "And if there is any other assistance I can give you in navigating London society, do ask."

Malcolm barked out a sound that was something between a laugh and a snort. "Lady Stanhope is quite well-versed at navigating London society," he said, piling his words with disdain.

"I enjoy the spectacle that people present is all," she said, fixing Malcolm with a sly grin. Let him take whatever meaning he wanted from that. It was his own fault if his mind went straight to the gutter.

"You enjoy it thoroughly," Malcolm agreed, eyes narrowing.

"We all enjoy what we're good at." Katya met his comment by arching one brow. She knew exactly the picture that look presented. She'd lived in her skin long enough to know how to convey heat with an eyebrow and sensuality with a twitch of her mouth. And she knew better than anyone else exactly what would cause Malcolm's blood to boil, in both senses of the word.

"Though it is possible to have too much of a good thing," Malcolm said, lowering his tone.

"Is it?" Katya feigned innocence. "I've never found that to be true. Have you, Sir Christopher?"

She glanced up at Christopher. The poor man's eyes had gone wide, as though he'd been caught between a river in full flood and a pack of rampaging lions. "I have no idea, Lady Stanhope," he said, then swallowed.

Malcolm opened his mouth to make what was likely to be some other witty reply filled with innuendo, but his expression collapsed into a genuine scowl. "Oh, God," he muttered, staring off across the hall. Immediately, he moved to take Cece's arm. "It's time for us to go," he said curtly.

"It is?" Cece asked. She glanced where her father was looking, and understanding instantly lit her face. "Ah. It is."

Katya turned to see what the fuss was. Her blood instantly froze in cold anger. At the other end of the hall, Lord Theodore Shayles had just made an entrance. The crowd had parted around him as he moved to intercept Alex and Marigold on their way out of the hall. Alex seemed to be holding his own, but Shayles was grinning like a wolf, which was never a good thing.

"Come along, Cecelia," Malcolm growled. "I don't want you exposed to a pestilence like that."

Cecelia agreed with a nod, and she and Malcolm marched off toward one of the doors at the opposite end of the hall from Shayles. Katya's heart sank, more because her game with Malcolm had come to an end than because of Shayles. She hated Shayles with a vicious passion, but a good half of that was because of all the wrongs the devil had done to Malcolm.

"What's Lord Shayles doing here?" Christopher asked.

Katya dropped his arm and stepped away, moving to stand with her daughters now that she had no need to toy with Christopher. "He's only here to gloat," she said.

"Is he?" Christopher frowned across the room. "I've never met the man. All I know is from the articles in *The Times* last year and the rumors I've heard."

"You're not missing out by not knowing him," Katya said. "The man is pure evil."

"He's so evil he isn't even intriguing," Bianca said, tilting her chin up at an angle that matched Katya's.

"The man truly is one to be avoided," Lavinia said in a voice laced with fear. She would know better than any of them. Shayles had arrived on her doorstep at Broadclyft Hall mere days after she and Armand had been married, and the trouble he had caused was still affecting them all.

"Oh, dear." Christopher stood straighter. "He's coming this way."

Katya's nerves bristled. Sure enough, Shayles had spotted them and was making his way across the hall. She had a split-second to decide whether to stay and fight or to take her daughters and run. Since the very idea of backing down from any threat a man presented left her cold, she straightened, squared her shoulders, and prepared for battle.

"Lady Stanhope, you're looking quite lovely this evening," Shayles said as he reached them. "And your daughters are downright delectable."

"You look at them twice and I'll have your testicles for Christmas ornaments," Katya growled.

Christopher flinched, staring at her with wide, offended eyes.

Shayles caught his expression and chuckled. "It seems you

have put off another conquest, Lady Stanhope." He clicked his tongue. "How many times have I told you that a more delicate approach is needed before moving in for the kill?"

Christopher blinked at Katya, as though seeing her in a new light. The overall effect made the poor man's face look even more idiotic, but there was a sharpness of thought in the man's eyes.

Shayles didn't see it. He continued to gloat and send Katya a look of victory as he offered Christopher his hand. "I don't believe we've met. Lord Theodore Shayles, at your service."

"Uh." Christopher cleared his throat and stared at Shayles's hand for a moment before taking it. "Christopher Dowland. That is, Sir Christopher Dowland, now that I've inherited."

"Inherited, you say?" Shayles's eyes lit with avarice. He reached into his waistcoat pocket and presented Christopher with a black card. "Allow me to invite you to my club."

Natalia made a strangled noise, but Katya reached for her wrist and squeezed it to stop her from saying more or getting involved. She glanced around for a way to get her daughters out of the room and as far away from Shayles as possible.

Fortunately, she didn't have to wait long before reinforcements arrived.

"Alone, are you, Shayles?" Peter deVere asked as he and Armand, Lavinia's husband, strode deliberately over to join their group.

"Where's my erstwhile cousin?" Armand asked.

Katya hid her interest in the answer to that question. Armand had a good point. Where *was* Lord Mark Gatwick? The man followed Shayles around like a shadow, though he rarely said much. And even though Lavinia had been convinced last autumn that Gatwick wasn't all that he seemed, Katya wasn't convinced the man's conspicuous absence meant he'd seen the light and disassociated himself from Shayles.

"Gatwick's chasing after some ridiculous painting on the continent," Shayles said, failing to hide his genuine irritation. "He claims not to think much of these Impressionists, but there's some ridiculous woman painter, Cassatt, or something along those lines, whom he's determined to acquire."

"Mary Cassatt?" Natalia brightened. "She's American, but she lives in Paris. She paints—" Natalia's words died on her lips as Shayles sent her an irritated scowl.

"Yes, well, she's the only woman I've ever known Gatwick to take an interest in," Shayles said with a sneer. "Must be because of his American relations."

Katya had heard whispers of Gatwick's relatives in the States, but only whispers.

"Why are you bothering these ladies, Shayles?" Peter asked, moving to stand between Shayles and Katya's daughters, his arms crossed.

Shayles glared at him. "I'm simply being social. Isn't that what we're supposed to do? Be social with our neighbors?"

"You are no neighbor of mine," Katya said. She turned to Bianca and Natalia. "Come along, girls. I think it's about time we go home."

"I think you're right, Mama," Bianca agreed, sending Shayles a withering look.

Shayles licked his lips, and if they'd been in a slightly less crowded arena, Katya was convinced he would have handled the unsightly bulge in his trousers as well just to infuriate her and throw Bianca off-guard. "Don't let me be the one to break up a party of friends," he said. "I'll go." He turned. "But you haven't seen the last of me. Sir Christopher, would you care to walk with me?"

"I...uh...." Christopher sent Katya a panicked look, but it

wasn't enough. Shayles steered him away, marching him across the hall.

"I hope Dowland has enough sense to stay clear of Shayles's machinations," Armand growled once they were gone. "He needs money more now than ever, and if what I've heard is right, Dowland just inherited a mountain of it."

"He did," Peter confirmed. "His estate isn't far from Starcross Castle. Dowland has one of the most productive farms in Cornwall, and a high-producing mine to boot."

"He doesn't look particularly bright," Armand said.

"Looks can be deceiving," Katya said.

The conversation lulled as they were all lost in their own thoughts.

Lavinia broke the silence a few moments later by saying, "Lord Gatwick is out of the country." They all turned to her. Katya was surprised by the seriousness in her expression. "He said he wanted to be out of the country when we used the information he gave us to bring Lord Shayles down."

"Could this be the time?" Bianca asked.

"I still don't trust Gatwick," Peter said.

Katya kept her opinion to herself. She wasn't certain if she trusted Gatwick either, but there certainly seemed to be a sense of frisson in the air. Malcolm had his contacts working on the information Gatwick had given Lavinia before Christmas—information about the corrupt policemen who turned a blind eye to the salacious and illegal activity of Shayles's club. The club was nothing more than an illegal brothel—one that specialized in dark, abusive practices.

"Either way," Katya said, clearing her throat to shake off the horrific memories the Black Strap Club raised in her, "I'm taking my girls home. Bianca, Natalia."

She started to go, leading her daughters behind her.

"Katya, wait." Peter stopped her.

Katya turned to him in question. Peter reached into his

pocket and took out a simple, folded piece of paper, which he handed to her. She opened it, read the hastily-scrawled words, and fought not to break into a smile. "Did you read it?" she asked Peter.

"I was told not to," he answered with a knowing grin.

"Good." Katya nodded, then faced her daughters. "Girls, will you be able to find your way home on your own? It seems I have an appointment to keep."

"I can take them," Peter said, his grin even more pronounced.

"Thank you." Katya smiled, pretending innocence, even though Peter probably knew what she was up to. Of all her friends, he was the most perceptive. Of the men, at least. "Go straight to bed when you get home," Katya admonished her girls. "We have a busy day ahead of us tomorrow."

"Do we get to come shopping with you and Cecelia?" Natalia asked, brightening.

"If you behave yourselves, yes," Katya said, then turned to go.

"Just as long as you behave yourself too," Peter chuckled as she started away.

Katya glanced back at him over her shoulder. "Since when have you ever known me to behave?"

The answer, of course, was never.

CHAPTER 2

*I*t was late when Malcolm arrived home to Strathaven House, but his night was just beginning. As soon as his carriage stopped, he hopped down, turning to help Cecelia alight and make her way up the stairs of the stately, Georgian townhouse.

"Thank you, Galston," he nodded to his butler and gestured for Cece to go on ahead. As soon as she had turned the corner into the drawing room, he slid closer to Galston and murmured, "I'm expecting a guest."

"Understood, my lord," Galston replied, his expression betraying nothing.

Malcolm nodded to him again, then strode across the hall and into the drawing room. Cece had taken a seat on the sofa nearest the fireplace and tucked her feet up under her. How any woman managed to look so comfortable in such restrictive clothing was beyond him. Young people seemed to be made of rubber compared to his tired, old joints.

"Shall I have Cook send a light supper up to your room?" Malcolm asked as casually as he could, inching toward the window that looked out on the square where his townhouse stood.

"Don't you want to have a bit to eat with me, Papa?" Cece asked. "We've so much to discuss after that session of parliament."

Malcolm parted the curtains, looking out onto empty, lamp-lit streets. It took him a moment to realize his daughter had addressed him. He let the curtains drop and turned to her. "It was a damned boring session and you know it," he said.

Cece didn't flinch at his curt tone or his mild cursing. He'd raised her by himself, and she'd heard much worse. "There was some useful debate tonight," she said. "Irish Home Rule seems closer than ever."

Malcolm snorted, crossing to the fireplace and tapping his hand impatiently against the mantle. "The Conservatives won't let Ireland go without a fight, I can promise you that."

"Home Rule sounds like such a sensible option, though," Cece said, leaning back and toying with a lock of her hair that had come loose from its fashionable style.

She had the same honey-blonde hair as her mother. She had Tessa's bright, blue eyes as well. If not for the stubborn set of her jaw and her feisty attitude—something most definitely inherited from him—he'd be tempted to wonder if Tessa had strayed.

An old ache squeezed his heart, but he batted it away before it could take hold and make him melancholy. Tessa was gone, and she'd taken that part of his heart with her.

"I'm not interested in Irish Home Rule," he said, his tone sharp once more. He took his pocket-watch from his waistcoat, glanced at the time, and slipped the watch back into his pocket. The minutes were ticking by fast. "You should be in bed by now," he told Cece with a frown.

Cece, imp that she was, glanced up at him with a lopsided

grin and eyes that weren't fooled. "Are you expecting something, Papa?" she asked. "A visitor, perhaps?"

"No," Malcolm answered, a little too quickly. "It's too late for company and you know it. You need your rest. You've a big week ahead of you."

"Yes, I do." Cece's face lit up, and she stood, crossing to join him at the fireplace. "I'm so excited and so nervous about it."

"Which is to be expected," Malcolm said, though in truth, he knew nothing about young women being presented at court. All he knew was that the moment he'd been dreading for the past eighteen years, the moment his darling little girl became a woman in the eyes of society, was upon him.

"I'm so grateful that Lady Stanhope has offered to sponsor me," Cece went on, the devilish light back in her eyes.

Malcolm's face heated. "Katya is a good friend."

Cece's grin was more lopsided than ever. "Of course she is." She schooled her features into a perfect mask of innocence. "She's been so kind to take me shopping and to make certain I have everything I need for my coming out. Why don't you invite her to stay with us at Strathaven Glen for a while?"

Malcolm laughed. "Katya hates the country, especially in Scotland."

"Does she?" Cece batted her eyelashes, overdoing the false innocence. "I think she would enjoy it in the right company."

Malcolm crossed his arms and stared at her. "Go to bed, Cece."

"What's the rush?" she asked, mimicking his stance. Yes, she was his daughter, for good or for evil.

"I'm your father, and I say it's time for you to go to bed," he said.

"Lady Stanhope, Bianca, and Natalia are staying the night

here on Friday anyhow so we can all travel to the palace together in the morning," Cece continued to argue. "Why not invite them to stay longer?"

"Because they already have a London residence," he told her. "And Stanhope House is perfectly adequate." He didn't need to add that Katya kept a second apartment in St. John's Woods for other purposes. He was beginning to see why as well. The longer it took Cece to go up to her room, the more of a risk of exposure he ran. Then again, it was fairly obvious he wasn't fooling Cece one bit.

"I think you and Lady Stanhope look dazzling together," Cece went on, the teasing light in her eyes growing. "I'm not going to live here with you forever, you know. You might want to think about bringing another woman into your life."

If she'd said the same thing five years before, he would have taken it as the not-so-subtle hint that it was. Under the circumstances, however, her words tugged at his heart-strings. "You'll always be my little girl," he said, cradling her sweet face in his hand. "No matter how old and mischievous you get." He bent to kiss her cheek, his throat tightening with sentimentality that would cause his friends to roar with laughter if they could see it.

When he straightened, Cece's eyes were glassy with emotion of her own. That only brought him closer to the edge of doing something unmanly. He sniffed, cleared his throat, and stood straighter, fighting to hide how much he wanted to pull his daughter into his arms and never let her go. If he could hold back the hands of time for just a little while longer, freeze the two of them in a moment where nothing would change and it would be the two of them against the world forever, he would. But time was merci-less, and even the sweetest of children flowered into adulthood.

He cleared his throat again and frowned. "Now, go to

19

your room. I want you fresh and lively as you face everything coming this week."

"You want to get rid of me for your own, nefarious reasons," she countered, picking up her skirts and heading away from the fireplace. "I'll go," she fired over her shoulder as she reached the door. "But you don't have me fooled, Papa. Not for one moment." She winked at him before sailing through the doorway. A moment later, he heard her foot-steps on the stairs.

He turned to stare into the fire, swallowing the lump in his throat. Love had never come easy for Malcolm, much less affection. But raising a daughter had broken open things inside of him that he never thought anyone would be able to crack. Not after all he'd been through. And Cece was right. He wasn't sure what he would do once she married and started a family of her own. Thinking about it made him feel old in a way nothing else could.

"Well, this is hardly the Casanova I expected to find, based on this note."

Malcolm jerked straight and turned away from the fire-place to find Katya standing in the doorway, holding his note, a sly grin adding heat to her striking features. His aching heart leapt in his chest, renewing his energy. He launched into action, striding across the room to her.

"Would you prefer something more like this?" he asked before taking her in his arms and kissing her with searing passion. He didn't stop there. He pivoted with her in his arms, pressing her back against the doorframe and leaning his body into hers. The bulk of her bustle served to thrust her hips forward, and he wedged himself between her legs, certain she could feel the evidence of what one sultry look from her did to him.

A whisper of relief washed through him as she responded to his brutish advances with equal passion. She hummed low in her throat as their mouths met, teasing and tasting, and raked her fingers through his hair. She lifted one knee just enough to signal for him to grab her leg and hike it over his hip as best he could with her restrictive skirts. He broke away from her mouth and trailed kisses down the lithe line of her neck to the low scoop of her bodice. She sighed in encouragement, and he cupped her breast, pushing it up to meet his hungry mouth. The temptation to lift her skirts, loosen his trousers, and take her right there in the hall was almost too much to resist, and if they'd been ten years younger, he would have tried it.

"Upstairs," he panted, breaking away from her instead.

Her eyes flashed with desire and her kiss-reddened lips spread into a naughty smile. He grabbed her hand and practically sprinted to the stairs, ignoring the slight ache in his knees. She followed without a word, doing her best to keep her footsteps as silent as possible, especially when they brushed past Cece's room at the top of the stairs. It wasn't the first time they'd had to sneak past without waking Cece, and, God willing, it wouldn't be the last.

As soon as they reached his bedroom at the end of the hall and slipped inside, silently shutting the door behind them, Katya whirled about and backed Malcolm into the wall. It was her turn to trap him with a kiss that left him senseless and burning with need. It didn't matter how many times they'd ravished each other or how much their bodies had changed since their first, fateful meeting seventeen years before. She worked with deft fingers to unbutton his waistcoat and shirt as he did his best to wriggle out of his clothes.

"You seem sad tonight," she said, breathless with passion, as she helped him tug his shirt over his head. As soon as his chest was exposed, she smoothed her hands across his muscles, teasing his nipples, before leaning in to kiss and nibble his shoulders. "What's wrong?" she asked as she returned to his lips.

He didn't want to think about it. He didn't want to think about anything but tearing Katya's clothes off and seeing her naked, splayed, and wet on his bed. "I want you," he answered, meaning it on too many levels. "I always want you."

She laughed, low and deep in her throat, and reached for the fastenings of his trousers. As soon as they were loose, she slid one hand inside to play with him. "I know," she hummed, sending unbelievable pleasure coursing through him. More potent still, she sank to her knees, tugging his trousers and drawers down with her, then drew his cock into her mouth.

The heady pleasure of moist heat and sucking threatened to pull him under as she toyed with him. She was beyond skilled with her tongue and capable of swallowing him deep. Every nerve throbbed with pleasure as the wet heat of her mouth sheathed him again and again. A younger man would have come in thirty seconds, but he was seasoned enough to enjoy the slower journey toward climax that came with age. And he and Katya knew each other well enough to know how to drive each other wild.

She pulled back, took a deep, gasping breath, then stood, shaking slightly with the force of her desire, and turned her back to him. Without hesitation, he fumbled through the row of buttons down her back, helping her out of her stylish gown with lightning speed. Once all the fastenings were loosened, they broke apart to finish discarding clothes on their own—something they'd learned was far more efficient than the so-called romance of stripping each other naked. Katya tossed her things over the large chair by the fire as she always did, and he gathered his clothes and shoved them haphazardly into the wardrobe before crossing to the bed and tearing back the covers. She joined him in bed a minute later, and he rolled her to her back. The two of them had perfected the routine of getting as close as possible as fast as possible into a science.

"Why are you so sad, Malcolm?" she asked again as he nibbled his way from her shoulder to her breast. He raked his thumb across her nipple, causing her to suck in a breath. She let that breath out on a sensuous hum as he closed his mouth over her nipple and stroked it to a point with his tongue. She wasn't about to let him ignore her question, though, no matter how much pleasure he brought her. "Is it because of Sir Christopher?"

He pulled away from her, narrowing his eyes as he stared down at her. "The man is a boob. I don't know what you see in him." It was likely that she saw nothing in him. Katya adored making him jealous and always had. And damn him, but jealousy made him hard in ways he didn't want to think about. "He could never make you feel the way I do," he growled, proving his point by skipping about twenty steps in their lovemaking routine to thrust inside of her.

Katya gasped, her eyes popping wide at the deviation from the norm. "If this is what I get for flirting with a passing stranger, then I should do it more often."

"Don't you dare," he growled, thrusting hard and deep. He reached for her leg, bringing it up over his hip so that he could increase the pressure of his thrusts. For a woman past forty, Katya was astoundingly flexible—something they routinely made full use of.

"I like you when you're on fire like this," she panted as he increased the pace of his thrusts, her words turning into impassioned cries.

"You just like to be fucked," he said, doing his best to give her everything she wanted. All the same, the agonizing whisper that hinted she liked it whether he was the one inside of her or not dampened the pleasure he felt.

His pace slowed, and the energy pulsing through him subsided somewhat. Katya obviously sensed it. She pushed him to the side, then rolled to straddle him, impaling herself on his cock and riding him without mercy.

"That's more like it," she said with a devilish sparkle in her eyes, her face flushed with need.

The sight of her body moving over him, still amazing even at her age, her full breasts with their large, pert nipples bouncing, and her face contorting with pleasure, fanned the flames within him into an inferno once more. She was everything he'd ever wanted, the only woman he'd wanted since the moment they'd met. She could reach into his soul, grab hold of his heart, and hold him in a state of arousal that drove him to blissful madness. He was completely at her mercy, and she knew it. But he doubted she felt the same way about him.

He spread his hands across her hips, meeting her movements with thrusts as she pleasured herself on him, and stroked his way up her sides to cradle her breasts. He knew her so well, knew that she was close to coming, and that it would be astounding for her. Thank God he'd read her signals right, sensed that she was in a randy mood, and sent her the note ordering her into his bed that night. He rolled her nipples between his thumbs and forefingers before pinching them with just the right amount of pressure.

She cried out as the muscles of her pussy clenched around him, milking him into his own orgasm. Her shattered look of ecstasy as she came kept him pumping until he was spent. The searing intensity of climax slowly gave way to the sated feeling of contentment that he'd grown to enjoy almost as much as the flash of orgasm over the years. Katya rode out the waves of her pleasure, then loosened, sinking to lie splayed across his chest, panting into the pillow beside his head.

The urge to sleep was almost overpowering, but he fought it. He reached awkwardly to cradle the side of her head, nudging her to face him. When she did, he surged into her and kissed her with a tenderness far more powerful than the lust they'd just spent in each other's arms. His heart swelled to fill the places that raw need had inhabited. He circled his arms around her and simply held her, brushing her lips with his own and wishing he could melt into her and be one with her forever.

Their light, bleary kisses continued until the heat of their bodies subsided enough that Katya reached for the bedcovers to envelop them in a cocoon of warmth.

"Tell me why you're so sad tonight," she said, her tone infinitely more patient and less demanding than before their lovemaking.

"I'm not sad," he insisted, rolling to his side and fitting her against his body.

"Malcolm." She pursed her lips and sent him a scolding look across the pillow. "I know you. I know when you're sad."

She did, and he wouldn't be able to get away with lying to her for long. "Cece was talking about her coming out earlier," he admitted. "It made me realize that she won't be mine for much longer."

The tender sympathy that filled Katya's eyes was enough of a reward to make him wonder why he hadn't confessed to her from the start. She smoothed a hand over his cheek, brushing her thumb across the stubble on his chin.

"My dear Malcolm," she sighed. "You're a sentimental old fool."

He intended to reply "I know," but the words that blurted past his lips were, "Marry me, Katya."

She stiffened, pulling away slightly, her gaze dropping.

"We both know it's inevitable," he went on, urgency

burning inside of him. "We belong together. We don't work when we're apart."

"We don't work when we're together either," she said in a voice so quiet he almost didn't hear it. He wished he hadn't. Her gaze flickered up to meet his. "You know that."

"No, I don't," he insisted. He cupped her backside, pressing his hips into hers. "We just experienced how well we work together."

"We know how to give each other pleasure," she said, her expression stern. "But we don't know how *not* to cause each other pain."

Malcolm frowned. "Life is pain. It's unavoidable. And it's easier to face when we're together." He wanted to add that he could only face the pain he knew was coming for him if she was with him, but he'd humiliated himself enough for one night.

She reacted as though he'd said it anyhow, smiling gently and kissing his tight lips. "Oh, Malcolm. There are so many things I wish I could tell you."

His frown deepened. "You can tell me anything. You've always been able to tell me anything."

She shook her head and stroked his cheek again. "No, I haven't. There are far more things I can't tell you than ones I can."

His body began to heat all over again, but with frustration more than desire. "What things?"

She let out an impatient breath. "I can't tell you."

"Why not?" he demanded.

"Because you wouldn't listen," she said, inching away. "You'd pretend to listen, but you wouldn't really hear."

"Is that what you think of me?" He pushed away from her, the cozy feeling of completion changing to an ache of emptiness inside of him.

"It's what I think of all men who try to learn all my secrets and toss me aside with all the other puzzles they've figured out," she snapped, propping herself up on one arm.

"I see," he growled, sitting up. "I'm just like every other man, am I?"

"I—" She blinked, sitting, her mouth hanging open for a moment. "No, actually. You aren't like every other man. Not even close."

Hope warred with anger and disappointment in his gut. "I'm special then?" he said, knowing there was too much sarcasm in his voice. "Not like all the others. I'm the only fool who's stuck around long enough to know just how replaceable I am."

"You are not replaceable," she said, glaring at him. "Far from it."

"Then marry me." He twisted toward her, cursing himself for sounding like he was begging.

"It wouldn't work," she said, turning away.

"Why not?" he demanded.

She snapped back to him, her eyes wide with indignation. "You know full well why not."

"Impossible woman," he hissed to himself before saying louder, "I have no idea why I've never been good enough for you."

She laughed as though he'd said something ridiculous. "You've always been good enough for me, but that doesn't change the fact that you—"

A sharp knock on the door silenced Katya before she could finish her thought.

"Papa," Cece called from the hall, her voice high with excitement. "Papa, a messenger's just arrived." She knocked again. "I told Galston I would fetch you."

Katya swore under her breath and dove off the far side of the bed.

Malcolm leapt from the other side of the bed and

27

snatched at his robe, hanging over the wardrobe door. "What messenger?" he called.

He threw on his robe and fastened the belt. Out of the corner of his eye, he spotted Katya scrambling on hands and knees to retrieve her clothes from the chair. She barely made it under the bed with the bundle of her things in her arms when Cece knocked one more time, then threw open the door.

CHAPTER 3

$\mathcal{K}$atya's knees and elbows would have bruises for days, but at least she'd made it under the bed in time. Not that she believed for one second Cece was fooled.

"Did I interrupt something?" Cece asked. Katya could see her feet and the hem of her gown a yard or so inside the door. Her voice held a teasing lilt.

"No," Malcolm answered, too gruff to be telling the truth. "I'd just gone to bed is all. What's this about a messenger?"

"Were you having a hard time falling asleep?" Cece asked on, more gloating than ever.

"The messenger?" Malcolm growled.

"Only, it looks as though you were tossing and turning quite a bit," Cece said, undeterred. "Your bedsheets are horribly tangled."

Katya let out a breath, but nearly burst into a fit of coughing as she breathed in a tuft of dust. She fought to hold her breath and keep still. Damn Malcolm's staff for not cleaning under the bed.

"Cecelia. What of the messenger," Malcolm said, raising his voice.

Katya watched Cece's skirts sway, as though she'd given up her prying for something more exciting. "Mr. Croydon just sent a messenger to the house," she said, her voice animated. "There's been a development in everything you've been doing to fight against Lord Shayles."

"What development?" Malcolm asked, the same eagerness in his voice that Katya felt.

Katya scooted across to Cece's side of the bed, no doubt picking up more dust as she did. It would be undignified for a woman half her age to hide, naked, under beds, listening in to conversations, but at the moment she didn't care. Anticipation surged through her, making her reckless.

"Inspector Coleman of Scotland Yard has just been sacked," Cece said.

Katya gasped, breathing in more dust. She couldn't help but cough that time, though she buried her face in the bundle of her clothes and prayed Cece wouldn't notice. Inspector Coleman was the name at the very top of the list that Mark Gatwick had given them—a list of the men protecting Shayles and his horrific club from the law.

"Coleman is gone?" Malcolm asked, nearly shouting. Likely he was attempting to cover up Katya's coughing, but shouting was even more suspicious. "When?" he went on. "How did it happen? Who's taking his place."

"I don't know," Cece said. "The messenger merely delivered the news of the man's sacking and said that Mr. Croydon wants everyone at his house within the hour."

"Right." Malcolm's bare feet moved across to Cece, and she turned toward the door. "Go to bed."

"I'm not going to bed," Cece protested. "I received the message, so I want to go with you."

"No," Malcolm snapped. For once, Katya agreed with him. "You're too young and naïve to be mixed up in anything having to do with Shayles."

"Papa," Cece said, stopping in the doorway, her feet pointing back to Malcolm. "I'm not *that* naïve."

"You're more innocent than you know," Malcolm insisted, pushing Cece into the hall, by the look of things.

"It's charming of you to think that, Papa," Cece said, her tone back to teasing.

"You and I need to have a talk when I return home," Malcolm said in a low growl.

"Yes, Papa, we do," Cece scolded him. "Perhaps Lady Stanhope could join us."

Katya winced. Cece most definitely knew she was there. But Malcolm was right when it came to how innocent Cece was. There were things in the world that the dear girl couldn't begin to imagine. But it was a hallmark of youth to believe one knew much more than, in fact, one did when one was newly arrived in adulthood. Katya dealt with that kind of youthful arrogance on a daily basis with all three of her children.

"Go to bed," Malcolm said at last, his tone brooking no argument.

Cece sighed. "I'll go to my room, but I won't sleep. I want you to tell me everything as soon as you get home."

Malcolm made an irritated sound. "Are all young women these days so impertinent to their fathers?"

Cece laughed. "Only ones raised by you, Papa."

Katya watched Cece's skirts sway toward Malcolm, indicating she'd kissed him, then swirl away as she marched down the hall. Malcolm stepped back into the room and shut the door.

As fast as she could, Katya slithered out from under

Malcolm's bed and stood. As she'd suspected, she was covered in globs of dust. Malcolm's frown transformed into a chuckle as he gave her a once over.

"Lady Dust Mop, I presume," he said, eyes dancing with mirth.

Katya let out a humorless laugh and glanced sideways at him as she tried to brush herself clean. "Explain to me again why you don't lock your door at night?"

"Because I'm in my own house," he said, crossing to help her banish the dust clumps. "It could be your house too if you'd only—"

Katya held up a finger to warn him. "We'll argue about marriage later. For now, we need to clean up and get over to Alex's house as quickly as possible."

"You're right," Malcolm agreed, launching into motion.

As Katya shook out her clothes in preparation for putting them back on, Malcolm crossed to his washstand and poured water from a large pitcher into a bowl. He soaked a rag, then handed it to Katya.

"I don't know why you haven't invested in installing proper water-closets in your townhouse yet," Katya said, using the rag to wipe away any remaining dust.

Malcolm shrugged, removing his robe and throwing it over the chair by the fire. "I'll get around to it." He opened his wardrobe and started to dress. Katya was a little jealous of his ability to put on clean clothes instead of the ones that had been worn half the day. It might be worth marrying Malcolm just to have fresh drawers at a moment's notice.

"It appears as though Lavinia was right," she said as she dressed in her rumpled clothes.

"About what?" Malcolm asked over his shoulder.

"She postulated that since Gatwick suddenly left the country, something must be happening to hurt Shayles."

"More likely he fled so that he doesn't end up splattered by the blood when the guillotine drops," Malcolm said in a grim voice.

Katya pursed her lips and stared at his back as he donned a fresh shirt. She had no great love for Gatwick, but neither could she explain away his behavior, the way he'd helped them in the past few months. Or rather, the way he'd helped Lavinia. Much though it galled her, Katya had to admit there was more to Mark Gatwick than met the eye.

"I'm eager to discover who the new Inspector is," she said as she and Malcolm finished dressing and headed for the door.

"It's likely to be someone just as corrupt and vile as Coleman," Malcolm grumbled.

Katya sent him a wry grin. "Are all Scotsmen as optimistic as you?"

Malcolm grunted in response and yanked open his door. He held up a hand to keep Katya from charging through, then peeked into the hall himself. The hall must have been empty, because he motioned for her to follow him.

Katya tip-toed through the upstairs hall and down the stairs to the entryway, where Mr. Galston seemed to be waiting for them.

"Your carriage will be in front shortly, my lord," he told Malcolm.

"Thank you, Galston." Malcolm nodded to the man.

"Papa."

Katya flinched as Cece appeared at the top of the stairs. She refused to look guilty or as though she'd been caught doing something naughty. Instead, she turned to face Cece with a mild smile.

"What are you doing?" Malcolm demanded, far less smooth. His face turned red, and he sent an embarrassed glance Katya's way before marching to meet Cece at the bottom of the stairs. "I thought you said you were going to your room."

"I changed my mind," Cece said with a smile. "Women are allowed to do that, aren't we, Lady Stanhope?" She sent Katya a grin that left no doubt about just how much the girl knew.

"We are," Katya answered, crossing her arms. "But changing one's mind should never be done for fickle reasons, or for the sole purpose of making others look foolish." When Cece's smug grin faltered, Katya added, "Perhaps we will spend some time in the coming week discussing the importance of discretion and forbearance as well as shopping for a new wardrobe. The former is far more indicative of womanhood than the latter."

Cece flushed pink and lowered her eyes. "Point taken, Lady Stanhope," she said in a softer version of the growl Malcolm used when he knew he was wrong. Cece turned to Malcolm. "I think I will go to bed after all, Papa. But will you tell me all about your meeting in the morning?"

"Yes, of course," Malcolm said, then gruffly kissed Cece's cheek. "Off you go," he added, pointing up the stairs.

Cece picked up her skirts and turned to head up the stairs. She glanced over her shoulder as she went, her sheepish look turning into a conspiratorial grin as she met Katya's eyes.

Once Cece's back was turned, Katya rolled her eyes and shook her head before letting her arms drop. "You're going to have your hands full with that one," she said as Malcolm rejoined her in the entryway.

Malcolm huffed a grim laugh. "We both are," he said. When Katya arched a questioning eyebrow at him, he went on with, "You know she has her sights set on Rupert."

"How could I forget?" Katya answered with equal foreboding. She supposed she would be delighted to have Cece as a daughter-in-law after all—as long as she and Rupert didn't rush into marriage before either was ready for it—but thinking about the tangled web of her relationship with Malcolm at the same time as contemplating one between their children made her head hurt.

"Your carriage is here, my lord," Galston announced, opening the door for them.

"Thank God for that," Malcolm said, taking the lead and marching out the door.

They remained relatively silent on the short journey to Alex's house. Alex and Marigold's London home was close enough to Malcolm's that they could have walked. But it was quicker to drive, and they were less likely to be seen. Katya wouldn't put it past Shayles to send his eyes and ears out into London to see what his enemies were up to. He must have known that Inspector Coleman had been sacked as well, and if he was smart—which Katya knew he was, damn him—he would be making preparations of his own.

"Cece knows all about us, you realize," Katya said at last, just as they reached Alex and Marigold's house.

"I know," Malcolm grumbled, scooting toward the door as the carriage came to a stop. "She wants you to marry me as much as I do," he added, opening the door and hopping out of the carriage before she could give him the cross answer she usually gave to his constant proposals.

Katya sighed and shook her head before following him out into the street, then up the stairs and into the townhouse. Alex's butler, Mr. Levins, held the door open and indicated that they were meeting in the large, front drawing room instead of one of the smaller, cozier rooms toward the back of the house. That was enough to make Katya forget her frustration with Malcolm's constant matrimonial pressure in favor of the problem at hand.

"It's about time you got here," Alex said with a knowing grin as Katya and Malcolm entered the room where all of their friends were already gathered.

He didn't seem the least bit surprised to find them arriving together. Neither did the rest of their friends. Armand and Lavinia were seated on a sofa that faced the curtained front window, holding hands. Marigold was pouring tea with the help of one of the maids. Peter stood by the fireplace with the anxious expression he always wore when Mariah wasn't with him. The fact that he was in London at all while Mariah remained in Cornwall, two months away from delivering their second child, was a minor miracle.

But what surprised Katya even more was that her son was there as well, cradling a glass of brandy as he sat in a chair across from Alex.

"Rupert, what are you doing here?" she asked, blinking at him.

"This is a matter of utmost importance, Mother," he said with an expression that was far too serious for his barely twenty years. "Mr. Croydon asked me to come."

A strange, painful lump filled Katya's stomach. She could remember the day Rupert was born like it was yesterday, a day that had been filled with tears of joy and sorrow for her. She'd kissed his scraped knees when he was a toddler, praised him for his childish drawings, sent him off to Eton, and gloried in his accomplishments at Oxford. She'd schooled him in the duties of the title his father had left to him when he was a boy of four and handed over the reins of those responsibilities to him only a year ago. And now she was caught between the ache of seeing the baby she'd cherished acting as a man and the anguish of having him replace her simply because he was a man and she was not.

"Katya, would you like tea?" Marigold asked.

Katya shook herself out of her burst of melancholy and turned to her friend. "I think whiskey is more in order," she said with a sharp grin that was intended to hide her true emotions. "But you can put it in the tea."

Marigold laughed and set to work fixing Katya's cup.

"What's going on?" Malcolm opted to dive straight into the issue at hand. "Coleman has been sacked?"

"Sacked and arrested," Peter confirmed, stepping away from the fireplace. "It turns out that the leads we gave Scotland Yard uncovered far more corruption than the way he was shielding Shayles."

"The leads Lord Gatwick gave us," Lavinia corrected him.

"All of Scotland Yard is having a fit because of it," Alex added, brushing over Lavinia's comment. "Tomorrow's newspapers are going to be splashed with headlines about lies, corruption, and cover-ups."

"Will it help us bring Shayles down?" Katya asked the all-important question as Marigold handed her a powerful cup of tea.

"It will if we can coordinate with the new chief inspector as soon as possible," Alex said. "But chances are he'll have much more on his plate than closing Shayles's club."

"Much more," Rupert added. "Coleman wasn't just protecting Shayles. It's as if the floorboards were pried up and a dozen rats scattered in all directions."

"We need to act fast to convince the new inspector that it will be worth his time to go after a peer," Peter said. "Shayles's title might not be an old or distinguished one, but the law has never been keen on going up against titles of any sort."

"He's only a viscount," Rupert said with the same sort of

youthful arrogance Cece had shown earlier, proving that the first flush of knowledge went straight to a young person's head. "We've got two earls, a marquess, a viscount, and one of the wealthiest men in England right here in this room."

"It's eighteen-eighty-one," Alex said. "Titles don't mean as much as they used to, and depending on who the new inspector is, they won't mean anything at all."

"I wouldn't be so quick to make that assumption," Armand said.

"Perhaps instead of debating the usefulness of titles, we should ask the obvious question," Katya said. "Who is the new Chief Inspector?"

"A man by the name of Jack Craig," Alex said, crossing to Marigold to take the cup of tea she was offering.

Katya exchanged a confused look with Malcolm. "I've never heard of him," Malcolm said.

"Neither had any of us," Peter told him. "He's young."

"Some of my friends know of him," Rupert said. All eyes turned to him. "He's barely thirty, but some say he's been working for the Metropolitan Police since they plucked him off the street for picking pockets as a boy."

Katya's brow shot up. "So he isn't an insider."

"Unless he feels a sense of loyalty to those who brought him up out of obscurity," Armand said.

"Even if he does," Malcolm said, an excited light in his eyes, "he won't feel that loyalty toward an impoverished viscount running a brothel."

"But it means he won't feel any loyalty toward the titled toffs fighting against Shayles either," Alex argued.

He had a point. Katya swallowed the rest of her whiskey-laced tea in a few gulps before saying, "I'll just have to speak to the man."

Malcolm narrowed his eyes at her. "And what if he isn't the sort to have his head turned by a pretty face?"

Katya grinned and batted her eyelashes at him. "Why, Malcolm, are you calling me pretty?"

"I'm calling you shameless," he said, squaring off with her.

"I take that as a compliment."

"You would."

She smiled seductively, wondering if it would be worth sparking Cece's meddlesome spirit by going home with Malcolm after they were done at Alex's meeting.

Alex cleared his throat. "I was actually going to suggest that the two of you seek a meeting with Craig together."

"Even better," Katya agreed. She and Malcolm could accomplish anything when they worked together.

"You'll have to go to Scotland Yard first thing in the morning," Alex went on. "The place is likely to be chaotic, and there's no telling whether you'll be able to get in to see Craig."

"The man will probably be up to his eyeballs in investigations," Peter agreed. "Rupert is right about the number of rats scrambling for new hiding places."

A twist of jealousy threatened to squash the pride Katya felt. "Craig won't say no to us," she insisted. She glanced to her son, arching an eyebrow. "Old age and experience beats youth and enthusiasm any day."

To his credit, Rupert grinned at her with as much pride in his expression as she'd always felt for him. "If anyone can woo Craig, you can, Mama."

It shouldn't have touched her so deeply to have him call her "Mama" instead of the more formal "Mother" he'd adopted around her friends. It shouldn't have brought a faint stinging to her eyes either. Perhaps she knew why Malcolm had seemed so sad earlier after all. Parenthood was the most wonderful and painful journey a person could go on.

"It's settled then," she said, tilting her chin up and sending Malcolm a challenging look. "First thing in the morning, as soon as the men of Scotland Yard are at their desks, Malcolm and I will pay Mr. Jack Craig a visit."

"And if the man is as smart as they say he is," Malcolm added, "he'll be exactly what we need to bring Shayles down once and for all."

CHAPTER 4

*I*nspector Jack Craig was a busy man. Malcolm took the fact for granted when he sent a messenger to Scotland Yard with a request to meet with him. But as it turned out, Craig was so busy that the best he was able to do was to meet Malcolm and Katya in passing between two undisclosed matters of even greater importance the next morning.

"But don't you see," Katya argued as she and Malcolm walked briskly down Oxford Street shortly before ten o'clock, "this is the perfect way to avoid any sort of suspicion this meeting might arouse."

Malcolm sent her a flat scowl, back itching with impatience. "Are you really willing to stake your reputation on the solidity of this idea?" he asked in a grumble.

"What are the two of you talking about?" Bianca asked as she scurried along a few steps behind them.

"They won't tell you," Natalia answered her. "It's probably the kind of thing Mama is constantly telling me I'm too young to hear."

"You are too young to hear it," Rupert answered her, sounding as put out about things as Malcolm felt.

Malcolm glanced over his shoulder at their entourage. Bianca and Natalia scurried a few feet behind him and Katya, eyes wide with excitement as they gazed around at the expensive shops and cafés lining the busy thoroughfare. Rupert escorted Cece a few feet behind them. The two of them looked entirely too cozy for Malcolm's liking. But since maintaining secrecy about their meeting with Craig involved pretending the whole family was on an outing to shop for Cece's coming out at the end of the week, there was nothing Malcolm could do about it.

"I still maintain this is a terrible idea," he told Katya, reaching into his waistcoat to check his watch. "They're going to be nothing but trouble."

"They'll be fine," Katya said, not sounding convinced herself.

"Oh! Mama, look at the hat in that window over there," Natalia gasped. "Wouldn't that be divine with my blue organdy?"

"Ask your brother," Katya snapped. "He's the one holding the purse strings these days."

Malcolm peeked at Katya with an arched brow. Chances were her short temper was due to the fact that she hadn't slept much the night before. Their meeting at Alex's house hadn't adjourned until close to two in the morning, she and her children had arrived at Strathaven House before eight, and heaven knew she hadn't gotten any sleep before the meeting was called. He didn't know why she hadn't just come home with him after the meeting. He'd offered. She'd refused.

"You have enough hats, Nat," Rupert said, laughing in a way that was sure to annoy his little sister.

Sure enough, Natalia huffed the same way Cece did when

Malcolm refused to buy some useless piece of frippery for her. "Mama, tell Rupert it's not fair for him to hold the purse strings," she said.

Katya barked a laugh, but there was little humor in it. Malcolm studied her with a sideways look again. The lines on her face betrayed more frustration than he'd picked up at first. The uncomfortable thought that it was unfair for Rupert to suddenly have control of everything that had been Katya's until a year ago itched at the back of Malcolm's mind. Sons assumed power when they came of age. That was the law and the way things had always been. But for a woman of Katya's strength, it must have been a bitter pill to swallow.

Hoping to comfort her, Malcolm swayed closer to her, reaching for her hand as they walked. He just about had it in what he hoped was a comforting grip when she yanked it away.

"What are you doing?" she demanded.

"Holding your hand," Malcolm replied with a scowl.

Katya made an impatient sound and shook her head. "You can't blithely hold a woman's hand in public. This is Oxford Street. Anyone could be watching and sharpening their gossip knives."

She had a point. "All right, then." He offered his elbow to escort her more formally.

"I don't need your support to walk down the street," she said with a sigh. "I'm perfectly capable of standing on my own."

Malcolm let his arm drop and his scowl grow. "God knows, we're all well aware of that."

She turned her head to stare at him with wide eyes. "What's biting at you this morning?" she demanded, as though she were a pot calling him black.

"You tell me," he said. "You've been peevish since...since I first met you."

43

"I deserve every bit of my attitude," she replied, eyes bright with anger.

"Oh, yes. Katya the Great, foiled at every turn by villainous men who want to put her in her place," he said, knowing full well his sarcasm would hurt her.

"You have no idea," she seethed.

"Of course not," he said. "You've never deigned to tell me."

She started forward again and picked up her pace. He kept up with her, if only to prove that she wouldn't get rid of him so easily.

"Don't worry, Kat," he said quietly once he was striding by her side. "Everyone knows that you're the one who puts men in their place. And that there's a line at your door every night, waiting for that privilege."

She stopped abruptly, pivoting toward him so fast Malcolm flinched. Fury lit her expression. "There's banter, Malcolm, and then there are insults. Kindly learn the difference."

"I'm just giving you something to smack me around about later," he said, in spite of the sharp regret that pinched his insides. He didn't mean to hurt her, but it was so easy when every step she took felt like she was stomping on his heart.

"Look at the two of you," Cece giggled as the children caught up to them. "Bickering like an old married couple."

"What an apt description," Bianca said, then leaned over to whisper something in Natalia's ear. Natalia laughed, clapped a hand over her mouth, and turned pink.

Malcolm was in no mood for their youthful high spirits. "We should have sent the lot of you to finishing school," he grumbled. "In Argentina."

"We?" Cece asked, batting her eyelashes.

"Rupert, take the girls somewhere for tea," Katya ordered, clearly at the end of her patience.

"Yes, Mama," Rupert said with a nod, facing Cece and his

sisters. "Right, you lot. In there." He pointed to a café a few doors down.

The young people went one way and Katya marched on in the opposite direction. Malcolm sighed, rubbed a hand over his face, and hurried after her. He could practically feel the heat of anger rippling off of her. The words "I'm sorry" hung on his lips, but pride wouldn't let them come out.

"Inspector Craig said he'd meet us in that café there," he said instead, pointing across the street.

Katya didn't say a word, didn't even acknowledge him. She paused at the corner only long enough to let the bustling traffic thin, and then marched across the street. Malcolm was nearly mowed down by a speeding wagon in his efforts to keep up with her.

"I'm not insulting you," he said when he finally caught up with her. "I'm merely stating fact. I thought you were proud of the number of conquests you've made."

Again, she whirled to a stop and glared at him. "Proud? Like a man would be proud of all the women he's bedded?"

Malcolm blinked. "Yes?"

She made a disgusted sound and marched on, yanking the café door open so hard he was surprised it didn't fly off its hinges.

"If you want to know why we're not married, Malcolm, look no further than your own arrogance," she said, dodging between tables and heading to the back of the café.

"I'm not the only arrogant one."

It was the last shot he was able to get in before a man in a simple suit stood from a table near the back to greet them. Malcolm's brow went up. Inspector Craig was as young as Rupert had said he was, and yet there was a distinct weariness in his dark eyes and a touch of premature grey at his temples. His appearance was at odds with the curt way he greeted Malcolm and Katya as they reached his table.

"Lord Campbell and Lady Stanhope, I presume," he said in a strange accent, like someone who had been raised on the streets attempting to speak in posh tones but failing.

"How do you do." Katya held out a hand, turning on all her charms. But there was still a hint of smoldering fury in her smile.

Craig took her hand and bowed as though he weren't used to the formality, then gestured for her to sit. As she did, he quickly shook Malcolm's hand. Malcolm sat as well, but Craig's gaze returned to Katya.

"I understand you have a matter you'd like me to investigate," he said.

Malcolm sat back in his chair and crossed his arms. A tiny bit of his nose was out of joint that Craig would assume Katya was driving their inquiry, but the fact that the man had sensed in an instant to whom he should speak, regardless of the fact Katya was a woman, raised Malcolm's opinion of him.

"The Black Strap Club," Katya said, getting straight to the point. "Have you heard of it?"

"Yes," Craig answered with a grim nod. It was hard to tell just how much Craig had heard.

"We want to bring it down," Katya went on.

"More specifically, we want to bring down its owner, Lord Theodore Shayles," Malcolm added.

"Viscount Shayles." Craig nodded. "Scotland Yard is aware of him."

Malcolm clenched his jaw. Clearly Craig was a harder nut to crack than Katya. "We believe he's been protected in the past by the man you've replaced and by several others in the Metropolitan Police."

Craig merely stared at him, his face implacable.

"The activities of The Black Strap Club are disgusting and abusive," Katya went on. "I've had contacts working inside for years, girls whose sole purpose has been to protect the innocent as much as they can, get them out when possible, and record the atrocities they've been forced to endure. Women have died there."

For the first time, Craig's expression showed emotion. "You have records?"

"My contacts do," Katya confirmed with a nod. "I'm sure I can find a way to get them to you."

"Do that," Craig said, then paused. His expression darkened. "The evidence of women won't be enough for my colleagues to act on."

Malcolm saw fury flash through Katya's expression out of the corner of his eye. He shared that fury, but knew Craig was right. "What will it take, then?"

Craig glanced to him. "Solid information. Testimony from someone the courts are likely to respect. Not just the courts. Lord Shayles is a peer, and if he is indicted, he will be tried in the House of Lords. I need someone on that level to provide evidence."

"A man," Katya said, her jaw tight.

"Unfortunately, yes." Craig turned back to her. "Though anything your insiders can provide will be helpful. Their testimony can be valuable, but you and I both know that, as much as we would have it otherwise, the law finds it too easy to throw out accusations made against men, particularly noblemen, by lower-class women. Particularly if they can label those women as whores."

Malcolm's brow shot up. Few people he knew would speak so freely and use such language in public. Craig watched Katya as if to see how she would react. When she showed nothing but determination, the corner of Craig's mouth tweaked in what could have been a smile. More importantly, a firm sort of confidence came to his eyes.

"So you're saying you need one of Shayles's clients to come forward with rock-solid evidence," Katya said.

"I am." Craig nodded.

Katya turned to Malcolm, one dark brow raised. Malcolm felt the implication of her look down to his core. Prickling heat filled him.

"My association with Shayles's club was nearly two decades ago," he said, "when I was newly returned from the Crimea and...troubled."

"I need someone who currently patronizes the club to come forward," Craig said, his expression holding no judgment for what Malcolm had just confessed. "Without that sort of testimony, I could have the club raided, but the chances of Lord Shayles being arrested would be slim."

All three of them were silent in thought for a moment. Ghosts of Malcolm's past knocked at the doors in his soul where he'd shut them away. He wasn't the man now who he had been after the war. Tessa had changed him, and, if he were honest with himself, so had Katya. Perhaps even more than Tessa. But Tessa was the one he fought for, even though she'd lost her battle eighteen years ago.

"What if we send someone into the club with the expressed mission of finding evidence that could bring Shayles down?" Katya asked at length.

"What, a mole?" Malcolm blinked at her.

"Yes." For the first time since their earlier argument, she looked at him, the light of determination in her eyes. "Someone new, someone whom Shayles doesn't already have under his thumb and whom he wouldn't be able to blackmail."

"Is there such a person?" Malcolm asked.

"I think there could be." The excitement in Katya's expression grew.

"I'm willing to listen to whatever ideas you have," Craig said.

Katya broke into a smile. "Sir Christopher Dowland."

Malcolm's gut clenched with jealousy. "What, that idiot you were flirting with yesterday?"

Katya let out an impatient sigh and glared at him before turning to Craig. "Sir Christopher Dowland is newly elected to Parliament. He hasn't been in London long. We've only just met ourselves, but that will work to our advantage. Shayles wouldn't know there was a connection between us."

Malcolm shook his head. "Dowland is a fool."

"Dowland *looks* like a fool," Katya corrected him. She turned to Craig. "He has the kind of face that makes you think he's a harmless buffoon, but, in fact, from everything I've heard, he's brilliant."

"Where have you heard this?" Malcolm asked.

"From Peter," she told him. "Dowland's estate is near Starcross Castle."

All Malcolm could do in response was hum. If Peter thought well of the man, then perhaps he'd misjudged him. And if he had....

"A new lord in London who is smarter than he appears to be," Craig said, leaning back in his chair and rubbing his chin. "One Lord Shayles doesn't know is associated with you."

"He's not associated with us," Malcolm said. Suspicion itched down his back, and he narrowed his eyes at Katya. "Unless you're more associated with him than you've let on."

"Now is not the time," Katya seethed.

"Look, I'll be honest with you," Craig said, holding up his hands to stop whatever scrap Malcolm and Katya could have gotten into. "Coleman was taking a lot of bribes from a lot of people. I have my hands full with cleaning up his messes. I wasn't an obvious choice to replace him, and I have a lot to prove. My job is on the line. The only reason I'm willing to consider acting against Lord Shayles and his club is because I have a personal interest in bringing pimps to justice." The sudden burst of unadulterated menace in the man's eyes was enough to convince Malcolm that Craig had a painfully specific interest. "If this Dowland friend of yours is willing to infiltrate the club and find evidence we can use to arrest Lord Shayles and close the club for good, I'll help you pursue that. But we would need to act fast and be discreet."

"Understood," Katya said. "I'm sure I can convince Sir Christopher to help us."

Malcolm wanted to ask how she was sure, but he wasn't a big enough fool to let his jealousy get in the way of what might have been their best chance in two decades to bring Shayles to justice.

"Fine." Craig nodded and stood. "Speak to your friend, then let me know the outcome. I'll be waiting."

Malcolm and Katya stood as well. They hadn't had a chance to order tea, so there was nothing to keep them from heading for the door and back onto the busy sidewalk, where they were greeted immediately by Cece and Rupert, Bianca and Natalia.

"Mama, really. Tell Rupert that he must give me a few pounds at least." Natalia accosted Katya right away. "I might not be the one coming out on Friday, but I still need new clothes."

"Oh, hello," Bianca said, but not to Malcolm or to her mother. Her eyes were fixed firmly on Inspector Craig, and they were filled with stars.

"Good morning," Craig nodded to her. He kept moving, but didn't seem to be able to pry his eyes away from Bianca in spite of his momentum. His expressionless face twitched into a devilish smile over his shoulder, and before he turned forward, he winked.

"For Pete's sake," Malcolm grumbled. Craig was exactly the sort of rough, dangerous man girls like Bianca Marlowe found attractive. He shot a warning look to Katya.

Katya was miles ahead of him. "No," she told Bianca, grabbing her arm and turning her away from Craig.

"Mama, who is that?" Bianca whispered, a pink flush coming to her face.

"No one you need to know," Katya replied.

"Oh, but Mama, you're wrong," Bianca said, twisting to glance at Craig's retreating back, even as Katya pushed her on. "I very much need to know him."

"No," Katya repeated.

"I'll make my debut next year," Bianca went on. "And then you won't be able to stop me from knowing whatever man I want to."

Malcolm raised an eyebrow, wondering if Bianca knew how her words could be taken and if Katya had had the same attitude when she was that age.

"I'll be able to stop you," Katya replied with a grim smile. "Don't give me a reason to."

Bianca huffed in frustration and broke away from Katya to walk on with Natalia. Malcolm picked up his pace until he was at Katya's side once more.

"Do you really think you can convince Dowland to stick his hand in a viper's pit to help us?" he asked.

"What other choice do we have?" she asked, a darker edge to her frustration than before the meeting. "The girls I have positioned in that hell of a club are depending on us."

Malcolm nodded. "We have to bring Shayles's villainy to an end."

"Then you have to trust me," she said, stopping.

The children were in front of them and continued walking, giving Malcolm and Katya space.

"I do trust you," Malcolm said, though it felt like a lie.

Katya saw right through him. She shook her head. "You see only what you want to see, Malcolm, and that doesn't reflect well on either of us."

"You're going to seduce him to get him to help us."

She pursed her lips so hard they turned white around the edges. Her eyes were like steel. "It always comes down to seduction with you, doesn't it?"

"It's what we have in common," he said, narrowing his eyes.

"There are other ways to live, Malcolm," she said, a surprising burst of exhaustion in her voice that hinted at her experience. "There are other ways to interact with people and to win them to your side."

"Maybe," he admitted, beginning to feel weary and ancient himself. "But it is a rare man who is willing to put himself into danger without getting something in return."

To his surprise, Katya laughed. "And you claim not to know why I haven't accepted your offer of marriage."

His frown darkened. "What does me wanting to marry you have to do with it?"

She shook her head. "If you knew that, we could stop having this argument. We could stop having every argument."

He was too baffled by her statement to answer.

"Mama, are you coming?" Rupert called from halfway down the sidewalk.

"I am," Katya called back to him. She turned, shaking her head sadly at Malcolm, then walked on.

Malcolm stood where he was, watching her retreating back and wondering how, after all these years, she could still leave him feeling like a confused amateur.

CHAPTER 5

*I*f she had been born a man, Katya was fairly certain she would have stopped at nothing to get Inspector Craig's job. If she hadn't already been serving in Parliament. Then again, the boredom of an early marriage to a husband who viewed her with indifference was what had led her to take an interest in the lives of those around her in the first place. That interest had evolved past gossip into the need to figure out what was truly behind the odd behavior of the aristocracy. That had, in turn, spurred her to find ways to covertly help the innocent and punish the wicked behind the scenes.

So in a way, if she'd never been palmed off on Robert in the constricting bonds of matrimony, she wouldn't have been strolling through Hyde Park in an expensive walking dress the day after her and Malcolm's meeting with Inspector Craig, pretending that she was merely there to chaperone her girls and Cece, and not seeking out a clandestine meeting with Sir Christopher Dowland.

Christopher was there, wandering aimlessly along the banks of the Serpentine. Katya had made eye-contact with him a few times, but couldn't tell if he had the first clue that she was signaling for him to approach. That was the beauty and fun of enlisting the seemingly bumbling man's help. No one would have suspected him of subterfuge. No one would have expected him to make it across the park without tripping over his own feet. And if she were honest, she wasn't entirely certain he'd live up to her expectations.

Katya paused to purchase a cup of tea from a man with a pushcart. The girls would appreciate them giving her a bit of space, and she needed an excuse to stay still long enough for Christopher to approach her. As she sipped the warm liquid, she watched her girls.

They clustered together near the edge of the water, tossing the leftover crumbs from breakfast that they'd brought with them at the ducks and swans. A grin tweaked the corner of Katya's mouth. The dear things were convinced they were grown, but to her, they looked as much like children as ever when they giggled and squealed as a particularly hungry swan chased after them. One could have argued that Katya should have scolded them and reminded them they were in public, where decorum was demanded, but she was loath to bring their innocent, halcyon days to an end the way hers had ended.

Her mind wandered back to her own, destroyed youth. The only thing that had made those confusing, miserable days bright was Malcolm's explosive arrival in her life. Even though their introduction had involved him quite literally falling at her feet in a drunken stupor at one of Robert's lascivious house parties. He had been different than the other pleasure-seekers. He had been in mourning for Tessa, Katya had been grieving the loss of her innocence, but somehow, together they were ridiculously happy. She still wondered where that happiness went.

"Good morning, Lady Stanhope."

Christopher's stilted greeting snapped Katya out of her thoughts. She turned to smile at him as he inched closer to her, holding a steaming cup of tea.

"Good morning, Sir Christopher. What a joy to see you here this morning," she said, taking a sip of her now cold tea.

For a moment, Christopher's already laughable face pinched in confusion. "I thought we were—" He stopped and let out a breath, his shoulders dropping. He squeezed his eyes shut and clenched his jaw as though inwardly scolding himself. "Sorry," he said when he opened his eyes. "I'm not used to *London society*."

The emphasis he put on the last two words convinced Katya he knew what he was doing after all.

"It's not that complicated." She grinned, sipping the last of her tea, then moving to hand the cup back to the vendor. "It's all just a muddle of greetings and partings with inconsequential conversation in the middle."

"All the same," Christopher replied, finishing his tea in one large gulp, then handing the cup to the vendor, "I'm not very good at it."

"Why do you say that?" Katya asked, holding out her arm in an invitation for him to escort her.

He picked up on that much, jumping to offer his elbow. Katya took it, and they strolled away from the Serpentine toward Rotten Row.

"I've lived my whole life in the country," he explained. "I managed my father's land before inheriting it. I've far more experience dealing with farmers and tradesmen than London's elite."

"Then why did you stand for Parliament?" she asked, surprised that she was genuinely curious about the answer.

Christopher shrugged. "I didn't, in a way. My father traditionally held the seat. The election campaign had already begun when he died. Before I knew it, my name had replaced his on the ballot, I won the election, and here I am." He shrugged again, the gesture serving as bookends to his situation.

"There are so many advantages in being an unknown in these waters," Katya said, searching for the quickest way to come to her point. The fewer people saw her walking with Christopher, the more likely he would be able to infiltrate the Black Strap Club without Shayles knowing he was a spy. She steered their steps toward a cluster of trees that would block them from full view.

"I have no issue with being unknown," Christopher went on. "I'm rather more concerned with being thought of as a country rube."

"London gossip can be cruel," Katya agreed with a nod.

"Especially when my own kinsmen whisper about me behind my back," he added in a voice so low Katya was convinced he was talking to himself. "They're not convinced I have a right to the Dowland name, considering the rumors that abounded about my mother." He shook his head and grinned crookedly at her. "But that's unpleasant talk for such a lovely day. I understand you have something you'd like me to do for you?" he asked.

"Yes. Something of vital importance." Katya let her soothing smile melt into a look that was pure business. "You met Lord Theodore Shayles the other day, but are you familiar with his club?"

A burst of color filled Christopher's cheeks, and he was suddenly unable to meet her eyes. "I've heard of it," he said, clipping his words.

Katya raised a brow. "Have you visited it?"

"No," Christopher answered immediately. "And I've no wish to. From what I understand, the place is an abomination."

The fierceness of his words was a paradoxical encouragement to Katya. Obviously, Christopher wasn't of Shayles's ilk, which meant that he would be the perfect candidate to provide honest, believable testimony against the club, as Inspector Craig had requested.

Katya patted his arm. "If you know the place is an abomination, then you know how necessary it is that it be shut down."

"Absolutely," he agreed enthusiastically. "I don't understand why Scotland Yard hasn't boarded up the place already."

"Because where Shayles and his club are concerned, the law looks the other way."

Christopher gaped at her with an expression of shock and dismay, as though personally hurt that the law could be corrupt.

"At least, until now," Katya added with a sly grin.

Christopher frowned. "How do you mean?"

"A few days ago, the Chief Inspector of Scotland Yard was removed from his position and arrested for corruption. He was the one who had been protecting Shayles's club. The man who took his place, Inspector Craig, is not on Shayles's payroll, and could, therefore, shut the place down for good."

"Thank God for that."

"However," Katya stopped him, "Inspector Craig requires reliable, insider information that would give the police enough fuel for a raid. He needs someone who has patronized the club to break the vow of silence that Shayles's customers maintain. Someone who would be willing to testify about what they have seen inside the walls of the club in court."

Christopher blinked. "But I've never been there before. How could I—" He stopped, his mouth hanging open, and turned to her. His eyes held understanding far beyond the ridiculousness of his features. "You want me to patronize the club, gather information, and take it to the police, to your Inspector Craig."

"Precisely," Katya said.

Christopher let go of her arm and took a step back, rubbing his hand over his face, brow knit in thought. Katya stood patiently where she was, watching the man's inner debate. His face betrayed his thoughts in a way that made her wonder if he was up to the job after all.

At last, he let out a breath and met her firm gaze with a serious one of his own. "You wouldn't be asking me if there were anyone else who could do this, would you?"

"No." Katya nodded. "You're a newcomer in town, an unknown. Shayles knows everyone associated with me and my friends, the group that has been seeking to bring him to justice for years."

"But he does know we've met," Christopher said. "He saw us together at Westminster the other day."

"And that wasn't enough of an interaction to indicate we're more than passing acquaintances."

Christopher winced, running a hand through his hair. "What sort of evidence would your inspector need?"

"Reports of the activities of the club," Katya said. "Documentation, if you can get it. I'm uncertain if Shayles has such a thing as a contract his customers sign."

"I wouldn't have to...do anything, would I?" he asked, writhing with discomfort. "To those poor girls, I mean."

"That would be up to you," Katya said, finding it sweet that the man wouldn't want to take advantage of the situation. "Chances are you would only need to spend an hour or so with a girl behind closed doors. I could give you the names of the girls who are my contacts on the inside, if you'd like."

Surprise lit Christopher's expression. "You're in contact

with those poor girls?" He shook his head. "Why not get them to testify?"

"We plan to, but the court gives more weight to a man's testimony, especially when the court trying Shayles will ultimately be the House of Lords itself." Katya couldn't keep the bitterness out of her voice. "My girls are there to keep the other girls from greater danger than they are already in, and to get them out when they can."

Christopher seemed to understand, but he also looked as though he might be sick. "When do you need me to do this?"

A burst of hopeful relief filled Katya's heart. He would help them. "The sooner the better. Tonight, if possible."

Christopher made a sound as though she'd asked him to wade into the sewers. In a way, she had. "I'll see what I can do. But, Lady Stanhope...."

Katya waited for him to go on, but had to prompt him with, "Yes?"

He winced, shifting uncomfortably. "I...I hope that you would be willing to do something for me in return."

Katya's stomach clenched, not over whatever Christopher would ask, but because Malcolm had been right. Christopher wanted something in return for his assistance. She squared her shoulders, ready for the worst. "What can I do for you?"

Once again, Christopher seemed unable to meet her eyes. His face turned beet red. "I'm new to my title, such as it is. It's not anything as grand as yours. It's small enough that I can still serve in Commons. But it does have a certain amount of responsibility to it," he rambled, dripping discomfort. "And as such, there are certain expectations on me. Marriage, for instance."

Katya's brow shot up. "I'm well past marrying age, Sir Christopher, and if you need an heir, which I assume you do—"

"No, no!" He glanced to her in alarm. "I wasn't proposing.

I just wondered if you could introduce me to some suitable young women who wouldn't be completely repulsed by me."

The innocence in his eyes and the implication that most women would be repulsed by him touched Katya's heart. She smiled, feeling a burst of maternal affection for the man, even though he couldn't have been more than ten years younger than her. She took his arm and resumed their stroll.

"Of course I'd be willing to make a few introductions for you," she said. "In fact, I can think of a few young women who would be lucky to have you." Victoria Travers, for one. Mariah deVere's younger sister had been holed up at Starcross Castle for more than a year, unwilling to reenter society after the debacle with Peter's horrid nephew, William. Christopher was just the sort of gentle soul a frightened doe like Victoria needed. And Christopher's estate was close to Peter's.

She was already making plans to bring the two young people together as she and Christopher turned the corner at the end of the trees, following the path as it arched toward the Serpentine again. Her matchmaker's smile vanished in an instant as she spotted Malcolm pacing at the water's edge, not far from where her daughters and Cece were giggling like fiends while staring at a pack of young bucks on the prowl. Malcolm saw them. His expression darkened.

"He isn't going to challenge me to a duel, is he?" Christopher asked, a note of genuine terror in his voice.

"No," Katya laughed. "But I might have to challenge him." She narrowed her eyes as Malcolm grew near. "All the same," she went on, letting go of Christopher's arm, "it would be better if we weren't seen together."

Christopher nodded. "I'll let you know what happens with…the thing." He turned and strode off in the opposite direction, sparing a final, wary glance for Malcolm.

Katya continued forward, meeting Malcolm at the intersection of two paths.

"I see your young conquest doesn't have the chops to face a real man," Malcolm said.

Katya rolled her eyes and took Malcolm's arm when he offered it. "Please tell me you're only saying that to maintain the illusion that my interest in Christopher Dowland was something other than the task we need him to do."

Malcolm grumbled, the sound neither confirming nor denying her statement.

"Honestly, Malcolm," she huffed. "Jealousy in a man of your age is unbecoming."

"Just as flirting with young men at your age is obscene."

She pursed her lips and stared sidelong at him. "Are you saying I couldn't have a man of Christopher's age if I wanted him?"

Malcolm remained silent, his expression darkening further. Because, of course, he knew she was fully capable of seducing any man she wanted. Young men of a certain ilk were particularly eager to learn from their elders. What Malcolm failed to understand, however, was that she didn't, in fact, want a dozen young, virile men in her bed. Quite the contrary.

"You're too competitive," she told him, facing forward and smiling at the sunlight glinting off the Serpentine. "That's always been your problem. You can't stand to feel as though you're capable of being bested in anything."

"That's not true," he argued. "I know where my strengths and weaknesses lie."

Katya laughed. "It eats away at you to think of anyone winning at your expense, whether it's a vote in Parliament or a woman's affections or even a hand at cards."

"Nonsense," he barked. She had a feeling he would have

used a far more colorful word if they'd been in private. "I'm fully capable of losing."

"Really?" Katya arched a brow at him. "Prove it."

They had reached Bianca, Natalia, and Cece at the water's edge. Katya held out her hand, eyes fixed on the reticule of breadcrumbs that Natalia carried. Natalia handed it over. Katya opened it and scooped out a small handful, depositing it in Malcolm's hands. She kept a bit for herself, then handed the reticule back to Natalia.

"Do you see that swan out there?" She nodded toward the center of the lake, where a particularly majestic swan paddled, eyeing the people on the bank with suspicion. "The first one to lure that swan to the side of the lake wins."

"That's completely ridiculous," Malcolm grumbled.

His grumbling stopped when Katya stepped away from him, scooting along the Serpentine's bank to get clear of the cluster of waterfowl waiting to be fed by passersby. "Here, swanny," she called out to the large bird. "I've got a nice handful of breadcrumbs for you. Here, swanny, swanny, swanny."

"Come here, you big bastard," Malcolm called out from the stretch of bank on the other side of the girls. He tossed crumbs out into the water, nearly hitting the swan as he did.

"Here, swanny," Katya called a little louder, casting her crumbs as far out into the lake as she could, nearly reaching the bird. "Lovely, fine, swanny."

The rest of the ducks and geese sensed something was afoot and swam madly to snatch up the crumbs that the large swan was suspicious of. He paddled this way and that, closer to Malcolm then closer to Katya. Katya was sure he thought humans were a strange and ridiculous lot.

"Where do you think you're going?" Malcolm snapped when the swan drifted closer to Katya's side. "My crumbs are better than hers."

"That's a good boy, swanny," Katya cooed, worried that she was running out of crumbs. "Come to mama."

"Good Lord, Mama. You realize it sounds as though you're propositioning that poor swan," Bianca laughed.

Katya straightened and glared at her daughter. As she did, Malcolm sent a flurry of tempting crumbs sailing at the swan. It turned its head and looked as though it would choose Malcolm over here.

"Oh no, you don't," she said, resuming her efforts to lure the swan to her.

The rest of the birds quacked and squawked and fluttered. The girls laughed uproariously along with them. More than a few pedestrians had stopped to see what was going on and were laughing too. But Katya was glad to look like a fool if it meant she could prove a point to Malcolm.

"There's a good boy," she cooed as the swan made a definitive break toward her. "Ha!" She turned to Malcolm with a triumphant grin.

A moment later, the swan let out a ferocious honk and sped toward her. The move was so unexpected that Katya reeled back with a yelp. The other birds parted, leaving the swan free to charge up the bank in pursuit of her.

With another outburst that was something between a shout and a laugh, Katya dashed to the side. She wished she'd brought a parasol to defend herself with, but as it was, her only option was flight. The swan charged after her, long neck extended, honking up a storm.

Malcolm had stepped away from the water's edge, so Katya ran straight toward him. "I've got you," he said, extending his arms as though he would fold her into a protective embrace.

Katya reached for him as well, but the moment they made contact, the swan charged. Instead of playing the hero and clasping her to his chest, Malcolm shouted a curse and leapt back, tugging Katya with him. The two of them turned and ran, bursting into laughter.

They didn't stop until they were on the other side of a stand of bushes that reached out into the water. Completely abandoning dignity, Katya laughed like a woman half her age, sagging in Malcolm's loose embrace. He snorted with laughter along with her, his face red with embarrassment and amusement.

"This proves nothing," he said, glancing back to make sure the swan wasn't still chasing them.

"It proves that we're a pair of old fools," Katya said.

Malcolm made a sound of agreement, slipping his arm around her waist. He met her eyes with bright joy and lust. "If we weren't in the middle of Hyde Park on a busy morning, I'd drag you into that bush and ravish you until you honked like that swan."

Katya laughed louder, the ache of arousal heating her. "As I recall, you're the one who sounds more like that swan when you come," she murmured close to his ear before backing to a respectable distance. Several people were watching them, and age and titles could only protect them from social scandal to a point. It wasn't as if most of London didn't know what was between them anyhow. All the same, neither of them would be invited to a church bazaar any time soon.

"Really, Mama, you're an utter embarrassment," Natalia said in imitation of Katya's scolding tone as she, Bianca, and Cece approached.

"What kind of an example are you setting, Papa?" Cece asked.

But it was Bianca who squinted off in the distance and said, "Is that Sir Christopher Dowland talking to Lord Shayles?"

Katya caught her breath. She and Malcolm turned in unison to glance across the Serpentine. There, on the path that led toward Kensington Gardens, was Christopher walking side-by-side with Shayles. It was too far to judge Christopher's expression, but Shayles had a hand on his back.

"I do believe the plan is working," Katya said, the thrill of victory zipping through her.

"Shayles's days are numbered," Malcolm agreed with a menacing grin.

CHAPTER 6

*T*he concept of waiting was one Malcolm had never mastered. Knowing that a dolt like Dowland was in the process of infiltrating The Black Strap Club, that an idiot of Dowland's kind was the one who might pip him at the post and bring Shayles down, made him impatient, short-tempered, and restless for days.

In moments of relative calm, he was willing to admit quietly to himself that Dowland probably was the ideal man for the job at hand. His frustration with the situation was most likely simple jealousy over the way Katya spoke so highly of the younger man. If he were honest with himself, he'd never been comfortable with the company Katya kept. He should have been the man standing by her side for the past fifteen years. He should have been the one warming her bed, not the parade of lovers she'd flaunted in his face. And yes, the argument that had nipped their original affair in the bud had been his fault, but surely fifteen years was more than ample time to be in a snit.

"My lord?"

Malcolm was jolted out of his thoughts as Galston stepped into the doorway of his study, holding a silver salver.

"What do you want?" Malcolm snapped, setting the large tumbler of scotch whiskey he'd been nursing on the mantle of the fireplace he'd been staring into and crossing to meet Galston at the door.

Unperturbed by his foul tempers as always, Galston presented the salver. "A message has just arrived."

Malcolm swiped the small sealed envelope with a bare nod to Galston. His pulse shot up. He knew the stationary well, was tempted to hold the letter to his nose to breathe in Katya's scent. Without pause, he ripped the envelope open and pulled out the message.

"Your presence is required at once."

A devilish grin pulled at the corner of Malcolm's mouth. He tucked the note into his jacket pocket. "Galston, have my carriage sent around in twenty minutes."

"Yes, my lord."

Galston nodded and retreated from the room. Malcolm shot out into the hall after him, passing him as they reached the front hall and charging upstairs, three steps at a time. He dashed past Cece's room, where she was busy packing a small trunk.

"Papa, whatever are you doing?" she called after him, poking her head out of her room. "My presentation at court is tomorrow."

"I've been called away," he said without stopping, hurrying on to his room.

"But there's so much to do," she continued. "Remember the change of plans? We're staying the night at—"

He shut the door, cutting off the rest of whatever complaint she was making, and stripped off his clothes as he crossed to his washstand.

As fast as he could, he tossed the clothes he'd been wearing aside and bathed in his washbasin, using the lemon-scented soap Katya liked. When that was done, he toweled off and threw open his wardrobe to pick out crisp, clean, and stylish clothes. Ones that were easy to remove. Katya's note had been clear. His presence was *required* at once. They both knew what that meant.

As soon as he was dressed, he dragged a comb through his hair, then left his room a mess as he dashed back into the hall. Galston would clean it up. That's what he paid the man for.

"You can't be called away at a time like this, Papa," Cece called after him once again as he whisked past her room and down the stairs. "We've far too much to do. The Queen—"

"I don't understand why all you young girls are so eager to kneel before that old harridan," Malcolm barked as he descended the stairs.

"Papa!" Cece scolded, fists on her hips as she glared down at him. "Your Scotch is showing. Don't say things like that outside of the house."

As he reached the door, Malcolm turned to send his daughter an impish wink. How he'd managed to produce offspring that loved an English queen so much was a mystery to him. He didn't have time to contemplate it, though. His carriage was at the door already when Galston opened it for him, and Katya was waiting.

The short ride seemed interminable. Malcolm tapped his foot against the carriage's floor the whole time, feeling far more self-satisfied than he should. It was one thing for Katya to come when he sent her a note letting her know he needed her, but it was far rarer for her to send for him. Their system had been in place for more than a decade, though, and had successfully enabled them to carry on like lunatic children— or perhaps not children exactly—without their friends knowing about it. Peter would probably shake his head and call him a damn fool if he knew how fast he jumped when Katya crooked her finger.

He was out of the carriage and at Katya's front door within moments, and was pleased when Katya's butler, Stewart, opened the door without him having to knock. Malcolm smoothed his hand over his hair one final time, breathed into his hand to check his breath, and put on his most seductive grin as he marched straight toward the stairs that led up to her bedroom.

"Malcolm, wherever do you think you're going?" Katya called to him from her front parlor.

Malcolm froze with his foot raised to mount the first stair. Prickles broke out on his skin as he turned to find her standing in the doorway, dressed in a plain afternoon dress, the bodice buttoned all the way up to her chin. Behind her, Malcolm spotted Dowland and Craig sitting on sofas that faced each other. Both men stared at him with surprised looks.

Heat rose up Malcolm's neck. There was nothing he could do to stop it from breaking out on his face. He hid his wrenching disappointment with a glower and marched straight past Katya and into the parlor, pretending he hadn't made an utter ass of himself.

"What's the meaning of this?" he asked, his voice gruff.

Katya studied him with narrowed eyes and a twitch to her mouth that said she knew exactly what was going on in his mind. The vixen had probably planned for him to make a fool of himself. "Sir Christopher is ready to make his report to Inspector Craig," she said. "I thought you'd want to hear it."

"I do," Malcolm grumbled, moving away from her to stand behind the sofa where Craig sat. His pride couldn't take the humiliation of standing next to Katya, knowing she was probably laughing at him.

Dowland looked like a confused stoat as he glanced from Malcolm to Katya to Craig, then back to Malcolm. "As I told Inspector Craig just now, I ended up visiting The Black Strap Club on two nights." His face was redder than Malcolm's, which was a strange kind of relief. "It's just as bad as you said it was," Dowland went on in an apprehensive voice. "The staff, if you can call them that, treated my first visit as though it were a special event of some kind. I was taken to an alarmingly decorated salon at first and given a complete menu of the services the place offered."

"A menu?" Craig said, sitting forward with a frown.

Dowland nodded and swallowed. "Some of the offerings were startling. Most of them were."

"Was it printed, this menu?" Craig asked, the excitement of discovering exactly what he needed pouring off of him.

"Yes," Dowland answered, wiping his mouth. "With illustrations for some things."

"That's new," Katya said, moving to sit beside Dowland. She rested a hand on his arm. It was probably a comforting gesture, considering how upset the man clearly was, but Malcolm hated it all the same. He needed comforting too, dammit.

He also needed to keep his head on if he was going to defeat Shayles at last. "Shayles will argue that was all a charade and that the menu was a joke unless you have evidence to back it up," he said.

"Oh, I have evidence," Dowland said with a doleful look.

"What evidence?" Craig scooted to the edge of the sofa, looking like he would either fall off the edge or spring to his feet.

"Screams, for one." Dowland rubbed a hand over his face, eyes squeezed shut. "We walked past a hallway, and I heard a woman screaming and begging for mercy." His voice faltered, and he drew in a long breath as though trying not to be sick.

"Go on," Katya prompted him softly.

Dowland shook his head. "I figured it wouldn't be enough for me to pick some poor girl and lock myself away with her for an hour," he went on. "So I pretended I was curious about some of the...stranger things on that damnable menu. Shayles himself was there, and he took me on what he called 'the grand tour'. We went down to what I can only describe as a dungeon."

"I've seen it," Malcolm growled. He'd rescued a young American woman named Noelle Walters from that very dungeon a few years before.

"Then you know how utterly hellish it is," Dowland said, glancing to him like they were comrades sharing a horrible secret.

As much as Malcolm wanted to despise the man for the way Katya sat so close to him and offered such sweet support, after a look like that, he rather liked the man.

"There was more than just the dungeon, though," Dowland went on. "The entire club is packed full of what looked to me like devices of torture."

"Photographs might sway a judge," Craig said as if talking to himself. "They would at least warrant an indictment."

"But the very worst of it was the women," Dowland said, more haunted than ever. He shook his head, his face contorting with misery. "I don't know which was worse, the ones who were trying to look appealing or the ones who cowered as if praying not to be seen. And they were young, too young. The cosmetics couldn't hide the bruises on some of them," he reported in a rush.

"I know," Katya said in her most soothing voice, stroking his arm. "Rest assured, my girls on the inside do whatever they can to help those unfortunate women."

"I've heard enough," Craig said in a surprisingly vicious growl.

He stood and began pacing, tension rippling off of him. His face was mottled with anger, and his blue eyes burned with fury. Malcolm would have bet his entire fortune that a woman Craig had cared for in the past had been abused in some way. He knew that kind of fury, had lived with it night and day since meeting Tessa and rescuing her from Shayles's clutches.

"We have to bring Shayles to justice," Malcolm said, meeting Craig's eyes and holding them. The time had come to lay all his cards on the table. "My late wife was once married to that bastard. He treated her no differently than he does the women in that club now. I was barely able to save her, but saving one woman from treatment like that is not enough. We need to save them all. I think you know that more than most."

A light of understanding shone in Craig's eyes. "I do," he said, communicating far more with two words than most men did with lengthy speeches. "And we will."

"So it was all worth it?" Dowland asked, glancing between Malcolm and Craig.

"It was," Katya answered, the softness in her voice turning to steel.

"I'll start the ball rolling immediately," Craig said, cutting around the sofa and heading to the door. "We need physical evidence from the club itself, as well as photographic evidence, and in order to get all that without Lord Shayles getting wind of the impending raid, we'll have to act fast." He turned back to them as he reached the door. "Very fast."

"How fast?" Katya asked, rising from the sofa and meeting Malcolm halfway across the room as he followed Craig into the hall. Dowland got up on shaky legs and followed them.

"Like lightning," Craig told her, absolute determination in his eyes.

An odd sort of excitement buzzed through Malcolm's

entire body. For nearly twenty years he'd been fighting against Shayles, putting everything he had into bringing the man to justice. His pursuit of the man had stopped him from taking holidays, interrupted relationships, and haunted his every step for almost half his life. Now, all of a sudden, he stood on the precipice of ending the war with a decisive victory. It seemed unreal.

"This may sound odd," Katya spoke into the sizzling silence that had followed Craig's single word, "but would you care to stay for supper, gentlemen?" She glanced to Craig and Dowland, sending Malcolm a final look as though she assumed he would stay.

"I wish I could," Craig said, some of his tension loosening, "but this needs to be dealt with immediately."

"Oh, but you must stay." Bianca practically leapt into the hall from around the corner of the doorway to a private, family parlor across the hall from the front parlor. Natalia peeked around the corner after her.

Malcolm rolled his eyes, wondering how much of the frightening conversation Katya's two wildcats had overheard and how long they'd been spying.

"Land sakes, you two," Katya exclaimed, pressing a hand to her forehead as though they'd given her a sudden migraine. "Am I going to have to lock you in chains and throw you in the cellar?"

Dowland made a strangled sound, his expression twisting with misery. Katya instantly looked contrite, but it was Craig's amused grin as he studied Bianca that caught Malcolm's attention.

"I'm tempted to stay for supper after all, if it means I have the pleasure of such lively entertainment," Craig said, the formal words sounding odd in his bastardized accent.

"Please stay." Bianca swept forward, making doe-eyes at Craig. "You could escort me in to supper and sit next to me. I promise I won't bite." She twitched an eyebrow, much the same way Katya had when she was that age and too young to know how obvious the gesture was.

Craig seemed to be eating the whole thing up. "I'm certain you're a brilliant conversationalist, Miss...."

"Bianca," Bianca informed him, sweeping even closer. "Lady Bianca Marlowe, at your service." She held out her hand, presumably for Craig to kiss.

Malcolm couldn't let the farce go on. "She's seventeen," he said, glancing from Craig to Katya.

Instantly, Craig's expression shifted from overt interest to embarrassed caution, and he pulled his hand back before he could touch Bianca's. He peeked at Katya. "I'm terribly sorry, my lady. I didn't realize."

"It's not your fault," Katya said, glaring at Bianca. "Go change for supper."

"But Mama," Bianca said through clenched teeth.

"Go," Katya told her in a warning voice.

Bianca growled in frustration, then turned a charming smile on Craig, as if the man hadn't just witnessed the entire childish exchange. "It was a pleasure to meet you, Inspector Craig," she said, curtsied, then did her best to march up the stairs with dignity. She might have managed it if Natalia hadn't dashed out of her hiding place to scurry up the stairs after her.

"So that's no to supper then?" Malcolm said with a sly grin for Craig.

"Not for a few more years at least," Craig answered. He nodded to Katya. "Good evening, my lady."

With a final nod to Malcolm and Dowland, Craig turned to go.

"I must decline your kind invitation as well, Lady Stanhope," Dowland said. "I'm afraid I don't have much of an appetite at the moment."

"Understandable," Katya said, taking Dowland's arm and escorting him to the door. "Another time, perhaps?"

"Certainly."

Malcolm stood where he was, trying not to seethe with envy at the way Katya fussed over the man as Stewart handed him his coat and hat and saw him out the door. As soon as Dowland was gone, Katya turned back to Malcolm wearing the smile he'd hoped to see from her when he arrived.

"We're so close," she said, crossing the hall and sliding easily into his arms. "So close I can taste it."

Her sudden burst of amorousness knocked Malcolm off-guard. "After all these years."

He leaned close, intending to kiss her, but the front door flew open again, revealing Cece, followed by Stewart and one of Katya's footmen carrying trunks. Katya leapt out of Malcolm's arms, and he stepped back, pretending he and Katya hadn't been about to light any fires.

"Papa," Cece scolded the moment she saw him, not a trace of surprise in her expression. "I tried to tell you that if you had just waited for me, we could have come here together." She shook her head and muttered, "Called away indeed," under her breath.

"What are you doing here?" Malcolm asked, more alarmed than he cared to admit.

Cece stopped a few feet in front of him and let out an impatient breath. "My presentation at court is tomorrow. Lady Stanhope is my sponsor. We agreed that the whole family should stay the night here so that we can all travel to Buckingham Palace together bright and early tomorrow morning."

Malcolm glanced to Katya in confusion. "Aren't you staying at my house tonight?"

Katya blinked at him. "You didn't remember? We decided

it was less of a hassle to have two people relocate to Stanhope House instead of all four of us packing into your house,
since the girls insist on not being left out." Katya rolled
her eyes.

The faint echo of something Cece had said to him a few
days before, deep in the middle of his preoccupation with
Dowland's part in their mission against Shayles, and in
possible connections between Dowland and Katya, came to
mind. "Of course I remembered," he said.

Katya shook her head at him. "Stewart can get the two of
you settled. Supper will be served within the hour." She
launched into motion herself, as though there were a thou-
sand things to do to prepare for what amounted to a small,
family meal. "You can keep yourself occupied until we eat,
can't you?" she asked him as Cece headed upstairs, Stewart
and the footman following her.

"Yes, of course," Malcolm said.

"Good."

Katya moved past him, her hand brushing his as she did.
A jolt of excitement coursed through him. Maybe the visit
wouldn't be without comfort after all.

As much as she enjoyed subtlety and the clever dance
of politics and society, few things filled Katya with as much
of a sense of contentment as a family dinner. Especially
when family included Malcolm and Cece. Between the six of
them—her and Malcolm, Cece and Rupert, and Bianca and
Natalia—there were always at least five conversations
happening simultaneously. Robert would have had a second
heart-attack if he could have seen the way his children
carried on at the table, the girls expressing their opinions as
loudly as Rupert. But Robert wasn't there, God rest him, and
what society couldn't see wouldn't hurt it.

"We should all sleep in my room tonight," Bianca suggested to the other girls with an excited gasp as they finished their pudding. "That way we can talk about all the gentlemen who are likely to ask Cece to dance at the ball tomorrow night."

"If you all pitch your tents in the same room tonight, none of you will sleep a wink," Rupert said. Katya detected a hint of temper in his words, probably at the thought that other men would want to dance with Cece.

"That's the point," Natalia told him, rolling her eyes.

"Young women apparently don't need sleep," Malcolm added, his expression surprisingly similar to Natalia's.

Katya hid her grin by taking a last sip of wine. "If you truly want to stay up all night and have dark circles under your eyes when you're presented to the Queen tomorrow, then by all means, do so with my blessing," she said with only a touch of sarcasm.

Malcolm grinned in approval at her across the table.

"You have a point, Lady Stanhope," Cece said with a sigh, then sent a covert smile to Bianca. "Although we could stay up for a bit to discuss a certain gentleman I saw leaving the house as I arrived."

Bianca burst into a giggle, Natalia following suit shortly thereafter. Rupert rose from the table with a sigh, throwing his serviette down.

"I, for one, want to be well-rested for tomorrow's activities, so I'm going to bed," he said.

"I think I might turn in early as well," Malcolm said, not quite meeting anyone's eyes. He stood and walked around the corner of the table to kiss Cece's forehead. "Sleep well, my darling." As he stepped away from her he added, "That's an order, by the way, not a suggestion."

"Oh, Papa," Cece replied with a laugh.

Katya stood as Malcolm reached her end of the table. "I

think I'll head up to bed as well," she said, doing a far better job of appearing innocent than Malcolm was. "You young things might be able to look fresh and vibrant after a night without sleep, but when you reach my age, it takes a great deal more effort."

"Mama, you're always beautiful and you know it," Bianca said with a sweet smile.

Katya's heart thumped with maternal affection for her daughter, but she arched a brow and said, "You're not going to the ball and you know it. Your presentation is next year, and I'm not willing to put up with wagging tongues if you show up at Spencer House before you're officially out."

"But Mama," Bianca deflated, looking more like a girl than a woman. "It's eighteen-eighty-one. Nobody cares about those silly rules anymore."

"Yes, they do," Katya told her. "So behave."

Malcolm had already moved into the hall, doing a poor job of pretending he wasn't waiting for her as he did, so Katya only gave Bianca one, parting look of warning before sweeping out of the room herself.

"When I'm out," Bianca grumbled behind her, "I'm not going to let a bunch of silly society rules keep me from doing exactly what I want."

"You will if you want to be received by anybody who's anybody," Cece told her.

"Smart girl, your daughter," Katya whispered as she caught up to Malcolm at the base of the stairs.

"Obviously," Malcolm whispered back as he took her hand and hurried up the stairs. "What brilliance has she displayed this time?"

"Warning Bianca that she can't flout all the rules if she wants to have a place at society's table," Katya said.

"I'm surprised you would think so," Malcolm said, as they

reached the top of the stairs and tip-toed down the hall. "You've never played by society's rules."

She turned to him with wide-eyed surprise as they reached the door to her room. "Of course I have. Rule number one is discretion. The finer ladies of society may whisper about me, but they can't prove anything."

She followed her bold statement by sending a covert glance down the hall to be certain they weren't being observed. As soon as she was satisfied, she opened her bedroom door as carefully as possible and whisked Malcolm inside. He chuckled as he went, shrugging out of his jacket as soon as Katya had the door shut.

"Observe," she told him in a voice that was still hushed, reaching for the lock. "This is how properly discreet women conduct their affairs." She arched her eyebrow and turned the lock until the tumblers clicked.

"I didn't expect Cece to come rushing into my room the other night," Malcolm argued, sitting on the edge of her bed to take off his shoes.

"Really, Malcolm," Katya shook her head at him as she crossed to her vanity and began pulling the pins from her elaborate hairstyle. "The first rule of illicit romance is to always lock the doors."

"You're full of rules tonight, Lady Stanhope." Malcolm rose from the bed, tossed his shoes aside, and crossed the room to her. He slid his arms around her waist and nibbled at her neck. "One would almost think you were in a mood for discipline this evening."

She laughed, loving the way his bold suggestion sent a thrill through her that was as fresh as the first time he'd snuck into her bedroom...when she was barely older than Bianca was now.

She turned to him, a strange sort of nostalgia making her

wistful. "We don't need games and ploys to be together," she said, resting a hand on his cheek.

"No," he agreed, mischief in his eyes. "But they are fun."

She burst into laughter, the sound far louder then she'd intended. Her gaze darted to the door, but Malcolm silenced any other noise that could have given them away with a kiss. His hands roved her side, knowing exactly what he wanted from her. She circled her arms around his shoulders for a moment, indulging in the delicious familiarity of his mouth. A new lover every night was exciting to a point, but at her age, she craved the tender and the familiar.

Their kiss ended only when they were both so aroused that clothing became a burden. With a sigh, she stepped away from him, reaching for the fastenings of her skirt. "Someday," she said as she turned her back so that Malcolm could undo her buttons, "they'll make clothing for women that doesn't require a second set of hands to remove."

"What a horrible day that will be," Malcolm replied.

Katya grinned and undressed as quickly as she could. Once her buttons were done, Malcolm stepped away to shed his clothes. He tossed them over the chair instead of folding them neatly, as usual, missing the chair entirely as he threw off his drawers.

"Really, Malcolm," she clucked, taking more care with her chemise and drawers. "Is it so hard to fold your things?"

"It's so hard. Let's leave it at that."

Of all the things that could turn her heart to butter and make her consider swallowing her pride to marry him, it had to be ribald comments like that. Heat flushed through her and her heart felt years younger as she crossed to the bed, where he was pulling back the covers.

"You're impossible, you realize," she said.

Instead of answering, when she drew close enough, he spun and sat abruptly on the side of the bed, tugging her off-balance and drawing her, face-down, across his lap. Before she could regain her equilibrium, he smacked her backside hard. The surprise sting was ridiculously arousing. He spanked her again, sending the ache between her legs into a full-fledged inferno.

"Malcolm, what are you doing?" she laughed in spite of the sting and the ache.

"You deserve a few more smacks for the way you've been flirting with Dowland this week," he said, trying to sound stern. She knew him too well to buy the act, though. There was too much humor in his voice.

"I was not fli—"

He brought his hand down hard on her backside, and she finished her sentence with a loud yelp.

A noise in the hall instantly made her swallow what was either going to be a shout of protest or a plea for more.

"Mama, are you all right in there?" Natalia's voice came from the other side of the door.

Malcolm tensed and cursed under his breath.

"I'm fine, sweeting," Katya called out. "I stubbed my toe on the washstand." She deserved a royal commendation for her acting abilities.

"All right, then," Natalia said. "Be careful. Good night."

"Good night, dear."

She and Malcolm remained frozen as they listened to Natalia's retreating footsteps, whispers from more than one of the girls in the hall, and finally, a door shutting. Then Malcolm smacked her backside again.

"Stop, stop, Malcolm," Katya said through a rush of embarrassed and relieved laughter. "One of them might be lurking on the other side of the door. You know they all suspect what we're up to."

"If they're listening," Malcolm murmured, "you'll just have to stay quiet as I do this."

He brushed his hand across her pleasantly hot backside, delving his fingers into the cleft between her legs. She gasped as he stroked the wet folds of her sex, the unusual angle of his attentions adding to her arousal. He was relentless in pleasuring her, and he knew exactly how to tease her into what promised to be a fast orgasm. He also knew just when to pull back, leaving her sweating and hungry for more.

"I doubt the likes of Christopher Dowland can make you feel like that," he purred.

His words were as good as a pail of cold water to douse her mood. She yanked away from him, standing with a sigh. "Would you kindly stop being a jealous prick?" she asked.

"As soon as you stop making eyes at every man that walks past you," he said, clearly still thinking they were playing.

She shifted to straddle his knees, then pushed his shoulders with her full strength. He lost his balance and splayed on his back, giving her the opportunity to position herself over him and pin him beneath her.

"For the last time, Malcolm. I am not the whore you seem to think I am," she said unable to keep the genuine anger from her voice.

"I never said you—"

She silenced his tired old protest with a kiss, but it was a kiss on her terms. She loved Malcolm, far more than she was willing to admit to herself most of the time. But the man was an ass more often than not.

He responded to her show of dominance by circling his arms around her and kissing her as though he was the one who had started it all. His cock jutted between them, a reminder that they both gained something from their ridiculous relationship. But that was the problem. She didn't want to do without him, without all the ways he made her feel, both physically and emotionally. Even without a ring on her finger, he could still hold what little power she had in the world hostage.

"What's wrong?" he answered as her thoughts sapped her energy. He rolled her to her back, sliding all the way into bed with her.

"Nothing," she said, looking away from him.

"You're angry with me," he said, positioning himself between her legs.

She cursed herself for wriggling her hips in invitation and for feeling so relieved when he pushed inside of her.

"I'm angry with the world," she admitted as they moved together. He felt so good inside her, like they could actually be one in life as well as in bed.

"I'll change the world for you," he said, stroking her leg and lifting her thigh higher against his hips. "If you'll let me."

She sighed and dug her nails into his back, closing her eyes so that she could block out everything but the bliss of making love. If she let him, Malcolm would trap her in a marriage as constrictive as the one Robert had caged her in. She could see the same masculine determination to tame, to control, and to make her submit in his eyes that she'd seen in Robert. But sometimes it felt so divine to give in to his will, to have him use her as he saw fit.

"I love you, Katya," he sighed, picking up his pace. The tension she could feel coiled in him drove her mad with desire and frustration. "I love you."

I love you too, she thought, tears stinging at her eyes. If only loving him didn't mean losing everything.

CHAPTER 7

*M*alcolm always slept better with Katya in his arms. In fact, he slept a little too well. The first rays of dawn were peeking through her curtains as he drifted awake the next morning. The house was already alive with thumps and footsteps, and all Malcolm could do was pray that it was the servants making the noise and not any of the children.

He scrambled out of Katya's bed as deftly as his sated, old body could manage, knees creaking as he searched the floor for his clothes from the night before.

"Why are you making all that noise?" Katya asked in half-asleep tones, rolling to her side to face him. She was even more beautiful disheveled from sleep—and other things—than she was in full, formal regalia.

"I need to get to my guest room before the children wake up," Malcolm whispered. He sat on the edge of the bed to pull on his socks, but was up again in a flash.

"All right," Katya sighed, settling against the pillow again and closing her eyes. "If you want to go through all the trouble."

Malcolm frowned at her. It was her reputation he was protecting by not being found in bed with her. Their children weren't young anymore, and the damned things had grown far too clever for their own good.

With his shirt, waistcoat, and jacket unbuttoned and his shoes in his hand, he unlocked Katya's door and tip-toed into the hall. As soon as he shut the door, he turned to find Rupert quietly shutting a door at the other end of the hall. Katya's son wore a robe, the hem of his pajamas peeking out at the bottom, and he hadn't yet shaved.

Malcolm felt a moment of panic as their eyes met—a sentiment that was reflected in Rupert's eyes. A split-second later, rage replaced guilt, and he nearly dropped his shoes.

"What the devil do you think you're doing, boy?" he growled, marching down the hall to stand toe-to-toe with Rupert. "If I find out you've interfered with Cece in any way—"

"This isn't her room, sir, it's mine," Rupert answered in a tight whisper. "How dare you suggest I would dishonor Cecelia that way?"

Malcolm wasn't sure whether to be embarrassed or not. "I know what it's like to be a young man in love," he said as justification. "But Cece is my daughter."

"And Katya is my mother," Rupert snapped.

Damn, the boy was quick. Carrying on with Katya had been much simpler when Rupert was tucked away in the nursery.

"She is," Malcolm nodded, fighting to keep the upper hand. "And she's perfectly capable of making her own decisions."

Before things could get even more awkward, Malcolm squared his shoulders and marched past Rupert to the unused guestroom that was supposed to be his. As he reached for the doorknob, he could have sworn he heard

Rupert chuckle. Once he was safely inside the room, he let his shoulders drop and made a face at himself in the mirror. He was far too old for these sorts of shenanigans.

It didn't take long for him to wash, shave, and dress in clean clothes. Katya's staff was highly efficient when it came to accommodating guests. Malcolm tried not to think about how often Katya had guests—particularly of a certain ilk— but he never had been any good at curbing his imagination, especially when it came to Katya. As much as he fought it, he couldn't help but wonder how long it would be before Christopher Dowland would be creeping down the hall in the early morning, pretending he'd been in the guest room all night.

"Don't be an ass," he told his reflection as he tied his tie and straightened his jacket. Katya was and always had been her own woman, and what she got up to on her own time was her business. Or so he insisted to himself. What he actually believed in his heart was another matter. If she would just stop being so stubborn and marry him already, things would be infinitely easier.

Thoughts of marriage were still foremost in his mind as he made his way down to the breakfast room, which was why he stopped short, his heart dropping to his feet, at the sight of Cece standing near the window in her elegant, white presentation gown, Bianca and Natalia with her. Malcolm barely noticed Katya's girls, though. His eyes were only for his own, darling angel.

"Good morning, Papa," she said with a radiant and excited smile.

Malcolm simply stood there and looked at her. He wasn't sure his heart could withstand her beauty. The girl whom he'd done his best to raise in a way that would make her mother proud wasn't a girl anymore. She looked more like Tessa than ever, with her honey-blonde hair caught up in a fashionable style, her blue eyes the same shape as Tessa's, and her smile freer than any Tessa had ever worn. There was no doubting whose daughter she was, though. Cece reminded him of everything he'd loved, everything he'd lost, and everything he continued to fight for.

"Papa, are you all right?" Cece stepped away from the window and her friends, coming to meet him in the doorway. "You look...well, honestly, you look as though you're about to cry."

"It's because I am," he answered in a strangled voice. "You look beautiful."

"Oh, Papa." Cece blushed and lowered her eyes, her modesty making her even more of an angel.

Malcolm opened his arms and stepped toward her to hug her, but paused. "I don't want to crease your gown," he said, lowering his arms and leaning in to kiss her cheek instead.

"Now you're going to make me cry," she said with a sniff. "I'm not finished getting ready, of course," she went on, stepping around the table to the side where Bianca and Natalia were taking their seats. "I still have to do my hair."

"What's wrong with your hair?" Malcolm asked, moving to the sideboard to fix a plate of breakfast.

"She still has to style it," Natalia informed him, as though she were an expert in all things pertaining to royal audiences. "Unmarried women wear two white ostrich feathers in their hair when they're presented to the Queen. And we have ever so many more decorations to go with those feathers."

"We bought special pins that day when we met Inspector Craig," Bianca said, a dreaminess in her eyes that wasn't for the pins at all.

"And while it's not the thing to wear cosmetics at court," Natalia went on, "we're going to try to figure out how to put a bit more rose in Cece's cheeks and lips."

Malcolm grunted and brought his plate to the table. A

moment later, Rupert strode into the room, looking far more presentable than he had earlier. He stopped short at the sight of Cece, looking as though he'd walked into a dream. That put the rose in Cece's cheeks, all right.

The moment was precious, but it ended all too soon when Rupert glanced sideways toward Malcolm. "Good morning, sir," Rupert greeted him, clearing his throat and avoiding Malcolm's eyes.

"Morning," Malcolm answered, far more interested in his plate than the breakfast fare warranted.

The girls glanced between the two of them with puzzled expressions, but quickly went back to fawning over Cece.

In spite of the awkwardness of that moment, breakfast was a far more agreeable experience than Malcolm was used to his meals being. Katya arrived last and made an entrance, of course.

"What a charming and well-turned-out bunch you are," she said, looking like a page from a French fashion journal herself in a blue gown that brought out the rich darkness of her eyes. She sat immediately at the foot of the table, opposite Rupert at the head, and reached for the teapot.

"Aren't you going to eat anything?" Malcolm asked her.

Katya made a noise, her eyes wide with wariness. "I'm far too anxious about today to eat a bite."

"Really?" Bianca said, sending a sly smile between her and Malcolm. "I'd've thought you'd worked up quite an appetite last night."

Malcolm nearly spit out the gulp of tea he'd just taken. Heat rose up his neck to his face, and he wasn't sure whether to avoid Bianca's impish grin or to take her to task for it.

Katya stopped pouring and glared at her daughter. "Hold your tongue or you'll be sitting out today's activities."

"Really, Mama," Bianca huffed. "You can scold and threaten me all you'd like, but you aren't fooling anyone." She

glanced to Malcolm to make sure he understood the statement applied to him as well.

Malcolm set down his cup and frowned. "I am astounded
at the level of insolence at this table. It might not be my place
to reprimand another's children, but really, girls. If you show
this kind of cheek in public, you'll be banned from society in
no time."

"I don't care about society," Natalia declared, tilting her
chin up.

"We're sorry, Papa," Cece rushed to apologize. Her color
was still high, though, and mischief sparkled in her eyes. "But
you really aren't fooling anyone."

"I just think it's hypocritical for Mama to spend the night
with Lord Malcolm when she won't even let me say hello to
Inspector Craig," Bianca said, stabbing at her sausage.

Katya was in the middle of stirring her tea and set her
spoon down with a loud clatter. "Enough," she snapped.
"Lord Malcolm is right. The two of you are behaving far
beyond the pale."

Bianca and Natalia shrank a bit in their seats, their smug
grins disappearing.

"No, Lord Malcolm and I aren't fooling anyone," Katya
went on. "Not in this house, at least. Yes, we're lovers. We
have been for decades."

"Decades?" Natalia blinked.

"You're not ignorant babies anymore," Katya continued.
"Heaven knows you haven't been raised in what society
thinks of as the proper way. I've always been free with information when you've wanted to know things, and so I'll tell
you this, if only so that you'll bite your tongues in the future.
People live all sorts of different lives. Sometimes they marry
and sail through their lives as happy as characters in a fairy
story. Sometimes they don't. And sometimes they find happiness when and where they can, even if it comes outside of

the prescribed norms. The secret of life is to know when to declare yourself and when to conduct your business in private. Do I make myself clear?"

"Yes, Mama," Bianca answered, meek on the surface, though Malcolm detected a spark of cunning in her eyes.

"Natalia?" Katya asked.

Natalia stared at her plate with a curious frown. At last, she took a breath and looked up. "What do you mean, 'decades'?"

Katya's righteous anger shifted into a tired—and perhaps slightly sheepish—sigh. She glanced to Malcolm, one eyebrow raised as though asking for help.

The corner of Malcolm's mouth twitched. "Don't look at me. I'm still waiting to see how far you're going to go to ruin my reputation in my daughter's eyes."

He spoke with enough humor in his tone that Cece merely laughed. "Oh, Papa. Your reputation isn't ruined at all. I've known you and Lady Stanhope were carrying on since I was twelve."

That had Malcolm's brow shooting up. "You have?"

"I've known since I was ten," Rupert said from the end of the table as he scanned the headlines in *The Times*, as uninvolved in the conversation as it was possible to be.

Katya didn't look surprised, but Bianca's jaw dropped in outrage. "Why didn't you tell me?" she asked her brother.

"It wasn't appropriate to discuss," Rupert said, turning a page of the newspaper.

"There," Katya said, picking up her teacup. "At last, some sense."

"This is so unfair," Bianca sighed.

"Did you meet for the first time before I was born?" Natalia asked, strangely quiet.

"Yes," Malcolm answered. There didn't seem to be any point in denying things now. In for a penny, in for a pound.

Katya wore a much more cautious expression, however. In fact, it bordered on alarm. "It was a long time ago," she said, sipping her tea as though thinking about it.

"My first wife, Cecelia's mother, Tessa, had recently died," Malcolm explained to Natalia. "Your mother was so kind and helpful as I dealt with that grief."

Bianca's eyes went wide, and she jerked to look at Katya. "You were still married to Father?"

Katya flushed, but there was a hardness about her face that wasn't embarrassment. "My marriage to your father was not a love match," she said in a tight voice. "We've discussed this before. And we will not be discussing it further at the breakfast table. Particularly not when we need to leave for Buckingham Palace within the hour."

Cece gasped, glancing to the clock that stood on the mantle at the far end of the room. "Oh, dear," she said, pushing her chair back and leaping to her feet. "I have so much to do and not enough time to do it in."

"I'll help you," Bianca said, standing as well. She hooked her arm through Cece's and started to rush her out of the room, sending Katya a disappointed look as she went.

"I'll help as well," Natalia said, rising more slowly. She followed her sister and Cece, but frowned at Malcolm as she left the room.

When only Malcolm, Katya, and Rupert were left at the table, Malcolm huffed out a breath and sagged back in his chair.

"Strangely enough, exposing my past to my daughter and looking like a fool for it wasn't on my calendar for things to do today," he said, though if he were honest, he wasn't sure whether to be angry or relieved that he wouldn't have to hide things anymore.

"They all knew," Katya said with feigned calm. And it was feigned. Malcolm knew her well enough to sense something about the conversation they'd just had was deeply unsettling to her. "It's better to have it out in the open, now that they're all adults."

"I wouldn't say Natalia is an adult yet," Rupert commented, turning another page of the newspaper. "I'll talk to her about keeping family business within the family."

Rupert didn't see the stung look Katya sent across the table to him, but Malcolm did. It was painful. Without notice or effort, Rupert had usurped what had been her duty since the girls were born. An odd pang formed in Malcolm's chest. Katya was a proud woman, God knew. He'd wrestled with her pride for years, but he'd never dented it. He'd never wanted to. Yet with one sentence, Rupert had reduced her to second-rate importance.

"Do you want me to talk to Stewart about bringing the carriage around?" Malcolm offered, searching for a way he could help.

Katya turned the same, stung look on him. "I'm perfectly capable of directing my own staff," she said, rising and marching from the room.

Malcolm sighed, taking one final bite of sausage before rising himself.

"Don't mind them," Rupert said, folding his newspaper. "Everyone's overexcited today because of the presentation."

Malcolm shook his head. "You have a lot to learn about being a true man, Lord Stanhope," he said, standing. "You've wounded your mother terribly."

Rupert blinked, startled. "I have?"

Malcolm sighed and shook his head before marching out of the room.

He wasn't able to find Katya, which worried him. Although it didn't worry him for long. Within minutes, the whirlwind of the girls was back, and preparations for departure got underway. Malcolm had his hands full keeping the girls from giggling themselves stupid and aggravating the staff while they did so.

Katya appeared just as they were about to leave the house and pile into the carriage. By all outward appearances, she was as elegant as always, but Malcolm was certain it was all a show.

"Are you all right?" he asked as they climbed into the carriage along with the girls. Wisely, Rupert had chosen to ride his horse behind them, but five people, even in an open carriage, was tight.

"I'll be fine," Katya replied as the carriage jostled into motion. "I just hate getting old."

Malcolm grunted and reached for her hand under the folds of their coats. "I know exactly how you feel, though I would argue that you're hardly old."

She smiled at him, and for a moment, the world was right again. The drive to Buckingham Palace was a pleasant one. The April sunshine was warmer than usual, which was a blessing. As they drew closer to the palace, more carriages transporting excited young women and their doting mamas could be seen. People were lining the roads near the palace to get a look at them all. When, at last, they joined the queue of carriages waiting to let debutantes out at the palace door, the crowds were smiling and waving.

"Mama," Natalia asked as the ripple of impatience was making them all restless. She'd been surprisingly silent through the whole ride, leaving Cece and Bianca to do the chattering.

"Yes, dear?" Katya turned to Natalia.

Natalia pressed her lips together, her brow knitting in a frown. "I've just been thinking."

"Always a good idea," Malcolm said, praying they'd make it to the front of the line soon.

Natalia glanced at him with a deeply assessing look, then back to Katya. "Is Lord Malcolm my father?"

Malcolm started to laugh.

Katya remained stony-faced and silent, color splashing her cheeks.

Malcolm's laughter died, and a slipping, swooping sensation filled his gut. His pulse kicked up, and suddenly he couldn't breathe. Eyes wide, he glanced to Natalia. He'd always thought she looked a great deal like Katya, with her dark hair and eyes. But there was something in the shape of her mouth and chin, in the stubborn determination she sometimes showed. He shifted to study Cece, whose mouth had dropped open in shock as the truth dawned on her as well. Yes, there was a resemblance there.

"Kat," he snapped, his voice barely more than a whisper. He glanced to her, numbness spreading through him at her downcast eyes and guilty expression. "Why didn't you tell me?"

The carriage jerked forward, bringing them to the front of the queue. Footmen in royal livery stepped forward to open the carriage door, one of them offering a hand to Cece.

"Kat," Malcolm repeated. "Look at me."

Slowly, with pain pinching her mouth and fear in her eyes, Katya glanced up at him. The truth was there in every guilty line of her face. Natalia was his.

CHAPTER 8

*I*t wasn't supposed to happen that way. Katya had spent years debating whether it should happen at all. Natalia deserved more than to be branded a bastard and treated as an object of rage, which was exactly the look in Malcolm's eyes now. That didn't stop Katya's stomach from twisting, or keep her from second-guessing the secret she'd held onto for sixteen years.

"My lady?" the palace footman prompted her, clearing his throat.

Cece and Bianca had already stepped down from the carriage, although they stood to the side, eyes wide. Natalia sat frozen in her seat, her face pale as she studied Malcolm with new understanding. Malcolm looked as though everything had vanished around him and that the two of them and betrayal were the only things left in the world.

It couldn't go on like that.

Katya took a breath, forcing herself to appear calm and in control of the situation in spite of the tempest in her soul. "Now is not the time, Malcolm," she said, moving to take the footman's hand and alight from the carriage.

"When is the time, then?" He followed her, helping Natalia down as he did.

The fire in his eyes was enough to melt a lesser man, but Katya had withstood much worse. Though it was harder to keep a hold on the belief that right was on her side.

"Cecelia is about to be presented to the queen," Katya snapped, rounding on him as he marched to within inches of her. "Kindly keep your fury in check."

"Like you keep everything you feel in check?" he bit back at her. "How much have you hidden from me over the years? What other secrets are you keeping?"

"More than you want to know," she hissed, darting a quick glance around.

Rupert had just dismounted and handed his horse over to one of the palace grooms. "What's going on?" he asked the anxious group of girls, all of them glued to the confrontation as though it were a play.

"Mama just admitted that Lord Malcolm is Natalia's father," Bianca whispered.

"He's what?" Rupert bellowed.

Several people waiting in line to enter the palace turned toward them. So much for discretion. Every tenant that Katya had built her life upon was shaking at its foundation, but she would not let the whole thing collapse.

"Lips shut, tongues bit," she told her daughters and Cece. "That's the first lesson all of you need to learn if you want to call yourselves grown women."

"Yes," Malcolm seconded with venom in his voice. "Bottle it all up. Keep those secrets locked away. Never give a man any reason to trust you."

"Malcolm," Katya snapped, glaring at him. His bitterness banished any guilt that lingered in her. His reaction was exactly why she'd kept the truth to herself. "Remember where you are."

He surprised her by clamping a hand on her arm and marching her to the side of the slow-moving line of debutantes and their sponsors entering the palace. "I had a right to know," he hissed once they were hidden from view by a parked carriage.

"You did not," Katya said through clenched teeth. "Natalia is my daughter. I brought her into this world, alone and in pain."

"You should have told me."

"You abandoned me to a life of isolation with a man I didn't love," she said with a startling burst of emotion, as if those agonizing days were yesterday instead of nearly two decades ago.

"Robert was your husband," Malcolm said, glancing away, guilt of his own pinching his features.

"And did your attack of conscience help either of us?" Katya asked. She shook her head. "Robert knew Natalia wasn't his, but he was willing to accept her as his own."

"And then he died." Malcolm turned his glare on her again. "You should have told me then."

"When I was newly widowed with three children under the age of five? I was nearly a child myself, not even twenty-three, and suddenly the duties of an earldom were on my shoulders."

"I would have been there for you," he insisted, his anger now mingled with regret. "I would have married you in an instant."

"And taken everything away from me all over again." She shook her head. "I'd already had my life wrenched away from me once. I'd had enough of being put in my place, relegated to an ornament in a man's household. I wasn't about to give up the power that had been handed to me just so you could soothe your guilty conscience."

"I loved you," he argued, passion of all sorts in his voice.

"You loved Tessa. I was merely a distraction from your grief. I always have been."

The truth Katya hadn't dared to admit to herself felt like a knife in her gut. Tears stung at her eyes, but she wasn't about to give in to them. She sucked in a breath and stood straight, marching past Malcolm with her head held high.

"Where are you going?" Malcolm demanded, striding after her.

"Your daughter—Tessa's daughter—is being presented at court, and it's my duty to accompany her," Katya answered without looking at him.

The girls and Rupert were waiting by the palace's grand entrance, looks of shock and worry in their eyes.

"Is everything all right, Mother?" Rupert asked, his formality clearly meant to intimidate Malcolm.

Katya laughed, half at her son's efforts to protect her from a man infinitely more powerful than him and half over the hopelessness of the situation. "Everything is fine, dear. Cecelia, are you ready?" She marched past the startled group into the doorway, turning back to beckon to Cece.

"I...uh...I'm ready." Cece sent a worried look to her father, started after Katya, second-guessed herself, then scurried back to a glowering Malcolm to kiss his cheek. "We'll work this out after the presentation, Papa," she said before hurrying after Katya.

The kiss didn't appear to do anything to soothe Malcolm's boiling temper. He glared at Katya with the look of anger that could only come from being betrayed by someone you loved with your whole heart. Katya wasn't foolish enough to think it was solely because of the revelation about Natalia. She met his eyes with implacable strength, knowing the entire history of their relationship had just boiled over. And there was nothing she could do about it.

"Watch after your sisters," she said, sending a look to Rupert.

Rupert nodded without a word, turning toward Malcolm as though he were a threat.

"My lady, you're needed," another of the palace staff said from inside the door.

"Yes, yes." Katya sighed and walked away from the debris of her life exploding to escort Cecelia into the palace.

"I'm sure Papa will calm down and view the situation rationally in time," Cece said as they joined the line of other debutantes being directed through the cavernous halls of Buckingham Palace. "He really is quite sensible. Except when he's upset."

"I'm sure you're right," Katya said, though she was anything but. She was willing to wager that she knew Malcolm better than his daughter did.

The two of them remained silent as they were ushered up a flight of stairs and into the anteroom where final preparations were being made for presentations. The mood of the room was excitement and joy, which formed a stark contrast with Katya's growing feeling of loss and grief.

"I have a sister," Cece said, her smile brightening as they stood waiting.

Katya blinked out of her anxious thoughts and managed a smile for her. "You do, in a way."

"I've always felt as though Bianca and Natalia were sisters of sorts," Cece went on. "I think I could get used to the idea of Natalia being a real sister."

"And Rupert being a sort of brother?" Katya asked, one brow raised.

Cece's smile dropped. "Oh, dear."

Instantly, Katya regretted the barbed comment. She regretted a lot more than that. "I'm so sorry to eclipse your special day, my dear," she sighed. "Today should be all about you."

"I don't hold any ill will toward you, Lady Stanhope," Cece assured her, resting a hand on Katya's arm. "Yes, it's exciting to meet the queen, but everyone knows that the purpose of coming out is to announce your availability on the marriage market. I have no need to do that." She blushed, glancing down modestly.

A whole new kind of fear rose up in Katya's chest. She placed a heavy hand on Cece's shoulder. "Please don't tell me you already have an understanding with my son."

Cece's blush deepened and she peeked up at Katya. "It isn't a formal understanding," she admitted. "He hasn't proposed or anything like that. But I believe we both know what we want."

"My darling, no." Katya gripped both of Cece's shoulders and faced her squarely. "You're only eighteen. Don't do that to yourself."

Cece blinked at her in surprise. "I would have thought…."

Katya shook her head. "I was given away in marriage within weeks of my eighteenth birthday, and I gave birth to Rupert before I was nineteen. I wouldn't wish that life on you for all the world."

"I'm sorry that happened to you," Cece said, her expression flashing between sheepish and determined. "But Rupert and I are in love."

"It doesn't matter," Katya said. "Listen to me." Cece met her eyes. "There is so much more to life than being someone's wife. That's what your father doesn't understand. You have a life of your own, and you deserve to live it. You have mountains to climb, oceans to sail, fields to plant and sew. You have a whole world to conquer."

"But there are so few things that a single woman can

accomplish," Cece argued, so like her father. "The law prohibits us from doing just about anything."

"Those laws can be changed," Katya insisted. "The more women stand up to defy them, the more we cherish our own lives and independence instead of depending on a man for our identity, the more we'll be able to change the world. I'm not saying you shouldn't marry Rupert," she rushed on. "I will rejoice when the day comes that I can call you my daughter in earnest, as confusing and muddled as that will be for all of us, what with your father and I. But don't be so quick to give up your youth and your power for the title of 'Mrs.' Once the babies start coming, and they will, sooner than you can imagine, your whole life will change. Live that life first. There will be time for the rest later."

Cece opened her mouth, but before she could reply, a steward near the front of the hall declared, "Ladies, the time has come."

He launched into an explanation of what the girls could expect as the procession line tightened and began to move forward. Katya and Cece moved with it.

"He will forgive you," Cece whispered as they drew near to the doorway of the throne room. "Papa will forgive you. As long as you forgive him."

MALCOLM WATCHED KATYA AND CECE RETREAT INTO THE palace, at war with himself over whether to charge after them and demand more answers or to charge off in the opposite direction, washing his hands of the whole thing once and for all. He didn't know what more Katya could say to him, or rather, he dreaded what other secrets she was keeping. Did she have more children hidden around the countryside? Ones that weren't his? Had she secretly married one of her numerous suitors behind his back? Or was he a damned fool for making her into more than a woman fighting to protect her children in his mind?

"Sir, if you could please step aside," the palace footman said, gesturing for Malcolm to move.

He did more than that, he swayed into motion, marching away from the palace entrance, through the line of carriages waiting to disgorge more debutantes or to travel on to the mews where they would wait, and headed for the gate.

"Where are you going?" Natalia shouted after him.

Malcolm winced, stopping a few yards into the courtyard, his boots crunching on the gravel. He wouldn't have stopped for anyone else, but Natalia was a whole new complication in his life.

Natalia followed his path, picking up her skirts and dodging between carriages to reach him. Bianca and Rupert followed closely behind. "You're my father," she said when she reached him.

"Apparently so." Malcolm didn't expect the awkwardness that crept up his spine, making him restless. "Sorry."

Natalia blinked. "What do you have to be sorry about? You didn't do anything." She blinked again, her shoulders dropping and her brow knitting into a frown. "Well, I suppose you did do something."

Malcolm writhed with discomfort. Most girls Natalia's age wouldn't have a clue about what he'd done to contribute to her birth, but Natalia was Katya's daughter, and Katya was far too free with knowledge.

He cleared his throat. "It was a long time ago."

"Sixteen years, I suppose," she said. "Or thereabouts."

"Quite," he said with a sharp nod, then glanced around for a way to escape. Nothing about the day, or about his life, had turned out the way he'd expected it to. He wasn't sure what he wanted to happen next, but standing around Buckingham

Palace waiting for a deceptive lover who didn't trust him with his own business was not it.

"You could be a little bit happy," Natalia said, a distinct note of disappointment in her voice.

Malcolm flinched. "I'm sure I will be, once I get over the shock," he admitted. If Katya was brutally honest with her girls, he could be too.

"I wonder why Mama kept me a secret from you for so long," Natalia went on, glancing to her brother and sister as they joined them. Their small group was drawing a great deal of attention from the stream of people attending the presentation.

"Probably because she knew he'd be an ass about it," Rupert grumbled.

Malcolm's eyes shot wide. "I beg your pardon?"

Rupert held himself with all the arrogance of a young man who had just come into his inheritance without a lick of experience to back up his attitude. "Mama tells you something wonderful and you fly into a temper. Of course she hesitated to tell you sooner."

"Is that what you think?" Malcolm asked with a humorless laugh.

"Mama wouldn't have stayed silent for so long without a very good reason," Rupert went on, holding his own.

Underneath his anger, Malcolm knew the boy was right. Katya never did anything without a reason. The bigger the secret, the stronger her reason. That didn't stop the fury from rising in him.

"You have a lot to learn about your mother, boy," he growled. "I'd wager there's a whole side to her that would turn your hair white if you knew."

"I am aware of the rumors," Rupert said through clenched teeth. "And I may know more than you suspect about whether or not they're true."

Malcolm wanted to challenge the whelp, but Bianca cleared her throat, looking decidedly worried.

"People are watching us, you know," she said. "Mama is always going on about discretion, and I don't think we're being discreet at the moment."

"No, we aren't," Malcolm admitted with a nod. "Which is why I'm leaving." He turned to go.

"You aren't going to just leave me like this, are you?" Natalia called after him.

A chill shot through Malcolm's blood. Her words echoed those of her mother nearly sixteen years before. He had walked out on her—walked out after Peter had informed him a nasty rumor was making the rounds that he was carrying on with a married woman mere months after Tessa's death. A rumor started by Shayles, who had been convinced Malcolm would return to his old ways. Once a bounder, always a bounder, Shayles had teased him. Hatred for the man had pushed him to try his hand at leading an upright life, but now Malcolm knew the greater price he'd paid for letting a rumor get under his skin.

"I have to go," he told Natalia, his words eerily similar to his excuse all those years ago. "You don't want me to stay right now." He started walking again.

"But—"

"Let him go, Nat," Rupert told his sister. "It really is for the best."

A bitter smirk twisted Malcolm's lips. That's what the boy thought, did he? Perhaps he was right. He'd only have mucked things up if he had stayed.

CHAPTER 9

alcolm pushed past the guards at the palace gate and stormed across Green Park, his feet taking him automatically toward Mayfair. He couldn't shake the strangling squeeze of betrayal that Katya's confession caused. She should have told him. That was all he could think about as he stomped past unwary bystanders, nearly plowing into a few of them in his temper. She should have told him right from the beginning, before Natalia was even born. If he'd known he would have…he would have….

His mind failed to conjure up what he would have done all those years ago, with Robert still alive, Katya firmly married to him, and Tessa fresh in her grave. He damn well would have done something, though. He would have done something if Katya had told him the truth after Robert's death. But no, she'd kept her secret and squandered her time jumping in and out of the beds of half the men in London. Had she done that simply to punish him for coming to his senses and leaving her to her husband?

His angry thoughts were still swirling when he found himself at the door of Peter's townhouse. He vented some of his frustration pounding on the door, then glaring at Peter's astonished butler.

"Is he in?" Malcolm growled, pushing past the man into the entryway.

"If you could wait here, I'll check—"

Malcolm ignored the man, storming down the hall toward Peter's study. "Peter," he shouted. "Where the devil are you?"

He rounded the corner into the study, finding it empty. At the same time, footfalls sounded on the stairs, so Malcolm returned to the hall.

"What in God's name are you doing, barging into my home and causing a racket?" Peter asked, coming down the stairs. He was in his shirtsleeves and looked as though he hadn't shaved that morning.

"Did you know Natalia Marlowe is my daughter?" Malcolm demanded with enough anger in his tone to suggest Peter had been in on the secret.

Peter nearly stumbled down the last two stairs, his eyes going wide. That was all the answer Malcolm needed, but Peter answered, "No," in an astonished tone anyhow. "She is?"

Malcolm's fury abated by a hair. At least he wasn't the only fool Katya had duped. "The girl figured it out based on…evidence." He wasn't about to explain that he'd spent the night in Katya's bed and been more or less caught by their children. The young people might have figured things out, but he and Katya had been damned sure to keep the nature of their association a secret from their meddling friends.

Another secret. Malcolm did his best not to flush with ironic guilt as Peter let out a breath and approached him.

"I take it Katya has known all along," Peter said.

"Evidently. Though how she can be sure it's mine with the way she carries on is…."

His words died on his lips at the censorious scowl Peter gave him. The bastard even crossed his arms and shook his head like a scolding father.

"Katya might have enjoyed herself, but she's never been careless," Peter said, striding past Malcolm and gesturing for him to follow down the hall to the study. "Otherwise there'd be far more little Marlowes running around London. Ones that couldn't claim even a shred of legitimacy."

"Are you defending her?" Malcolm snapped, heading straight to Peter's liquor supply as soon as they were in the room.

"No, I'm...." Peter let out a breath and rubbed his forehead. "Yes, I suppose I am."

"You're defending that deceptive tart?" Malcolm sloshed scotch over the lip of one of Peter's tumblers.

"Good God, Malcolm. Listen to yourself." Peter crossed the room to snatch the decanter from Malcolm's shaking hands, pouring himself a small glass. "You're insulting the woman we all know you love, and why? Because she hurt your feelings?"

"My feelings have nothing to do with it," Malcolm growled, immediately hiding his lie by gulping scotch. The liquid burned its way down his throat but only served to turn his stomach more. "I had a right to know about my own child."

"I'm sure you did," Peter said, putting the stopper back in the decanter with a clink. "But it's all water under the bridge now. Why are you really angry with Katya?"

"Because she's a lying bitch," Malcolm snapped, but the ache in his heart told him that there was a world of other reasons, each more painful than the last, that had been building up for over a decade.

Peter sent him a flat stare. "Katya is Katya. Yes, she can be a bitch, but can you blame her? Look at what she's up against on a daily basis." He gestured toward the window, as though the male hordes of London were waiting on the other side to put all women in their places. "She wouldn't be who she was if she didn't fight tooth and nail for her pride. And I mean that in terms of a lioness protecting her young as well." He pointed at Malcolm with his tumbler, then took a sip.

"I have only ever loved that blasted woman, and look how she's treated me?" Malcolm grumbled, pacing as the scotch slowly took effect.

"How has she treated you?" Peter asked with a wry grin.

"She refuses to marry me," Malcolm admitted. He hadn't told any of his friends about his numerous proposals and Katya's refusal to answer them. And yet Peter didn't look the least bit surprised. "She continues to defy me and make a fool of me, in public and in private."

Peter chuckled. "You do a fairly good job of making a fool of yourself."

"She flaunts her conquests in my face when I love her more than any of them ever could," Malcolm nearly shouted, the words sharp with emotion.

Peter finished his scotch and set his tumbler back on the tray. "So you're telling me that you're angry because a woman whom you love but have no binding claim to continues to live her own life and enjoy herself, and that she has gone to great lengths to protect her children from what would certainly be a social disaster if it were widely known? This is what has you so irate?"

Malcolm turned away from his so-called friend, downing the last of his scotch with an exasperated gulp. He was being an ass. His own children—both of them, God help him— were being more rational about the situation than he was. If any of his friends behaved as he was, he'd laugh them into oblivion. But it was *his* heart on the line, dammit. He'd sacrificed everything for love—with Tessa and with Katya—and he'd come up a loser both times.

"All I've ever wanted is someone who would love me with as much devotion as I love them," he murmured, half hoping Peter wouldn't hear him.

"Katya does love you," Peter said in an equally somber tone. "She always has. But she loves you on her terms, not yours. If you had accepted those terms from the start, your story would have been a very different one."

Malcolm clenched his jaw, wanting anything but for his friend to be right.

"Tessa loved you too," Peter said, quieter still. "No matter what happened at the end."

Malcolm squeezed his eyes shut, but he couldn't block out the horrific scene of her deathbed—the pain she'd been in after a difficult birth, the hysteria that had overcome her when she lay there bleeding to death, and her final, horrible words. It hadn't been fair. None of it had been fair. He'd come within a hair's breadth of ruining his name and fortune to extract Tessa from Shayles's clutches and to help her to obtain a divorce, and within a year, she was gone.

He would still exact his revenge for that, for the life Tessa deserved but never got, but first things first.

"There are certain things a man deserves to know," he said, turning back to Peter. "Who his own children are, for example. How would you feel if Anne had had a child that she didn't tell you about?"

Peter's expression hardened to cold stone. "You know full well Anne was incapable of bearing children and that trying to bear one killed her," he said in a hush.

"I'm sorry." Malcolm hid his slip-up by returning his tumbler to its tray. Peter's first marriage had been a source of heartbreak for him for twenty years. "I wasn't thinking."

"The trouble is, Malcolm, you never are." Peter shifted his

stance as though shaking off the demons of his past. "You say you love Katya, but you demand she change to suit you."

"I do not," Malcolm argued.

Peter merely raised a doubtful brow at him.

"I just want her to be honest with me, to stop humiliating me by running around with every young buck who strikes her fancy," Malcolm went on.

Peter crossed his arms. "And who does she have her sights set on now?"

"That dolt, Christopher Dowland."

Peter let out a breath and shook his head. "He's far too young for her. Besides, the only man she's looked at with genuine interest for years is you."

Malcolm scowled at his friend, inclined to think Peter was a trusting fool. Katya looked at every man who crossed her path with interest. And who knew whose bed she was in when she wasn't in his?

At the same time, a nagging doubt whispered at the back of his mind. Was she really as big of a flirt now as she'd been fifteen years ago? She smiled and flirted, all right, but it had been ages since rumors of her proclivities had found their way to him. But why would he hold on to such certainty about Katya's lack of loyalty toward him if she wasn't so loose with her affections?

"Look, friend," Peter cut through the gloomy silence of his thoughts. "I'm just packing to head back to Starcross Castle for a week. Mariah is due in a month, and in spite of my duties in Parliament, I intend to be there for this child as I was with the first one if I possibly can."

"Yes," Malcolm sighed, rubbing a hand over his face in an attempt to clear his thoughts. "Go. Be with your wife."

"And what do you intend to do?" Peter asked. "Nothing stupid, I hope."

Malcolm glared at him. "Of course not."

Peter didn't look convinced. All the same, he thumped Malcolm on the back with a grin. "You love Katya, Katya loves you. Leave the past in the past and move forward. You've gained a daughter out of the whole mess, and you should probably spend some time making up for lost years with her."

Malcolm agreed with his friend, but age-old doubts continued to nag at him as he left to make his way back to Buckingham Palace. He hadn't made it more than halfway before shoots of anger poked up through emotions he could only describe as confusion. This was all Shayles's fault. He wasn't certain how, but every horrible thing in his miserable life could be traced back to Shayles. The day he'd met the man at university had been the darkest day of his life, worse than the war. Without Shayles, Tessa wouldn't have needed rescuing, nor would dozens of other unfortunate girls. Without Shayles, Katya wouldn't have been so determined to meddle in politics and put herself in danger by infiltrating his club with girls on her payroll. Without Shayles....

He let out a breath halfway through Green Park, letting his shoulders drop. It always came back to the same thing. Whenever anything didn't go the way he wanted it to in his life, he laid it at Shayles's feet. The man was guilty as sin and the devil combined, but that didn't mean it was his fault whenever things failed to go the way Malcolm thought they should.

He changed direction, heading toward his club instead of back to the palace. The last thing he needed was to face Katya, her children, and his daughters when his thoughts were in such turmoil. He needed solitude and a place to stew in peace. A meal and another glass of scotch wouldn't be amiss either.

By the time the sun began to set that evening, he'd successfully avoided anyone he knew and come close to swallowing his anger. Close. All that flew out the window when, of all people, Galston marched into the club with an anxious look on his face.

"What are you doing here?" Malcolm asked him, setting aside the newspaper he'd been pretending to read while lost in his thoughts.

Galston breathed a sigh of relief as soon as he saw his master. "We've been looking all over for you, my lord," he said.

"We?" Malcolm frowned and crossed the room to deal with his butler off to the side, where half of the other men in the room weren't watching them like old women looking for gossip.

"Your daughter has been concerned about your where-abouts all day," Galston reported.

Malcolm came close to asking which daughter, but thought better of it. He sighed and headed for the hall that would lead to the club's front door. "Where is she now?" he asked.

"If Lady Stanhope's words were true, they should all be at Spencer House for the ball."

Malcolm scowled. If Lady Stanhope's words were true. The man had said a mouthful.

Malcolm didn't bother returning home with Galston to change into more suitable clothes for a ball. He piled Galston into the carriage he'd come in to fetch him, against Galston's protest that Malcolm should be the one to take the carriage while he found other means to return home. After that, he headed on foot to Spencer House, half hoping a footpad of some sort would attempt to accost him. He was in the mood for a fight.

No one impeded his progress, though, and long before he was ready, Malcolm arrived at Spencer House. And within minutes of entering the crowded, overheated ballroom, Cece spotted him.

"Papa," she scolded, dodging a few gray-haired men who seemed to think ogling freshly-debuted young women was a spectator sport. "Where have you been?" Her words were as angry and clipped as...well, as his would have been, under the circumstances.

"What I do with my time is none of your concern," he grumbled, kissing her cheek. "You look lovely. How did the presentation go?"

Cece wasn't about to be side-tracked. She huffed in frustration and hooked her arm through his, dragging him deeper into the room. "Now that you've had your temper tantrum, it's about time you apologize to Lady Stanhope for embarrassing us all this morning."

Malcolm's brow shot up. "What kind of insolence is this? Why, if we weren't in public, I'd turn you over my knee and give you—" His threat died on his lips as the image of spanking Katya's delicious, round backside sprang up in his mind instead of a father disciplining an unruly child. His face heated, and he writhed with discomfort.

Blessedly, Cece didn't have a clue where his thoughts had gone. "Sometimes, Papa, I think you're more of a child than the rest of us put together. And if I am insolent, I learned it from you."

"I am not—"

His words were cut short as they slipped around a cluster of chattering women and Malcolm nearly ran headlong into Katya.

"—and I won't be pushed around by a boy barely out of short pants," she was in the middle of complaining to Rupert. She turned at that moment, her eyes going wide as she came close to falling into Malcolm's arms.

"There," Rupert said. "Right on time. The orchestra is playing a waltz."

"Yes, a waltz," Cece said, shoving Malcolm's back and nudging him closer to Katya. "Go."

Malcolm frowned at his daughter, then at Katya, his eyes narrowing.

Katya let out an impatient sigh. "Oh, very well. Since the two of you won't leave us alone until we've danced." She held out her hand to Malcolm. "Let's get it over with."

Jaw tight, Malcolm took her offered hand and practically yanked her toward the center of the room, where couples were forming to dance. The cheery strains of a popular waltz filled the air, and Malcolm tugged Katya into a stiff, close dance position. He swayed into the steps, leading with far more force than was strictly necessary, staring firmly over her shoulder.

"You're still pouting, I see," she said without her usual teasing charm.

"You say that as if I have nothing to be upset about," he grumbled.

"You have plenty to be upset about," she said. He glanced to her, surprised she would agree. "Knowing you," she added with a sting.

He responded by jerking her through a particularly tight turn and deliberately knocking her off balance. She, in turn, stepped on his foot.

Their dance continued in combative silence, until Malcolm hissed, "Have you no pity at all in that cold heart of yours?"

"Oh, so you want to be pitied, do you?" She stared at him with implacable eyes.

"No," he snapped. "You know what I mean."

"Actually, Malcolm, I don't," she huffed. "All I know is that you're more impossible than usual when you're hurt."

"I'm not hurt," he insisted.

"Really?" Clearly, she didn't believe him.

"I'm furious," he said, barely able to speak to her. Her proximity and the heat of her body was having a sharp effect on him, but that only served to fan the flames of his anger. "All this time, I thought you loved me as I love you, when, in fact, you couldn't care less about me."

She missed a step in the dance. Thankfully, they were near the edge of the dancing mob and were able to stop to glare at each other without blocking other couples.

"I've never heard such a load of rubbish in my life," she hissed. "It's always the same with you, isn't it? You don't trust me—"

"No, I don't," he cut her off before she could continue her rant.

She straightened, looking wounded. A part of him instantly regretted his words, but the rest of him was too angry to care.

"What reason have you given me to trust you?" he went on. "You kept an entire child from me," he whispered.

"For her sake, not yours."

"All the same," he argued. "How can I forgive that?"

"The same way I can forgive you for being a jealous pillock," she growled.

"Do I have reason to be jealous?"

She huffed, and if he wasn't mistaken, stomped her foot under her ball gown. The picture of righteous fury she presented was so paradoxically appealing that he was ready to declare himself a madman and drag her into an unused room for a quick shag up against a wall. But before she could throw some new insult back at him, her expression changed to puzzlement as she stared past Malcolm's shoulder.

Malcolm twisted to see what had distracted her. Cece and Rupert were pushing their way through the party guests toward them, worried looks on their faces. Behind them marched Inspector Craig, looking extremely out of place in plain clothes and a bowler hat. Dancers and debutantes stared at them in their wake.

"Mama," Rupert spoke first when they reached Malcolm and Katya. "Inspector Craig needs to speak with you immediately."

Malcolm and Katya both turned to Craig, who stepped forward as though the room were empty.

"Lord Campbell, Lady Stanhope." He nodded to each of them. "I thought you would want to know that we're moving on The Black Strap Club."

"When?" Katya asked, blinking.

Craig answered, "Now."

CHAPTER 10

*E*xcitement swooped into Katya's gut as Inspector Craig nodded to her and Malcolm, then turned to cut his way back through the ballroom, heading for the door.

"Wait." She rushed after him, glad to shove aside the miserable emotional tangle that was her argument with Malcolm for the moment. "What do you mean *now*?"

Inspector Craig paused to study her, then gestured for her and Malcolm to follow him out of the ballroom and into Spencer House's entryway. Rupert and Cece brought up the rear, looking as though they weren't supposed to be there.

"My superiors have decided the time for a raid is now, before Lord Shayles or any of his associates suspect such a thing is coming. It's thought he may still have protectors in high places, so we must act before they get wind of our action."

"Then let's be on our way," Malcolm said, pushing past Inspector Craig and making for the door.

"Hold up there," Inspector Craig darted into Malcolm's path, holding up his hands. "This is a police operation. I only came here to inform you of our actions because it was on the way and because I felt I owed it to you to inform you what was going on."

Malcolm glared at the man in spite of his implacable expression. "I'm going with you."

"I am as well," Katya added, head held high.

Inspector Craig looked as though he was second-guessing stopping by Spencer House at all. "I can't allow civilians to interfere with police action," he argued.

"Without us, you would have no action," Malcolm told him, looking as though he wanted a fight.

Katya knew him well enough to see he would use his fists to break past Inspector Craig if he had to. "We can stand here arguing about it or we can get ourselves over to Kensington as quickly as possible," she said.

Inspector Craig clenched his jaw and stared at Malcolm for several long, anxious moments. "Don't get in the way," he said at last, turning and marching out of the building.

Malcolm followed him, but Katya turned to Rupert. "Take care of Cece, and mind your sisters once you get home. I think it would be best not to tell them what's going on until it's over."

"Agreed," Rupert said with a sharp nod.

Cece looked worried enough to burst into tears and clung to Rupert's arm. Katya felt sorry for her, but there was only so much she could do to shield the young people she cared about from the perils of the world. She sent Rupert a final, cautious smile before hurrying to join Malcolm and Inspector Craig.

They said little as they piled into the plain, unmarked carriage Inspector Craig had waiting. Katya sat on the opposite seat from the men, attempting to study their faces in passing flashes of lamplight as they sped through streets crowded with carriages taking revelers to and from parties and on to Kensington. The momentary semi-calm sent

Katya's thoughts spiraling back to her argument with Malcolm.

Their argument never seemed to end. It had been going on forever, or so it felt for her, and it was always the same thing. Only now, after all the time that had passed, Malcolm seemed to be on the edge of understanding everything that was truly at stake. He continued to be as stubborn as the day was long, though. Of course she hadn't told him about Natalia's paternity. Malcolm was a man of passion, and he would have destroyed her world and his if he'd known from the start. Natalia's world too, and Katya wouldn't have that. All the same, it was torture to see him in such pain, torture to know that his anger and frustration was born out of a desperation to be loved, and torture not to be able to explain as much to him and have him understand. Men were as distant from their hearts as England was from Bombay most of the time, but their lives would be so much easier if they'd simply admit their shortcomings once in a while.

The Black Strap Club sat one street back from the western end of Hyde Park, close enough to see Kensington Palace from its upper windows. Katya held her breath as they drew near, but let it out in a confused puff when Inspector Craig had his carriage turn onto a small street more than a block from the club.

"What are we doing here?" Malcolm asked in reflection of Katya's confusion as Inspector Craig opened the door and hopped down.

Malcolm alighted after him, leaving Katya to help herself down, something she was more than happy to do. The scene that revealed itself through the dark around her sent a chill down her back. At least two dozen men dressed in the dark uniforms of the Metropolitan Police stood in the shadows, absolutely silent. The air crackled with readiness.

Inspector Craig marched straight toward a pair of

uniformed officers that stood apart from the main group. "Everything ready?" he asked in a clipped Cockney accent, all attempts to sound posh falling.

"Yes, sir," one of the men answered.

"As I'll ever be," a third man said in a fine accent with a hint of a Cornish lilt.

Katya blinked, then squinted through the darkness to be sure she was hearing and seeing correctly. Along with the policemen stood Sir Christopher, dressed as though he had been to one of the many balls taking place that night.

But before she could greet him, Malcolm marched toward the man. "You," he said, a menacing note in his voice. "What are you doing here?"

A streetlight near the closest intersection flickered to life, allowing Katya to see Christopher's startled look and Malcolm's scowl more clearly.

"Inspector Craig asked me to help with tonight's operation," Christopher said, his surprise at Malcolm's question making him look like the last person anyone would want taking part in a delicate raid.

"Nonsense," Malcolm snapped. "You have nothing to do with this. Go home."

"Sir Christopher is here on my insistence," Inspector Craig told Malcolm, holding a hand at Malcolm's chest level to stop him from charging Christopher, which it looked like he was about to do. "He's gained Lord Shayles's trust, is recognized by the guards at the club's doors, and will make it much easier for the rest of us to gain entrance to the club."

"I can do all that," Malcolm insisted.

"No, you can't," Katya told him. "Shayles wouldn't let you within a hundred feet of the club if he knew you were around."

Malcolm turned to her, glaring. "I should be the one to lead this."

"The police have the operation well in hand," Inspector Craig said.

"I've been pursuing Shayles for nearly twenty years," Malcolm nearly shouted at him. "I've given up my life to defeat that man and his disgusting ways. I refuse to stand on the sidelines and to let that idiot take my place at the front of the charge."

A surprise burst of agreement squeezed Katya's chest. "He's right," she said, inching closer to Malcolm's side. "This is Malcolm's fight as much as anyone's." And if he was denied the opportunity to be present when Shayles was apprehended, his pride would never recover.

Inspector Craig blew out a frustrated breath and rubbed the back of his neck. He glanced to his men waiting in the shadows, then to Christopher, then back to Malcolm and Katya. "We don't have time to stand around arguing about this. If you can stay out of trouble and do as you're told, then you can be a part of things."

"You're damned right I can," Malcolm said, standing straighter.

Inspector Craig gave him one last irritated look before turning to address his men in a quiet voice. "You know the plan. If everyone sticks to their jobs and goes where they're supposed to go, this should be a quick and tidy operation. Hormel, take your unit around through the mews. Willoughby, off you go to the west side. The rest of you, with me. Let Sir Christopher walk ahead as though he's a client."

"I'll walk with him," Malcolm insisted.

"You'll hang behind with the rest of us," Inspector Craig told him, shaking his head.

"I can go with Sir Christopher," Katya offered. "Shayles hasn't banned me from the club. Quite the contrary. He's been trying to get me to participate for years."

Malcolm clearly wanted to make a comment on her statement, but Inspector Craig beat him to it.

"You're staying here, Lady Stanhope," he said. "In the carriage. Josephs, stay with her."

"I'm doing no such thing," Katya insisted as Inspector Craig turned to gesture to her would-be guard. When he looked as though he would argue with her, Katya went on with, "I have girls in that club who know me, who are under my supervision. I want to make sure they're safe, as well as the rest of the unfortunate young women forced to work for Shayles."

"That club is no place for a lady," Inspector Craig said.

Katya laughed out loud. "I know that better than you do, son." She rushed on before he could counter her with, "I either go in with you or I stand on the corner, screaming bloody murder and alerting everyone that they're about to be raided."

She had no intention to do anything of the sort, not after all the trouble they'd gone through, but Inspector Craig didn't know that. Dirty tricks were never the best way to get what was wanted, but desperate times called for desperate action.

"Fine," Inspector Craig said at last, clearly aggravated. "But the same rules apply to you that apply to him." He gestured to Malcolm. "Stay quiet and stay out of the way."

Katya agreed with a nod. It must have been good enough for Inspector Craig. He had one last, quiet word with one of his men, and within minutes they were in motion.

"I'd tell you to listen to Craig and stay behind, but I know it wouldn't do any good," Malcolm grumbled as they fell into line with the policemen speeding through the shadows.

"So you have learned something in all these years after all," Katya replied, too tense with anticipation to grin or tease him further.

"I've learned that you're as stubborn as—"

"You?" Katya finished his sentence. "We both already knew that."

"Quiet," Inspector Craig cautioned them as they crossed the street and made their way along the side of the club.

Christopher was already at the door, knocking in a peculiar pattern to gain entrance. The door opened and he stepped inside as Inspector Craig's men strode closer, as if they were merely uninterested passersby. One of them climbed the steps after Christopher, stopping the unseen attendant from closing the outer door. Katya knew from her girls that there was a second, inner door that would be much harder for anyone who wasn't on the inside to get through, but before she and Malcolm had reached the steps leading to the entrance, there was a shout, and in a coordinated burst, Inspector Craig and his men surged forward.

Within seconds, everything was movement and pandemonium. Katya was caught up in it as she and Malcolm stormed the club alongside the police. As soon as they stepped into the outer foyer, it became obvious that whoever was attending the inner door had opened it to allow Christopher in, and once that barrier was breached, the club was infiltrated by sheer force.

"Where is Lord Shayles?" Inspector Craig was in the middle of demanding from the sinister, wiry butler as Katya hurried into the heart of the club.

"He's not here, he's not here," the butler insisted.

Katya didn't believe him for a moment, but she wasn't interested in Shayles. She searched the front hall for a familiar face, finally spotting Bess, one of her girls, peeking around a corner to see what was going on.

"Bess." Katya marched right toward her. "The police are here. We need to get the girls to safety immediately."

"Yes, Lady Stanhope," Bess said, her eyes going wide. She

dashed around the corner, and Katya followed her deeper into the club.

Malcolm roared into The Black Strap Club, fists balled, ready to fight anyone, including Craig, who would keep him from exacting his final revenge on Shayles. He was immediately assailed by old memories of his early days, right after returning from the Crimea, when his mind and heart had been so damaged by the devastation he'd witnessed and been part of on the battlefield that he was willing to do anything to distract himself. The scent of the place hadn't changed—candle wax, exotic spice, sex, and fear. It sent a chill down his back that had him trembling with bottled-up energy.

But his own fear burst wide open when he saw Katya disappear around a corner.

"Katya," he called, starting after her.

He stopped dead when he heard Craig saying, "Arrest every man you find in this building. High and low, I don't care. And find Shayles."

Teeth on edge and heart beating in his throat, Malcolm turned away from the hall Katya had run down to march up to Craig's side. "I know where he hides," he said.

Craig glared at him, but the man's frustration was eclipsed by determination. "Take me there."

It had been decades since the dangerous days when Malcolm had called Shayles a friend, since Shayles had first purchased and refurbished The Black Strap Club, but Shayles didn't change the way he thought or his core actions. Malcolm launched ahead of Craig and his men—barely noting that the idiot, Dowland, followed with them—taking a small set of spiral stairs that led down. Shayles left the grandeur of his club for his customers, saving the under-ground warren of passages and dungeons for himself.

"What the devil?" a man asked from one of the dank side caverns as the parade of policemen whipped past. A middle-aged lord Malcolm knew all too well from the halls of West-minster stepped into the doorway, naked and erect. A woman's pleading cry came from the room behind him.

"Arrest that man," Craig said with barely a sideways glance. "Help the woman. Arrest every man you find down here." Disgust and fury were thick in his tone, but he marched on.

Within seconds, the dungeons exploded with shouts and panic as half a dozen dungeons were split open and their occupants dragged out into the hall. Shouts and thumps sounded from above as well. Malcolm could only imagine that the entire club was disgorging every manner of evil. He only hoped the men Craig had brought with him were enough to sweep up the mess.

"Down here," Malcolm said, pushing on to a small, arched door at the end of the hall. "This is where he hides."

Craig pushed ahead of Malcolm as they reached the door, three burly men behind him. He didn't stop to knock, and a fiery sort of fury blared from him that gave Malcolm pause. Craig tried the handle of the door, and when it seemed to catch, he took a half step back and kicked the door so hard it clattered off its hinges.

The sight that met them in the small dungeon room was everything Malcolm could have hoped for and more. Shayles was there, and he was engaged in an act so foul—and with a young woman who was barely more than a child—that half of Craig's men turned away. One burst into a sob. But it wasn't the act Shayles had been caught in or the age of the girl, or even the humiliation of Shayles being completely naked, it was the way the bastard's eyes went wide with fright and his body snapped rigid with fear. They'd caught the blackguard completely by surprise.

"Lord Theodore Shayles," Craig said, gesturing for his men to grab Shayles and hold him, "You are hereby under arrest, by order of Her Majesty and the Metropolitan Police."

CHAPTER 11

"*Y*ou can't arrest me," Shayles shouted, attempting to pull himself together, but looking ridiculous as he scrambled for something to hide his arousal. He edged sideways, to where his clothes were strewn over a wicked-looking iron chair with leather straps in key places. "I've done nothing wrong."

Malcolm barked a laugh. "Nothing wrong? Look at you, man. Look at that poor girl."

Shayles barely spared a glance for the weeping, shivering girl. One of Craig's men had thrown his jacket around her shoulders and was trying to coax her to get up and leave the dungeon with him. She was too traumatized to move.

"Since when was it a crime to pass the evening with a willing partner?" Shayles asked, chin tilted high. He continued to creep toward the side of the room.

"Check that girl's age," Craig ordered, crossing the room to intercept Shayles. "Interview her. I'd wager she isn't here willingly."

Shayles sneered. "You can't believe a word a girl like that

says. She's trash, you know. She parted her legs for a scrap of—"

Shayles never finished his sentence. Craig threw a punch that snapped his head to the side, bloodied his lip, and jolted him out of the grip of the officers holding him. Malcolm wasn't sure which surprised him more, the usually cool Craig losing his temper or the fact that he himself hadn't been the one to throw the first punch. The former was satisfying, but the latter made him unaccountably angry.

Craig turned to Dowland, rubbing the hand he'd used to punch Shayles. "Sir Christopher, can you positively identify this man as Lord Theodore Shayles."

"Yes, I can," Dowland said, looking a little green around the gills as he stepped forward.

"And can you confirm that he offered you a variety of illegal services, as detailed in the document you presented to Scotland Yard—" Shayles's eyes went wide with alarm, "—including service by underage girls and practices that could be classified as torture?"

"Yes," Dowland answered, then swallowed and glanced away.

A creeping sense of wrongness slithered down Malcolm's back at the exchange. Craig should be turning to him for that kind of confirmation. He was the one who had spent the greater part of his life in the last several years making the case against Shayles. But for all Craig and Dowland were concerned, he wasn't even in the room.

It was Shayles who noticed Malcolm, appealing to him with, "You aren't going to let them do this to me, are you?"

Malcolm was so taken off-guard by the pleading in Shayles's question that he was slow to respond with, "You've brought this on yourself."

"How long have we known each other?" Shayles went on, forgetting his sideways pursuit of clothing to approach

Malcolm. "Since university," he answered his own question. "You and Gatwick were some of my closest friends, some of the first members of this club."

Malcolm's chest tightened as it filled with rage. "I know what you're doing, Shayles, and it won't work. You won't implicate me in this mess." Though he stopped short of defending Gatwick's innocence. Who knew if Gatwick was innocent or not? "I have had nothing to do with this filthy hellhole for decades and you know it."

"We shared such good times," Shayles went on, a clever spark in his eyes. "Very good times." He glanced to Craig. Craig shifted to study Malcolm with narrowed eyes. "You met your dear wife, Tessa, here."

Even though he was standing in the middle of the room, Malcolm felt backed into a corner. "Craig knows all about Tessa," he told Shayles, then turned to Craig. "He treated her no better than that poor girl." He nodded to the shivering form that Craig's man was carrying out of the room. "I got her out of this place and helped her to obtain a divorce."

"And that's as far as your association with the club goes?" Craig asked. "You know your way around awfully well."

Malcolm wanted to throttle the inspector as much as he wanted to put a bullet in Shayles's brain for the agony he'd caused Tessa, and every other woman unfortunate to fall into his clutches in the last two decades. "That was a long time ago," he growled. "Before this place turned into a nightmare."

"Lord Campbell," Craig began with brittle respect. "Perhaps you should wait outside while we continue with police business."

Behind Craig, Shayles burst into a wry smirk.

Malcolm saw red. "I've devoted my life to this. How dare you shut me out when the hour of triumph is here?"

"I understand your desire to see justice, Lord Campbell,"

Craig began, approaching Malcolm in a way that was designed to back him toward the door.

"I will be a part of this," Malcolm shouted.

"Yes, I've heard that before," Shayles muttered, loud enough to catch Craig's attention. When Craig turned to him, Shayles went on with, "Strange how you've known about the club for decades, and yet it's only now that Mr. Craig here has accosted me."

Malcolm's eyes went wide with fury. "I've been working to clear away the corruption within the police force that has shielded you for so long, you miserable shit."

"One must question how hard you have tried," Shayles drawled, crossing his arms. Even naked, he had the easy stance of a man who was winning his point.

Craig let out a frustrated breath and rubbed a hand over his face. "We'll sort this out when we're through here." He turned back to Shayles. "My men are rounding up your clients and getting the girls to safety as we speak. Put some clothes on." He turned away from Shayles, who had gone white with sudden fear. "Gather up as much documentation as you can find," Craig went on. "Bring in the photographers to document—"

He didn't get any farther. As soon as he turned his back, Shayles leapt toward the chair where his clothes were. He didn't reach for them, though. Instead, he tore at a small cabinet on the wall, wrenching open the door and pulling a series of levers.

For about five seconds, there was a sinister hiss. Malcolm frowned and glanced around. It came from the narrow pipes that lined the floor and ceiling of the room. The faint scent of gas filled the air before a second, louder whoosh filled the air, followed by a booming explosion. In an instant, the room was on fire.

"The place is rigged," one of Craig's men shouted.

"Get out," Craig shouted. "Get everyone out of here as fast as possible. Don't let him out of your sight." He thrust an arm in Shayles's direction before leaping toward the door.

Malcolm shot into motion. Shayles's dungeon room ignited like a tinderbox. The hem of his trousers was singed as he passed by one of the leaking gas pipes. There was no telling how long they had to claw their way back to ground level before the entire dungeon exploded.

His flight was made worse by the rush of panicked men who jumped into the halls from the side rooms. Screams echoed around the dungeon caverns as Shayles's clients pushed their way toward the narrow staircase and up to the ground floor. Craig's men were caught between trying to arrest them, save the unfortunate women who had been abandoned in the dungeon rooms, and getting to safety.

"Evidence," Craig shouted somewhere behind Malcolm. "We need evidence."

Malcolm would have laughed, if the smoke filling the crowded corridor wasn't choking him. Shayles wasn't stupid. He must have known a day would come when his wicked endeavors would be discovered. The entire building must have been piped with gas that was set to explode. It was a wonder the whole place hadn't burned to the ground by accident before.

The thought brought Malcolm up short as he reached the top of the stairs and dashed out into the club's main hall. Everything was on fire, even on the ground floor. But the genius of the system was instantly forgotten as a much greater thought rushed to the front of Malcolm's mind.

"Katya," he shouted, sprinting across the hall to the corridor she'd disappeared down. Dowland followed on his heels, but he hardly noticed. One thought superseded all else: Katya was in danger.

· · ·

HER GIRLS HAD PLAYED THEIR PARTS WELL. KATYA HADN'T BEEN able to inform them of the raid, not when it had been organized so swiftly, but her girls were always alert. Those that could had abandoned their clients to let Inspector Craig's men into the building at the first signs of the raid. By the time Katya made it upstairs to the halls that held private rooms, the building was swarming with policemen who were in a mood to arrest anyone and everyone male, regardless of how lofty their title or position in society.

"Lottie," Katya called out when she spotted one of the girls who had been working covertly for her for the longest amount of time. "What's the situation here?"

Lottie skittered to a halt at the end of a hall where three blustering men in various states of undress were being carted out of rooms by policemen.

"Lady Stanhope," she exclaimed in surprise, then changed direction to meet Katya. "Are you responsible for this, m'lady?"

"Only indirectly," Katya said. She glanced up as a woman screamed, only to find one of the policemen yanking her into the hall, looking as though he would arrest her as well. She swore under her breath. "I was afraid of this." She left Lottie to march down the hall to the officer. "Keep your hands off the girls. They're innocent victims in this whole enterprise."

The officer stared at her with shock and indignation. "They're prostitutes," he argued. "They're no better than the blokes."

"You ignorant dolt," Katya scolded him, her voice shaking. "Most of them are here against their will. They are victims, not criminals."

The officer gave her a look of such condescension that it was all Katya could do to keep from slapping him. "Begging your pardon, ma'am," he began.

"That's Lady Stanhope to you," Katya cut him off, turning

back to Lottie. "Gather up as many of the girls as you can find and get them to safety. I don't trust this lot to treat you with the respect and compassion you all deserve."

"Yes, m'lady." Lottie bobbed a quick curtsy before dashing off, hollering for the girls to follow her.

"You're interfering with official police business," the officer yelled at her, an edge of uncertainty in his eyes when she didn't immediately back down. "Inspector Craig will—"

"I'm here with Inspector Craig's full authority, and I will not—" She stopped abruptly, sniffing the air. The sharp scent of gas had suddenly filled the hall. Faint hissing came from all around her. "What the devil?"

Seconds later, an explosion reverberated through the hall that nearly knocked her off her feet. It was followed by a second explosion that threw her against the wall as a sudden ring of flames roared around her. The suddenness of the heat enveloping her knocked the air from her lungs and filled her with panic of a sort she had rarely experienced. Screams and shouts erupted around her.

The raw instinct to survive took over after the initial thunder of the explosion. Everything around her was on fire —the walls, the floorboards, the ceiling. The hallway had become a tunnel of flame. She dashed for the end of the hall where Lottie had headed.

"Lottie," she called out, her voice strange and choked. "Get the girls out."

"I am, m'lady," Lottie's voice came through the fiery hallway.

The burst of relief it brought was short-lived, though. Katya backpedaled, rushing for the end of the hallway where she'd entered from the staircase. But once she reached it, instead of fleeing downward to get to safety, she charged up.

"Get out," she cried when she reached the top hallway. "Get out at once."

She threw open the door nearest her, hoping to find someone she could help get to safety, but the room behind the door was filled with fire. Male and female screams echoed through the conflagration. She raised a hand to shield her eyes from the intensity of the flames as she peered down the hall, praying that the girls were making it to safety, but not sure how they could. They knew the building far better than she did, though. They must have known ways out.

She, on the other hand, didn't. The danger of her situation hit home, and panic filled her. She turned, fleeing back down the stairwell.

"Katya! Katya!"

The sound of Malcolm's voice searching for her was a beacon she could latch onto. "Malcolm," she shouted in return, dissolving into wild coughing.

"Katya, where are you?"

The stairwell was filling with smoke so swiftly that she couldn't see more than a few steps in front of her. The roar and crackle of the entire building burning around her drowned out almost all sound. All the same, she continued to push forward, nearly falling down the stairs in her haste.

"Malcolm," she shouted as she reached the first-floor landing, although her voice was little more than a croak.

"Dear God, if anything happens to you...." Malcolm's shout seemed far too distant and faded. "I'm coming, my love, I'm coming."

"Malcolm," Katya gasped.

"I've got you."

A pair of arms closed around her, and her head spun as she was lifted. But it wasn't Malcolm's arms around her, and it hadn't been his voice to reassure her. She blinked through the blinding smoke, barely able to make out the surprisingly heroic features of Christopher as he carried her through the burning front hall toward the door.

"What are you doing, man?" Malcolm's voice joined them a moment later. Even through a fit of wrenching coughs, he sounded like fury itself.

"I'm getting Lady Stanhope to safety," Christopher said, coughing himself.

"But, you...but, she...."

Malcolm didn't finish his protest. The three of them burst out of the front door—which was ringed with flames—and into the chill of the night street. The contrast was so sharp that Katya instantly began to tremble in Christopher's arms. She clasped her arms around his neck and hugged him tight. There was as much pandemonium outside as there had been inside. A fire brigade had just arrived, and men were shouting orders. Dozens of spectators had gathered to watch from the park across the street, where Christopher took Katya. As soon as they were well out of the way of the flurry of activity, Christopher stopped.

"Are you well, my lady?" he asked.

Katya attempted to reply, but all that came out was coughing so vicious that it made her gag.

"What are you doing to her, you fool?" Malcolm demanded.

Katya was too busy feeling as though she would cough her lungs right out of her body to pay much attention to him...until her world tipped off-balance once again as Malcolm wrenched her from Christopher's arms.

"I'm not sure that's—" Christopher started.

"Mind your own business, you usurping buffoon," Malcolm growled.

He tried to clutch Katya tightly, but between coughing and indignation, she pushed away from him.

"What...in blazes...are you doing?" she managed to wheeze, doubling over. Her ball gown was singed all over and burnt through in several places. She hadn't been aware of it catching fire or of someone putting it out, but she wasn't surprised.

"My whole life," Malcolm raged between coughing fits of his own. "Bringing Shayles down has been my whole life. And you robbed me of that."

It took Katya a moment to realize he was shouting at Christopher, not her.

"Inspector Craig asked—" Christopher began.

"All I've ever wanted was to make that man pay for what he did to Tessa," Malcolm raged on. Katya straightened enough to see the mad fury and grief in his eyes. "That was *my* victory. Mine! Not yours. And Katya…." His words faded into a coughing fit that ended in retching.

"Malcolm, hush," Katya wheezed.

"Lady Stanhope needed help," Christopher defended himself. "You were distressed yourself and—"

"Christopher saved me," Katya tried to explain, her head throbbing and her lungs burning.

"It's always going to be someone else instead of me, isn't it?" Malcolm demanded of Katya, ignoring Christopher entirely. "I'm never going to be the hero in your eyes."

"That's not true," Katya said, although her words were without the true emotion she felt behind them.

"I was never good enough for Tessa either," Malcolm raged on. "I was her way out, but nothing more. I can't even avenge her without someone else taking the credit." Two, clean, damp lines cut through the caked soot on his face, from his eyes across his cheeks.

The pain Katya felt through her body and soul doubled. "Was Shayles arrested?" she gasped, coughing hard enough to turn herself inside out.

"He was," Christopher told her.

"This is my battle, not yours," Malcolm shouted, agony sharpening his voice. "Stay out of it." He pushed Christopher aside and gripped Katya's arms, his eyes reflecting the fire of the club burning down as he stared at her. "I'm never going to be what you want, am I? I'm never going to be young enough or clever enough or...or just enough, am I? I've wasted my entire life chasing you and trying to bring Shayles down. I could have lived. I could have made something more of myself, but I'm just a lonely laughingstock with nothing to show for it. Tomorrow, the papers will rave all about how brave Sir Christopher Dowland was and how his efforts brought an end to Shayles's evil. He wasn't even involved until last week. And what will they say about me?"

"I'll insist that your name is mentioned as one of the key operators in this," Christopher said.

If Katya could have warned him to keep his mouth shut, she would have. But between her coughing and the sorrow that burrowed so deeply into her soul that it left her paralyzed, she couldn't summon up a word.

"This is not your battle," Malcolm bellowed at Christopher. "This is not your war. You interloper. This is my life, my love, and you stole it from me."

"I didn't—" Christopher clamped his mouth shut before he could say more and make it worse.

Malcolm took a step back, the red-orange light of the fire illuminating him. He was a man of passions in the best of times, but the sheer agony in his expression was enough to sap the last of Katya's strength. She tumbled to her knees in the damp grass, clutching her stomach as she coughed. Christopher leapt to crouch beside her, holding her up, but she tried to push him away. The help he thought he was offering was only making things worse. In that moment, Katya needed to be miserable, needed to feel pain. Because she couldn't shake the horrible feeling she was as responsible for Malcolm's misery as Shayles or Tessa or anyone else. She could have been more open with him. She could have told him about Natalia, told him all the reasons she'd refused to marry him. She could have told him about Robert and the way her life had been stolen from her. But pride had kept her silent. Teasing him had been more enjoyable than being honest with him. She'd taken the easy way out for too long.

At last, after a long silence filled with the crackle of fire and the crash of part of The Black Strap Club caving in, shouts and screams and mayhem, none of which were half as potent as the desperate rise and fall of Malcolm's shoulders as he stared at her, Malcolm wiped his face and shook his head.

"What have I been doing all these years?" he asked in a voice so calm and quiet it sent a chill down Katya's spine. "Why have I wasted so much time?"

No answers came. Malcolm turned to the crumbling club, heaving a sigh, shoulders slumping. He shook his head again, then turned and walked away.

Katya opened her mouth to call out to him, to beg him not to go, but her heart wasn't in it. She didn't feel as though she had the right anymore. Instead, she clutched her stomach and bent over, coughing and retching as her lungs and her stomach convulsed, as her world dissolved around her.

"My lady, let me take you to a hospital," Christopher said, closing his arms around her and attempting to lift her.

"No," Katya croaked, pushing him away. She tried to stand, but Christopher had to assist her.

"Really, Lady Stanhope. You're quite unwell. You need to see a doctor," Christopher insisted.

"I just want to go home," she sobbed, shocked at how weak she sounded.

"But there's a hospital not far from here," Christopher said.

Katya shook her head and pushed against him, but she

couldn't extract herself from his support. "Please. Just take me home."

Christopher made an uncertain noise, glancing around as if someone else might come to help them. There were masses of people on the scene, but everyone was busy watching the club burn down.

"You're friends with Viscount Helm," Christopher said at last. "He used to be a doctor. Could I take you to his house?"

Katya shook her head. "Take me home." She sagged against Christopher, making it possible for him to lift her at last. "But you can send for him to come to my house," she conceded.

It was the last thing she would concede. It was the last order she would give as well. In the blink of an eye, age had caught up with her. All she wanted to do was go home and hide under her covers until the pain within her stopped, but she feared it never would.

CHAPTER 12

"My lord, what happened?" Galston greeted Malcolm as he stormed through his front door.

"Nothing," Malcolm grumbled, brushing past the man and down the hall toward his study. There was a large decanter of scotch waiting for him there, and he intended to drink most of it.

"But your clothes, my lord," Galston said, following him down the hall.

Malcolm glanced down at his scorched and sooty clothes and paused. He was close enough to a mirror to peer at his black and sooty reflection. The fire seemed like a minor detail in the travesty of his evening. The destruction of The Black Strap Club was nothing to the desolation of his life's work. His friends would laugh at him, call him childish for raging against the way things had turned out, and tell him to be happy that Shayles was captured at all, but to see a newcomer take credit for everything? To see Dowland rescue Katya and carry her to safety? To see the way she clung to Dowland? She could deny her involvement with the young dolt all she wanted, but Malcolm had seen the connection between them with his own eyes.

"My lord?" Galston prompted. "Would you care to change into something a little...cleaner?"

He'd lost his battle to bring Shayles to justice. He'd lost Katya in the process. He wasn't going to lose anything else.

"Later," he said, turning fully toward Galston. "Go up and pack my things. All of my things. Send one of the footmen to find out when the first train to Glasgow departs in the morning. I'm going home."

Galston's eyes betrayed his surprise, but he quickly schooled his expression and bowed. "Yes, my lord."

As Galston headed upstairs, Malcolm stormed down the hall and into his study. He needed that scotch to bring him the oblivion he craved. With any luck, he could sleep the whole way home on the train. With even more luck, some thief would steal his wallet, his identity, and his entire, miserable life.

"Papa?"

Malcolm stopped short inside his study as Cece rose from one of the leather couches near the fireplace. Her ball gown was rumpled and creased, but her tired face popped into a look of alarm.

"Oh my, Papa. What happened to you?" She flew across the room, reaching for him.

Malcolm dodged her, too miserable even to let his daughter comfort him. "Mind your gown," he said, his voice heavy with defeat. "I'll ruin it." He marched past her to the table holding his liquor. "What are you doing here anyhow? I would have thought that ball would go on until morning."

"I wasn't enjoying myself." Cece followed him to the table. "Not after Inspector Craig took you and Lady Stanhope away."

Malcolm's hands shook as he poured his scotch, but at the

mention of Katya's name he flinched so hard the lip of the decanter smacked against the tumbler, ringing like a crystal bell. "You should have stayed and enjoyed yourself," he grumbled.

"How could I?" Cece took the decanter from him and finished pouring. She stopped before the tumbler was even halfway through, handing it to him. "I've been so worried about you. Especially since news of the fire reached me."

He glanced up at her in surprise. "Who told you about the fire?"

She fixed him with a flat stare. "It's all over town already," she said. "Rupert and I had just made up our minds to leave the ball when someone ran in off the street to tell one of the footmen at Spencer House there had been a series of explosions near Kensington Palace that had caused a massive fire. I think he might have assumed the palace was on fire, but Rupert and I knew better."

Malcolm huffed humorlessly, which caused a fit of coughing. He steadied it with a gulp of scotch, or at least tried to. In actuality, the liquor made his coughing worse.

"Dear Papa." Cece tried to slide closer and rub his back, but Malcolm pushed her away.

"Leave it to gossip to get the story even more wrong than it already is," he croaked.

"What is the real story?" Cece asked. The innocence in her eyes was almost painful. She was young and likely still believed life would treat her fairly and give her everything she desired. She had yet to learn that the world was a cruel place, where the people you loved didn't love you in return and where justice could only be had with a price.

"We raided the club, as Craig had planned," he forced himself to tell her. She had a right to know. In an indirect way, Shayles and his club were part of her story too. "The raid was a success. Shayles was caught unaware and arrested.

But he must have known this day would come. His entire club was piped with gas. Somehow he managed to open all the valves and set the place on fire."

Cece gasped, pressing a hand to her chest. "How could he do that? What would have happened if there had been an accident before? Didn't he care at all for the people who might have been caught in a disaster like that?"

"No," Malcolm said. "Shayles never cared for anyone other than himself. And he must have been desperate." Malcolm narrowed his eyes, trying to remember as much as he could about the moments in the dungeon. The pipes were shiny copper. They must have been newly installed. Shayles had released the gas in his dungeon and perhaps other rooms nearby, but someone else would have had to take similar action in the rest of the house. Shayles had had accomplices, which could explain why the house exploded in stages instead of all at once. Either way, mountains of evidence had likely been destroyed, which was precisely what Shayles would have wanted.

Malcolm slammed his tumbler down on the table. As likely as not, Shayles had destroyed his club as yet another way to rob Malcolm of the victory he'd been striving for.

"There's more, Papa," Cece said, resting her hand over his on the table. "I can see it in you."

Malcolm glanced sideways at his daughter. She looked so much like Tessa, so much like the woman he'd rescued but failed to win, sought justice for, but failed to avenge. Why shouldn't he be honest with her?

"I've been a damned fool and I've wasted my life running after something I'll never get," he said, the smoke he'd inhaled turning his voice into a wolfish growl. "All those years, and in the end, it was Christopher Dowland who played the hero and enabled Craig to arrest Shayles. Christopher Dowland." He spat the name like a curse.

143

"I'm sorry, Papa," Cece sighed, squeezing his hand. "That must have been difficult for you. I know how much you've been longing to defeat Lord Shayles."

"Oh, it's more than that." He straightened, facing Cece, then turning away, uncertain where he wanted to direct the full force of his anger. "As the club was burning and coming down around her, who did Katya turn to? Christopher Dowland. She clung to him like he was her savior."

Cece's brow knit in confusion. "Did she say why?"

"They're lovers, obviously," Malcolm growled, then fell into another coughing fit.

Cece rubbed his back, and he didn't have the energy to push her away. "I really don't think they are," she said quietly. "As far as I know, they're barely acquainted."

"You didn't see the way she looked at him," Malcolm argued, part of him feeling like a mad idiot for justifying it all to his eighteen-year-old daughter. But Cece was there for him. She might very well be the only person to ever fully be there for him when he needed her. But with her attachment to Rupert, Katya's son, how much longer would that last? He would lose once again.

"I can imagine that the peril of the fire was alarming and confusing," she said, failing to sense the darkening of his mood. "Perhaps Lady Marlowe was terrified. Perhaps she latched onto the first person to offer her help."

"I should have been the first one to offer her help," Malcolm shouted, startling Cece into stepping back. "I should have been the one protecting her." The ache of guilt that squeezed his heart came as a surprise. He pushed it away, latching onto anger once more. Anger was far easier to feel than the shame of failure. "She's been making a fool of me for years, but I'm not having it anymore."

He poured himself another glass of scotch, splashing the liquid over the tray, then downing far too much in one gulp.

The result was a mess on the table, scotch streaking his sooty hands, and a coughing fit that caused him to retch and left his throat raw.

"Papa, you need to clean up and go to bed." Cece surged forward to slide her arm around his back in spite of the soot in an attempt to steer him toward the door. "I'm sure everything will seem better in the morning."

"No." Malcolm shook his head, but his energy was draining as fast as a gutter in the rain, so he didn't push her away. "We're going home."

"We are home, Papa," she said.

"Home to Strathaven Glen," he clarified. "Immediately. On the first train. So go pack your things."

"Scotland?" Cece stopped short, staring at him with wide eyes. "Are you saying we're going to Scotland?"

"Yes. Go pack," he growled.

She continued to study him with alarm. "It's not like you to retreat to the country when things go wrong."

"Maybe that's what I should have done all along," he said. Part of him felt like he should argue with her. Part of him felt like he should stay and continue the battle. But too much of him was done. He'd lost. It was over. "We're going home," he repeated. "And we're not coming back."

"Very well, Papa," she said as they continued forward. Her voice was hollow and sad, which raised more guilt in Malcolm.

"I'm sorry," he said when they reached the stairs. "What am I thinking? You've just had your coming out. You should stay in London with your friends. You should enjoy your life. We can find someone for you to stay with." Up until hours ago, he would have assumed she'd stay with Katya, but that door was closed forever now.

Cece shook her head and valiantly straightened her back

as they mounted the stairs. "You're my father, and I'll stand by you no matter what."

"You don't have to," he said. He needed to grow accustomed to the feeling of being alone anyhow. "Stay here."

"No," she argued. "I'm going with you."

There was no sense in arguing. Cece might have looked like her mother but she had his stubborn streak. Malcolm knew full well no one could argue him out of doing something he insisted on doing, and the same went for Cece. If he were honest, he was relieved she would stay with him.

Cece also inherited his cleverness, though. Not more than half an hour later, as Malcolm walked from his bedroom to the dressing room where one of his footmen had drawn a hot bath for him, he caught Cece slipping an envelope to one of the other footmen. Her expression was sharp with conspiracy, leaving no doubt in Malcolm's mind that the envelope was a letter, most likely for Rupert Marlowe, informing him of everything that was going on.

Malcolm sighed and dragged himself on to his bath. Let Cece and Rupert conspire all they wanted. They couldn't change the facts. He'd spent his whole life giving his heart to the wrong people. Katya didn't think any more of him than she did her other lovers. Their children could plot, but nothing they did could make love blossom where there were only thorns.

BY THE TIME SHE REACHED HOME, EXHAUSTION LIKE KATYA had never felt before overcame her. She should have climbed out of the carriage Christopher hired on her own. She should have told him to go home and take care of himself. She should have done a lot of things, but by the time Christopher carried her over the threshold, alarming Mr. Stewart beyond measure as he did, she realized it was too late.

"She told me to send for Viscount Helm to treat her," Christopher explained to her butler as Stewart directed him to lay Katya on a sofa in her private parlor.

"Right away," Stewart said, turning to leave the room.

"Mama, is that you?" Rupert's voice rang from the hall. As soon as he entered the parlor, his face flooded with alarm. "Mama, what happened?"

"I'm all right," Katya insisted, instantly contradicting herself with another round of coughing that left her wracked and spent.

By the time she recovered from her fit, Christopher was already explaining things to Rupert.

"...entire place in flames. She was lucky to get out alive, but Craig told me her efforts saved the lives of numerous young women who would otherwise have been trapped inside."

Katya blinked, sagging into the soft comfort of the sofa. She didn't remember Christopher talking to Inspector Craig at all. She didn't remember much after Malcolm had stormed off.

Malcolm. Thoughts of him hurt more than her lungs and the bits of her that had been licked by flames. It was shattering that he'd come so close to being the instrument of defeat for Shayles, only to have his moment of glory ripped from him. She was certain there was more to the story and that she would hear it in time, but the look in his eyes, the bitterness and the heartbreak of believing himself to have been pushed aside for a younger hero at the last moment killed her. She knew too well what it was like to be pushed aside for someone younger, and in so many ways.

"Mama! Good heavens, what happened?"

Katya was robbed of the luxury of wallowing in her own sorrow as Bianca and Natalia scurried into the room. They both wore dressing gowns over their night clothes, had their hair tied up in rags, and wore looks of extreme worry.

"I'm all right," Katya wheezed. "It's just a little smoke is all."

"Rob has been sent to fetch Viscount Helm," Stewart reported from the doorway.

"Good. Thank you, Stewart," Rupert said, then turned his attention to Katya. "News of the fire reached us at Spencer House," he said. "I wouldn't be surprised if rumors were flying through London as we speak. What really happened?"

Katya opened her mouth, but coughed instead of forming words. She gestured to Christopher.

"The raid was a success," Christopher began.

Katya closed her eyes and submitted to Bianca and Natalia's hugs and petting instead of paying attention. Everything had gone right—at least, as far as nabbing Shayles—but she felt as though she'd experienced a crushing defeat. All she wanted to do was sleep.

Sleep is what she did, she realized with a shock, when her eyes snapped open again. More lanterns had been brought into the parlor, and Armand had arrived. She must have slept for half an hour at least. No one had bothered to move her, and no one had bothered to go to bed. Christopher had left, though.

"Awake at last?" Armand asked, smiling at her—an expression that was clearly designed to hide his true concern —as he sat on the edge of the sofa beside her.

Katya answered him with another wracking cough that left her weak and shaky and feeling as though her lungs were balls of smoldering embers.

"Don't try to talk," Armand said, resting a hand on her forehead. He placed a long listening device on her chest and bent to listen at one end. His brow knit into a frown. "Your lungs are severely irritated," he said. "Which is to be expected from someone who was caught in a fire but managed to escape."

"What can we do about it?" Rupert asked. He hovered behind the sofa, looking as though he would perform surgery on Katya himself if it could help her.

"Rest and fresh air are the only things that cure the effects of inhaling smoke," Armand explained. "You'll likely continue to cough for weeks to come and to taste smoke as well."

"Isn't there something else that can be done?" Bianca asked, as doggedly determined to heal Katya as Rupert was.

Armand turned to her, no doubt to explain at length, but Stewart stepped into the room and cleared his throat.

"Lord Stanhope, a letter has just arrived for you," he said.

Rupert pried himself away from Katya's side and rushed to take the envelope Stewart held.

"What is it?" Katya asked, anxious to direct attention away from herself, but sounding so much like an aged frog that her girls hovered even closer to her.

Rupert opened the envelope and withdrew a single piece of paper. The note must have been short, because within seconds, his face fell into an irritated frown. "Of all the stupid…." He started, but didn't go on.

"What is it?" Bianca asked. "Who would send you a letter at three o'clock in the morning?"

Katya's brow flew up. Was it that late?

"It's Cece," Rupert told them, returning to the sofa. Katya didn't like the look of uncertain sympathy he gave her. "She says that her father has ordered her to pack her things, and that they're leaving for Scotland on the first train this morning."

"That bloody—" Katya started, but a violent coughing fit stopped her from expressing just what she thought of Malcolm running away.

Being stopped from expressing her knee-jerk reaction

caused her to think twice, though. Malcolm never picked up and ran away when things were difficult. Quite the contrary. He stayed and fought, even when he shouldn't. Even when it drove everyone around him to distraction.

Something was horrifically wrong. He'd been so upset after the fire. Katya had been upset herself, but the calm of home and the circle of her loved ones had eased her back into the complacency of her routine. Her heart sped up and her mind raced all over again as the implication of Malcolm returning to Scotland hit her, like the fire breaking out all over again. And yet, with the rise in tension, her coughing grew worse, preventing her from speaking.

"Why would he do that?" Natalia asked, her lower lip turned down in a pout. "Less than a day after learning I'm his daughter."

Armand turned to her with a look of shock. Katya wanted to explain and to tell Natalia to hold her tongue, but her lungs prevented her.

Instead, Rupert was the one to scold, "Natalia, hold your tongue. We do not discuss family matters in public."

"But we're not—oh." Natalia blushed after glancing to Armand, then whispered, "Sorry."

Katya gave up trying to speak and sank back into the sofa. Her coughing gradually subsided, but her lungs and her heart continued to burn.

"We can't just stand by and let them get away," Bianca said, crossing her arms. "Rupert, you need to get us tickets to Scotland too."

"Yes." Natalia leapt up from where she'd been kneeling beside Katya's sofa. "We have to go after them. Lord Malcolm is making a terrible mistake."

Katya shook her head, barely managing to whisper, "No. Leave it alone."

Her children ignored her.

"It will take some time to pack," Rupert said with a thoughtful frown. "We might not be able to catch the same train as them, but we can get ourselves together at least in time to catch one that departs before noon."

"Yes, exactly." Bianca rushed to his side. "We have to do this."

The pain in Katya's chest took on a different feel. No one had heard her protest. Her children were dragging her into a wild scheme she didn't want to be part of. Once again, Rupert was assuming the role she'd held for years, leaving her as much of a nothing as she'd been when she was married off to his father.

"No," she insisted, willing herself to be heard. They turned to her. "If Malcolm wants to lick his wounds in Scotland, let him."

"Mama, you can't be serious."

"You can't just give up like this."

Bianca and Natalia spoke at the same time, flying back to the sofa to appeal to her. Armand was forced to stand and move to the side so they could crowd into his place.

"You have to fight for the man you love," Bianca insisted.

"Yes. It's what any good heroine would do," Natalia agreed.

Katya squeezed her eyes shut and shook her head. "Life is not a fairy story," she whispered hoarsely.

"Your life is," Natalia insisted.

"Fresh air is the accepted cure for your current condition," Armand added. Katya opened her eyes to peek up at him, furious that he wore a grin, as though this were just another game and not a turning point in her and Malcolm's lives. "Scotland is full of fresh air. London is not."

"The air in London is terrible," Rupert said. "Everyone knows that."

"Yes, Mama," Natalia went on. "And if we go to Scotland, I can see where that part of my family comes from."

Katya frowned. She was going to lose the argument, and there was nothing she could do about it. At least if she traveled to Scotland, she could give Malcolm a piece of her mind for running out on her. And she could explain away the mountain of misunderstandings that seemed to have grown up between them.

"Fine," she sighed, coughing. "We'll go to Scotland." Though whether it would do any good was beyond her.

CHAPTER 13

*S*trathaven Glen sat in a dreary valley, surrounded by unattractive trees and piles of rocks, nudged up against the border of the Highlands, but not a part of it. Malcolm found a certain degree of wry humor in that. His ancestors weren't the great and noble Campbells who had made a name for themselves in the freedom struggles of the past. They were the money-hungry, bloodthirsty traitors who had sided with the English against their kinsmen and been rewarded with second-rate land and a title that didn't actually mean much.

It was fitting, really. He'd been no more successful than any of his forbearers, and now, like them, he was returning home to sulk with his tail between his legs.

"We should really do something about the house," Cece said at luncheon the day after their late-night arrival. She sat to Malcolm's right, stirring a bowl of cold stew and trying to hide her distaste.

"There's nothing wrong with the house," Malcolm's nephew and heir, Gerald Campbell, said as though Cece had insulted his mother.

Malcolm remembered Gerry's mother. He would have insulted the feckless chit too. His late, lamented brother hadn't been much better. They were all rotted fruit on the withered branch of the family tree.

"Do forgive me, Cousin Gerry," Cece said with a diplomatic smile. "I was merely going to suggest that some of the furnishings and decorations be updated. It's rather dark and medieval in here, you must admit."

Gerry shrugged, stuffing sausage into his mouth and looking rather like he was eating his own kind. "It gives the place character."

"Perhaps we could light a few more fires?" Cece went on. "Or throw more logs on the ones already lit? Installing a coal stove might help."

"Where do you plan to get the money for your improvements, Cousin Cecelia?" Gerry snapped, his piggy eyes full of avarice. Piggy eyes, piggy face, piggy body. It described Gerry to a tee. Malcolm wasn't sure how he was so closely related to the man. "You're certainly not taking it out of my inheritance, I can tell you that," he laughed, focusing on his food.

Malcolm sighed and shifted in his chair. Perhaps drinking himself into oblivion in preparation for the trip hadn't been such a good idea. Everything hurt. His eyes stung, his head throbbed, his stomach churned, and every muscle in his body felt as though it'd been wrung out. Not even the coffee he'd had the dreary estate's cook scare up for him was helping.

"At least it stopped raining," Cece went on. "It seems that every time I've visited Strathaven Glen it's been raining. It's rather like a gothic novel."

"There you go, then," Gerry said with a nod.

Cece blinked. "I beg your pardon?"

Gerry shrugged. "The estate is like a gothic novel. There's no need to rush about, changing the aesthetic, when we already have a solid identity."

Cece let out a short, impatient breath. "I'm saying that it doesn't have to be this way. If we replaced all the drapes with something lighter, kept them open so sunlight reaches the rooms, and traded the outdated carpets for something newer and more brightly colored—"

"I fail to see the point," Gerry cut her off, his mouth full. "It's an unnecessary expense. Carpets are meant for walking on and chairs are meant for sitting, nothing more. Besides," he added with a sideways look to Malcolm, who was rubbing his pounding head and barely paying attention, "it's not as though Uncle does any entertaining here."

"But he might," Cece said, a hint of mischief in her eyes that made Malcolm wince. "You never know who might drop by unexpectedly." She darted a glance toward him and broke into a nervous smile.

Malcolm sat straighter, reaching for his coffee but not replying. The letter he assumed Cece had sent off to Rupert the night before their departure must have begged the man to come rescue her from the specter of horrible, Scottish weather. He supposed he should alert his butler, Mackay, to prepare a room for Rupert. But at the moment, he wasn't inclined to move, let alone make preparations for guests.

"If there's nothing to spare to purchase new drapery and furniture," Cece went on, her expression hinting that she didn't believe for a moment money was a problem, "perhaps we could have the staff engage in spring cleaning. I would be willing to wager that if the carpets were taken out and beaten properly, they'd brighten up in no time."

"So now you're ordering my servants about?" Gerry gaped incredulously at her.

"They're Papa's servants, not yours," Cece corrected him, her jaw tight.

They might as well have been Gerry's, for all Malcolm cared. Strathaven Glen had always held a distant second place

155

to Strathaven House in London in his heart. If such things had been allowed, he would have foisted the title and estate off on Gerry and retired to London as a simple gentleman of means instead of a bloody marquess. The title had never done him much good anyhow, and Gerry was clearly champing at the bit to get his hands on it. Malcolm would do everyone a favor if he climbed to the top of the miserable house's highest roof and jumped off to speed things along.

The errant suicidal thought jolted Malcolm out of his thoughts and he sat straighter. Things weren't that bad yet. He'd pack everything up, including Cece, and embark on a world tour before ending things. In fact, leaving the country for sunnier climes didn't sound like a half bad idea. The islands of the Caribbean were nice this time of year, weren't they?

"Excuse me," he said, standing and tossing his serviette onto the plate with his uneaten lunch. Without another word, he started out of the room.

"Where are you going, Papa?" Cece rose and followed after him. "You haven't eaten a thing."

"I'm not hungry," Malcolm said as he marched into the hall.

"That's no excuse not to eat," Cece kept on his heels. "You hardly ate any breakfast and you barely touched anything on the train yesterday. Well, except whiskey. You aren't going to drink yourself into your grave, are you?" she asked, her tone far too chipper to be serious. "That may be a romantic reaction to a broken heart, but it's hardly your style."

Malcolm stopped abruptly in the front hall, whipping to face her. "I do not have a broken heart," he snapped.

Cece saw right through the lie. She crossed her arms and fixed him with a hard stare. "Then I suppose we're here for the view?" she arched one eyebrow.

The expression was so much like Katya that an ache formed in his heart. He turned away, striding on to a hallway that branched off the main hall.

"You're right. The estate has been neglected. It needs improvements," he said, knowing she would follow him.

"That's not why we're here either," she said.

They reached a long, dusty room that passed as a library. One side was set with tall, dirty windows, most of which were covered by thick drapes. Even the uncovered windows let in very little light. A fire filled the huge hearth, but the deep chill in the room hinted that, until they'd arrived the night before, the room had been abandoned and neglected. Malcolm crossed to one of the pitiful bookshelves, took down the first book that came to his hand, and took it to the sofa closest to the fire. He sat, pretending to instantly be absorbed by the book, but Cece didn't go away. She stood in front of him, her arms crossed.

"You love Lady Stanhope," she told him. "You always have. I know the two of you have had a falling out—"

"Mind your own business," Malcolm snapped.

Rather than doing as she was told, Cece's back snapped straight in offense. "You are my business, Papa, and if you ask me, you need quite a bit of minding."

Pride and sullenness warred in Malcolm at his daughter's tart reply. He should have known he couldn't get away with anything around her. "There's nothing you can do," he grumbled, pretending to read once more.

Cece sat on the sofa beside him. "I will admit that I don't know everything there is to know about you and Lady Stanhope. You say she has other lovers, but I would be willing to stake my life that you're wrong about that."

Malcolm glanced sideways at her, hope swelling within him. He pushed it down before it could take over. Cece was eighteen. What did she know of the kind of life women like Katya lived?

"I don't blame you for being upset that someone else might take the credit for everything you've worked so hard for," Cece went on. "And I'm not going to tell you to be happy with the outcome, no matter who accomplished it. But Lady Stanhope wasn't responsible for that, I'm sure."

"You weren't there," Malcolm said. "You didn't see."

"See what?" Cece asked. "Did Lady Stanhope demand that you stay in the carriage while Inspector Craig conducted his raid? Did she shove you aside at the last moment and personally hand credit to someone else?"

Malcolm snapped his book closed and turned to her. Only, instead of being angry, his tone was appreciative when he said, "Katya wasn't there when Shayles was arrested. She'd run off into the house to alert the women she had working for her to what was going on." He paused. "She probably saved lives."

"And you're angry with her why?" Cece stared hard at him.

"She put herself in danger," Malcolm insisted. "And you didn't see the way she clung to that buffoon Dowland when he brought her out of the fire."

"Clung to him like someone who had come within a hair's breadth of losing her life in a fire, perhaps?"

Malcolm scowled. All of the arguments that had whipped him into a fury days before felt flat now. The sickening sensation that he'd been wrong about everything crept through him. He hated being wrong.

"It doesn't change things," he said at last with a sigh, letting go of his anger and feeling only gloom in its place. "Katya and I were never going to work. I wasted too many years figuring that out. She doesn't want me the way I want her to."

Cece shook her head. "If you would just ask her to marry her, I'm sure—"

"I've asked her several times," he said, louder than he should have been with Cece. For her part, Cece blinked in surprise. "I've asked her two dozen times at least over the years. Every time, she's said no or not answered me at all. And now, to find out she's been keeping Natalia a secret from me all these years?" He shook his head and pushed himself to stand, needing to move. "My darling, I know you're young and have a lot still to experience, but women in love do not keep secrets or refuse the proposals of their beloved."

Cece watched him pacing for a few seconds before saying, "I'm not so sure about that. I can think of a lot of reasons a woman would keep things from the man she loves."

Malcolm paused to stare incredulously at her. "Is there something you're not telling me too?"

"No, Papa," she laughed. "I tell you everything."

It was a tiny consolation, but enough to push Malcolm into pacing again.

"I've been wrong about nearly everything for most of my life," he said. "So it's time to start a new life, a life free from the embarrassments of the past." He reached a table at the end of the room and set his book down, then said, "I think I might travel. Australia feels like a good idea."

Cece wasn't impressed. "Running away to the other side of the world isn't going to solve anything. It would just make you more miserable." She stood and met him in the middle of the room. "In fact, the only times I've seen you truly happy are when you're with Lady Stanhope. Surely there must be a way to mend fences between the two of you."

"Is it a woman?" Gerry asked from the door.

Any comfort Malcolm was tempted to feel at Cece's words vanished in an instant. He broke away from her and

continued pacing as Gerry entered the room, smiling oblivi-
ously at both Malcolm and Cece.

"Did a woman chase you up here?" Gerry went on.
"Because if it is about a woman, I find the best course of
action is a night on the town. Glasgow has some of the finest
whiskey and lightest skirts in the north." He followed his
comment with a loud, snorting laugh.

Malcolm sent an apologetic look to Cece. Perhaps
bringing her to his ancestral home was a bad idea after all.

He was about to suggest the two of them go for a walk—
something he was loath to do, but that would guarantee
Gerald wouldn't follow—when Mackay appeared in the
doorway.

"My lord," he announced. "You have visitors."

SCOTLAND WAS A BAD IDEA. THEN AGAIN, KATYA WAS
convinced that leaving her house was a bad idea. Rupert had
only been able to obtain tickets that would allow all four of
them to travel in the same first-class compartment later in
the day, which meant they'd had to stop overnight in York.
She'd coughed like a consumptive the entire way, which had
caused people to stare at her as though she were an invalid
on death's door. She was used to drawing attention, but not
that kind.

The hired carriage that took them from the station in
Glasgow out into the country was an exercise in torture.
There were enough holes and rocks in the road to shake
Katya's insides like an earthquake, and considering the fire,
her insides weren't in the best of shape to begin with.

"Ugh, I hate Scotland already," Bianca said after she'd
been bumped against the side of the carriage for the dozenth
time.

"Don't say that," Natalia argued. "My people come from here."

Katya rolled her eyes at her daughter, but she knew if she said anything it would only result in another coughing fit. Malcolm's people were no more hers than Robert's family were to Rupert. Yes, they shared blood, but not much else. Robert's kin barely acknowledged her family's existence.

"Is that the castle?" Natalia asked as they rounded a particularly rocky stretch of road and approached Strathaven Glen.

"It's not a castle, it's just an estate," Rupert said. He looked just as put out as Katya felt, but the eagerness in his eyes hinted that he was looking forward to the journey's end.

"I suppose Cece told you all about it," Bianca said.

"In fact, she did," Rupert told her, then glanced out the window.

They all pressed their faces to the window, looking out at the antiquated form of Strathaven Glen. All except Katya. She'd seen the estate before. More than seen it, she'd spent a great deal of time there over the years, mostly when her children were too young to travel. Old feelings of guilt over leaving them with their nanny and the servants so that she and Malcolm could carry on welled up, but she quickly dismissed them. She didn't have the energy for old regrets. Not when her new ones were so fresh.

The carriage crunched across the gravel in front of Strathaven Glen's front door, then stopped. The driver helped the ladies down, then waited for Rupert to pay him. Part of Katya felt she should have handled the transaction, but most of her was relieved not to have to worry about it. She waited for Rupert to be done before approaching the front door, breathing in the fresh, Scottish air.

Of course, it made her cough, but somehow her fit wasn't as bad as they had been. If Armand was right about the benefit of country air, she would be extremely put out. There was something humiliating about her friends being right while she was wrong. Then again, she would have to get over thoughts like that if she had any hope of moving on.

As soon as Malcolm's butler, Mr. Mackay, opened the door to find her and her brood standing there, his face lit up.

"Lady Stanhope," he said with a smile. "It's been too long."

"Hello, Mackay." Katya managed a weak smile. She'd always liked Mackay. He looked older now, but then, so did she. "Is Malcolm at home?"

"For you, my lady, I'm sure he is." Mackay took a step back. "Please come in."

The whole lot of them bundled into the house. Mackay showed them to one of the nicer parlors, but within minutes, his happy smile had faded. The man wasn't a fool. He had known Katya well enough all those years ago, and she was sure he could sense something was wrong now. He bade them wait in the parlor, then disappeared, presumably to fetch Malcolm.

"I bet this place is haunted," Natalia said, awe in her voice as she looked around the room.

Katya huffed a laugh, surprised that it didn't make her cough, and sank into a sofa near the fireplace. She held her hands up to warm them, but the room had a distinct chill to it.

Within minutes, Malcolm charged around the corner into the room, Cece and his odious nephew, Gerald, behind him. Whatever Malcolm was expecting to find, it wasn't Katya. He stopped so suddenly that Gerry nearly barreled into his back.

"What are you doing here?" he asked, his surprise seeming to melt into a flash of hope before solidifying into anger.

Katya was too tired to charge into battle with him. "Ask them," she said, nodding to her children, then coughing.

"Viscount Helm suggested country air would be the best cure for Mother's lungs," Rupert explained. He stepped subtly between Katya's sofa and Malcolm's glare as if he could protect her.

"Is that so?" Malcolm inched to the side so that he could deal with Katya directly.

"And we insisted on coming," Natalia added, the only one in the room who was excited. She practically bounced to Malcolm's side. "I want to see where my ancestors come from."

"Are you a Scot too?" Gerry asked her, sweeping Natalia with a look that filled Katya with fury.

"Yes, I'm—"

"Natalia," Rupert cut her short. "What did we talk about before?"

Natalia's face went pink and she took a step back, whispering, "Sorry."

Gerry's smile grew as he glanced from Natalia to Bianca. "Who are these lovely young women?"

"My daughters," Katya told him with as much force in her voice as she could manage, which wasn't much.

"Oh?" Katya had intended to put the man in his place, but his eyes gleamed with mischief. "And do they take after their mother?"

"If you so much as look twice at these girls, I'll have your hide for boots," Malcolm growled.

Gerry flinched, backing away from Malcolm. "Sorry, Uncle, sorry. But everyone knows what Lady Stanhope is like."

"Get out." Malcolm glared at Gerry.

"I didn't mean anything by it." Gerry held up his hands, moving toward the door. "I mean, she came with that young buck, didn't she?"

"Lady Stanhope is my mother," Rupert barked, staring at Gerry with undisguised disgust.

"Oh, dear." Gerry's flabby face went pale, and as soon as he'd backed far enough away, he turned and darted out of the room.

"I see your heir is as charming as ever," Katya croaked, then cleared the smoky taste from her throat.

"He's Lord Malcolm's heir?" Bianca yelped, visibly offended.

"He's my brother's son," Malcolm answered, "and since I have no son of my own, he'll inherit all this someday."

Bianca made a disgusted sound and moved closer to the fire to warm up.

Malcolm approached the sofa, where Katya was ready to pass out with exhaustion. "What are you really doing here?" he asked, eyes narrowed. "Come to gloat?"

"No, Malcolm, I—" Katya was unable to finish her sentence. She burst into a coughing fit that had her gasping the way she had right after the fire. Her eyes watered, and fury at being in such bad shape made her tense, which worsened the coughing.

It wasn't until she realized Malcolm had rushed to sit on the sofa beside her, hands outstretched to help her, that she stopped coughing.

"You really are sick," he said, anxiety pinching his expression.

"I didn't want to come," she whispered. Speaking any louder would only set her off again. "This lot and Armand forced me. I just want to go to bed."

"I'll have a room prepared at once," Malcolm said. He straightened and glanced toward the door. "Mackay."

"I'll have Mrs. Bruce prepare rooms immediately, my lord," the intrepid butler replied before Malcolm could give the order.

Malcolm proceeded to glare at Rupert. "You shouldn't have dragged her all the way up here."

"It's my fault, Papa," Cece answered, standing close by Rupert's side. "I told him we were coming here and begged him to follow."

The look in Malcolm's eyes wasn't surprised. He studied Katya with a doubtful, sideways look.

"Truly, I had nothing to do with it," she said. When Malcolm didn't answer, she went on with, "Really, Malcolm. Do I look like I'm in any condition to resist the combined force of our offspring?"

"No," Malcolm answered slowly. He stood, crossing to Rupert. "If you truly brought your mother here so that the country air could restore her, then I'll give you all rooms and order my staff to help the process along. But that's it." He turned to Katya's girls. "If any of you attempt to meddle in business that isn't yours, you'll regret it." He finished by sending Cece a pointed look.

Cece glanced to Rupert as though she had a whole library of stories to tell him. Katya was certain the two of them were up to something, but she was too wrung out to wheedle it out of them. She leaned against the back of the sofa and shut her eyes.

"You can wait here until Mrs. Bruce has prepared your rooms or you can sit outside," Malcolm said.

"Here is fine," Katya said, her eyes still closed.

"But, Mama," Natalia started.

"Leave your mother alone," Malcolm told her.

Katya opened one eye to peek at him. He wore his usual grumpy frown, but there was something older about him, something defeated. And there was a reluctant sort of concern in his eyes when he shifted his glance to meet her one-eyed gaze.

A burst of warmth filled Katya, but she shut her eye and

leaned her head back to block it out. The last thing she needed was more emotion where Malcolm was concerned. She was in his house, but she would do no more than Armand had ordered her. She would rest and breathe country air. Whatever was going on in Malcolm's head, he had made it clear it was none of her business. As far as she was concerned, that was fine with her.

CHAPTER 14

"*Mama* really should come for a walk with us this morning," Natalia declared at the breakfast table the next day. "It was such a relief to ramble over the hillsides after spending so much time on trains yesterday. And she is supposed to be getting country air."

Malcolm kept his focus on his plate as he wolfed down enough sausages and eggs to feed an army. His appetite had come back the evening before, and it was as if his stomach were making up for lost time. He was far more inclined to eat than to engage in conversation on the one topic he didn't want to talk about, but that wouldn't leave his thoughts.

"Mama is also meant to be resting," Rupert said from the opposite end of the table. As an earl, he deserved to sit in the place of honor at the foot of the table, but that didn't stop Gerry from sending the young man sour looks. Someday, as Marquess Campbell, Gerry would out-rank Rupert, but not yet.

"We could walk sedately," Natalia suggested.

"I doubt you are capable of doing anything sedately, Lady

Natalia," Gerry commented with a wink that made Malcolm want to walk to his end of the table and smack him.

His murderous intent must have shown on his face. Cece —who was seated at his right hand—reached out to tap his leg under the table.

As it turned out, Malcolm didn't have to murder anyone.

"I would rather be lively than boring, Lord Campbell," Natalia told Gerry, her expression saying that boring was exactly what she believed him to be. "Few people can keep up with me."

Malcolm's mouth twitched into a half-grin, which he quickly hid. Katya had trained her girls well. He wouldn't even need to inform Gerry that Natalia was his half-cousin at the rate Natalia was going.

"Where is Lady Stanhope this morning?" Cece asked, most likely deliberately shifting the direction of the conversation.

"Mama was still asleep when I checked on her earlier," Bianca said. "Or at least pretending to be. There was something a little too deliberate about the way she was breathing."

"If Lady Stanhope needs to stay in bed for a while, we should accommodate her," Cece said with a compassionate smile.

"I've heard Lady Stanhope has been very accommodating herself over the years, if you know what I mean," Gerry said, following his comment with a long, snorting laugh.

Silence fell over the rest of the table, and five sets of eyes —including Malcolm's—stared daggers at the buffoon.

As soon as Gerry noticed the scrutiny, his laughter stopped and his mouth dropped open. "What?" he said with an oblivious blink. "Everyone knows her reputation. She's a notorious—"

At the last moment, he seemed to realize who he was

addressing. His face mottled red and pink and he quickly lowered his eyes and sawed at the ham on his plate.

The silence continued for several more seconds before Rupert cleared his throat and turned his attention back to his sisters. "Mama is recovering from the effects of the fire. She needs calm and quiet for her lungs to heal. So you are not to pester her. Don't you agree, Lord Malcolm?"

Rupert sent Malcolm a look that was clearly intended to include him in the circle of people who were forbidden to disturb Katya.

"Quite," Malcolm grumbled, standing at his place to reach for the silver teapot to refill his cup.

"Where is Mama anyhow?" Natalia asked as things began to settle again. "She should have come down to breakfast by now. There are so many things to do in Scotland. I found out yesterday from one of the tenants that there's a spring dance next week."

"For the tenants," Gerry said, studying Natalia incredulously. "Our kind want nothing to do with that."

"Is the dance fun?" Natalia asked, mimicking Gerry's superior tone.

"If you call reels and jigs fun," Gerry sneered.

"Well, I do." Natalia nodded, then turned to Malcolm. "Can we go to the dance, Lord Malcolm?"

"I have no idea," Malcolm sighed, contemplating something stronger than tea. Then again, after his overindulgence a few days before, he was inclined to swear off liquor for a while. "You'll have to ask your mother."

"I would if she were down here," Natalia said. There was a pause as they continued eating, then Natalia huffed and said, "Where is Mama? She really should be down by now."

"If she wants to stay in her room, she wants to stay in her room," Rupert said, sounding as though his patience was wearing thin.

"Perhaps Lord Malcolm should take a tray up to her," Bianca suggested, a mischievous sparkle in her eyes.

"I think that's a brilliant idea," Cece agreed, exchanging a not-so-secret grin with Bianca. "What do you think, Papa?"

Malcolm turned a flat look on his daughter. "I think people should look to their own concerns before meddling in others'."

"Some people need reminding of thing things that are their concern," Cece shot back.

Malcolm stared at her, proud of her spirit but irritated that it was directed against him. "And some people need reminding that curtsying in front of a fat old lady doesn't make them an authority on all things."

"It doesn't?" Cece blinked, humor sparkling in her eyes in spite of her expertly innocent mask.

"We could prepare a tray for her," Bianca offered, standing and circling around the table to the sideboard, where platters of breakfast were still laid out.

"Yes, and you could take it up to her with the teapot," Natalia added. "I'm sure none of us need more tea."

"I might," Gerry said, looking wounded at the thought of missing out on any part of the meal.

Natalia ignored him as she jumped up to join her sister. "Make sure you put a whopping amount of butter on her muffin. Mama loves butter."

"I'm sure she does," Gerry murmured. He must not have realized how loud his comment was until he glanced up to catch Malcolm glaring at him. At once, he turned bright red and cleared his throat.

"Mama will be so pleased that you stopped to think of her health and wellbeing," Bianca prattled on as she filled a plate. "That's all she really wants, you know. Someone to care for her wellbeing."

Malcolm only barely managed to suppress a laugh. Katya

no more wanted someone fussing over her than he did. And even if she were inclined to accept pampering, her daughters would surely beat him to it.

"It's useless to take a tray up to her," he said. "She's likely to turn me away at the door."

"Nonsense," Natalia said. "She'd never turn you away. She loves you."

Malcolm's brow shot up, not so much over the comment, but because Katya herself appeared in the doorway of the breakfast room just as Natalia said it. A pink flush painted her otherwise pale face, and her dark eyes seemed particularly luminous as she stared at her daughters, then past them to Malcolm.

"Mama, there you are," Bianca greeted Katya, setting the plate she'd been loading on the sideboard. "We were getting worried."

Katya dragged her eyes away from Malcolm as Bianca skipped over to kiss her on the cheek. "I had a bit of a lie in is all," she said, her voice still hoarse from the smoke. "Nothing to worry about."

"We were just preparing breakfast for you," Natalia said, picking up the plate Bianca had set down and carrying it to the empty seat on Malcolm's left. "And we saved you a seat."

Katya glanced to Malcolm, but the surprise and emotion in her eyes were veiled by suspicion.

"I had nothing to do with it," Malcolm was quick to inform her. "Any plotting at this table is strictly the realm of the young."

Katya hummed instead of answering as she moved to take her seat. Malcolm couldn't tell if it was because that was all she had to say or because her throat was sore. She remained silent after she sat. True to Malcolm's earlier speculation, Bianca and Natalia hovered around her, pouring her tea—and nearly knocking Malcolm's cup over in the process—

cutting her ham, and generally treating her like an invalid. The tight expression of tested patience on Katya's face was a dead giveaway of just how much she loathed the fuss.

"We were just talking about how you should come on a walk with us today, Mama," Bianca said as she returned to her seat.

"And about how the tenants will be having a dance next week," Natalia rushed to add. "Can we go?"

Katya took a long drink of tea before answering, proving to Malcolm that her throat—and probably lungs—were still bothering her. "I would slow you down," she said. "Walk on your own."

"Oh, but Mama—" Natalia started.

"Perhaps that would be best," Cece interrupted her. "We could all go for a ramble together. Papa can stay behind to keep Lady Stanhope company."

"But—Oh!" Natalia's face brightened. She exchanged an impish grin with Bianca.

Malcolm rolled his eyes. Subtlety was evidently a skill that came with age. He stole a sideways peek at Katya to see what she thought. Katya's face was a mask of indifference, but the lines around her eyes and mouth betrayed that she was just as annoyed with the young people's machinations as he was.

"I have business to attend to away from the house," he said, taking a last bite of buttered bread and pushing his chair back to stand. "Especially if my tenants are planning an event."

"Oh, but Papa." Cece reached for him.

As it turned out, she didn't have to. Mackay entered the room with a folded piece of paper in his hand.

"A telegram has arrived for you, my lord," he said, bringing the paper to Malcolm.

Malcolm took it with a frown and resumed his seat to

read the contents. The message was from Craig, and it left his heart beating faster.

"What does it say?" Katya asked in a near whisper. She knew him well enough to read his expressions and to tell something was afoot.

"It's from Craig," Malcolm told the entire table. "Shayles has already been convicted by a Grand Jury. The date for his trial before the House of Lords has been set. It's to be in a month."

"So soon?" Rupert asked.

"Isn't he going to be tried at the Old Bailey?" Natalia asked with a confused frown.

"No, dear," Katya answered with a slight croak. "Shayles is a peer, and as such, he has the right to a trial in the House of Lords."

Malcolm folded the paper and stood once more. "I'm certain there's some sort of underhandedness involved."

"I thought it took months for trials like that to be organized," Bianca said.

"Usually it does," Rupert answered. "But seeing as Parliament is already in session, which means a sufficient number of lords are already on hand to make at least a twelve-person majority, I suppose they're attempting to fit it in before recessing for the summer."

"I'm sorry, trial?" Gerry asked, looking to everyone for answers.

"Lord Theodore Shayles was finally arrested a few days ago," Natalia informed him, back straight and chin held high as she divulged the information. "Mama and Lord Malcolm have been after him for ages."

"Good Lord." Gerry fumbled his cutlery in his haste to stand. "I must send a telegram at once." He tripped over the carpet and nearly knocked his chair over in his haste to flee the room.

Malcolm squeezed his eyes shut and pinched the bridge of his nose. He hoped Gerry was only in a hurry to spread gossip and not to cover up indiscretions related to The Black Strap Club. Either was possible.

"If you will excuse me," he said, nodding to the table in general before taking the telegram and heading out of the room.

Katya continued eating her breakfast as though nothing were out of the ordinary—which stung Malcolm's heart, whether he wanted it to or not—but Natalia leapt up from her chair to follow him.

"Are you just going to leave Mama alone like that?" she asked once they were out of earshot of everyone else in the hall.

Malcolm paused in the front hall and turned to her. "Your mother is her own woman and can do as she pleases."

"But you love her, don't you?" The innocence in Natalia's eyes was almost painful.

"Whether I do or not is of no consequence to you," he told her with a frown, then cut off whatever she was in a rush to say by holding up his hand and saying, "I appreciate your concern, but there are forces at work which are well beyond your comprehension. You don't understand the full story, and your meddling is only making things worse. So please, I beg of you, stop."

Natalia had tried to interrupt his speech several times, but as he concluded, she snapped her mouth shut and lowered her head. "We only want the two of you to be happy."

Guilt lashed Malcolm and he sighed. "I know. But please, let us handle this our own way."

He stopped any further protest by leaning toward Natalia and kissing her forehead. It felt good and natural. She was his daughter, after all, whether Katya had intended it to be a secret or not. But even that sliver of happiness had a sharp edge to it. Katya should have told him.

That thought brought the rest of his anger piling back on him. He stepped away from Natalia with a frown, turning toward the front door. He needed a walk to clear his head and remind him of what was really important, and he had yet to be convinced that a lying, faithless woman—no matter how much he loved her—should have any place in his heart or his life anymore.

KATYA DETESTED IDLENESS, AND CONVALESCENCE WAS nothing but idleness. She wanted to move and be active, to run, even, if only to settle her jangled nerves. But anything more vigorous than a moderately-paced walk set off a coughing fit that left her even weaker than when she'd started. The situation was so depressing that by early afternoon, she'd retreated to her room, traded her day dress for her nightgown, thrown open all the windows, and climbed back into bed.

Sleep eluded her, though. Her body may have been useless, but her mind was racing as if it were after the blue ribbon. Shayles must have pulled strings to have his trial so soon, which meant he still had friends on the inside. Inspector Craig was new to his position and might not have the time he needed to put together a case. His telegram didn't say who would be prosecuting the case, which meant there was no way to know if Shayles would face a competent barrister or some bumbling peer with skeletons in his closet. In spite of everything, Shayles could still walk free.

Beyond that, Malcolm was clearly still upset. Katya didn't know if she wanted to sit him down and demand he tell her what was behind his sullen attitude—other than the obvious myths he persisted in clinging to about her attachment to Sir

Christopher and other men—or wash her hands of the whole thing and move on at last.

The idea of walking out of Malcolm's life left her feeling as though she had a lead weight in her gut, though. It was just a pity that the thought of sticking by him until he came to his senses made her burn with frustration. No matter what she did, she would be miserable.

Her thoughts were running in circles for what felt like the hundredth time when there was a knock at her door. She let out an impatient breath and rolled under her covers to face the door. Assuming it was one of her children, she snapped, "What do you want?" Her throat tightened, but for a change, she didn't cough.

At least, she didn't cough until the door opened, revealing Malcolm. The shock of seeing him sent her into a brief coughing fit. He shut the door behind him, but didn't move any farther into the room.

"Are you certain you're all right?" he asked in his gruffest, most impatient voice.

Katya willed herself to stop coughing—with only moderate success—and dragged herself to sit. "Why aren't you coughing like your lungs are scorched?" she asked.

He shrugged. "I was that first day. I still cough occasionally. I wasn't fool enough to run as deeply into the house as you were."

"I wasn't going to let those girls burn," she told him, frustrated that she had to speak softly when she wanted to shout at him.

"You very well could have burned yourself," he snapped.

"Don't start with me, Malcolm," Katya sighed, sagging back against the pillows and hugging the coverlet to her chest. "Is that what you came here to do? Yell at me for risking my life to save others?"

"No." He approached the bed but stopped a few feet away.

"I came here to—" He pressed his lips together and looked away. "Why are these windows open?" he demanded, lurching into motion and crossing around the bed as though he would shut them.

"Leave them alone. Armand told me to get fresh air," Katya said, her annoyance growing by the second. "What do you want, Malcolm?"

"I want—" He marched close to the bed once more, only to hold back a second time. Katya could see the agony of his thoughts in the lines on his face and the tension in his body. "I don't know who you are anymore, Katya," he snapped at last.

Katya sighed, clenching her jaw and closing her eyes. "I'm the same person I always was."

"And I have no idea who that is," he said, moving closer. "I thought I did, but the woman I knew wouldn't keep secrets like you have."

Without opening her eyes, Katya said, "I didn't tell you about Natalia because I knew you'd overreact, and I didn't want her to be labeled a bastard."

"I had a right to know," Malcolm insisted.

"Malcolm, I don't have the strength for this argument right now."

"And am I supposed to continue to wait for my due?" he asked, sitting on the side of the bed. There was more hurt than fury in his expression, which made Katya ache all over. "Fat lot of good that's done me."

"Malcolm." Katya shook her head.

"Am I going to have to wait for you the way I had to wait to bring Shayles to justice? Is someone else going to sweep in at the last minute and steal you away from me as well, or has someone already done that?"

She glared at him. "Will you please drop this ridiculous

obsession with Sir Christopher? He's not my lover. I don't have any lovers."

"Not even me?" Malcolm's eyes went wide in offense.

"You're not acting like much of a lover right now," she growled.

"Oh no?"

He surged toward her, grabbing her arms and pulling her close. His mouth slanted over hers in a demanding kiss. In an instant, heat rushed through her, and the familiar pull of desire threatened to break her resistance. Malcolm was amazing when he was angry. Some of her most exciting memories of him were of times when he'd been so furious with her that he'd left marks. Part of her was ready to submit to him in every way, but that was the problem.

Her self-respect was saved by a violent coughing fit that split the two of them apart. As an added measure, she used what little strength she had to slap his face.

"Now is not the time," she managed through wracking coughs.

He pulled back and stood, straightening his clothes. His expression showed regret, but all the same, he hissed, "When is the time? When do I finally get my rest, my peace?"

"As soon as you stop holding on to the wrong things," she wheezed.

"Is it so wrong to want what's mine?" he shouted.

"I am not yours," Katya managed to raise her voice in reply. "I am my own. And until you realize that, you will never understand why I didn't tell you about Natalia, why I've refused to marry you all these years. You will never understand."

"Oh, I understand, all right," he said, marching around the bed and heading for the door. "I understand that you are a selfish, heartless bitch who has strung me along like a child's toy for almost twenty years."

"Malcolm," Katya tried to shout, but her strength was draining as though someone had smashed the bowl that held her together.

"I'm through with being your toy," he said, grabbing the doorknob and wrenching the door open. "I'm through with loving you until I have nothing left in my heart. It was all a waste anyhow. I should have learned my lesson with Tessa and given up on love entirely."

"Malcolm."

Her plea was useless. Malcolm shot out into the hall, slamming the door behind him. In his wake, a sob rose up from Katya's damaged lungs. It shocked her. She hadn't wept for years. She was too strong for that, too proud. But once the floodgates were open, the tide poured through, and she was helpless to stop it.

CHAPTER 15

*K*atya could only keep to her room for a few days before her absence from the activities of the house looked more like sulking than recovery. Barely speaking to anyone and sleeping twice as much as she usually did managed to bring actual improvement to her lungs, but her heart remained broken and her spirits shattered.

Her period of seclusion gave her the time to pick apart everything Malcolm said to her—not just during their brief battle in her bedroom, but over the course of their lives. He was angry that she hadn't told him about Natalia. He still believed she was a faithless harlot who kept a stable of lovers. Her refusal to marry him wounded him. None of that was a revelation. But a new complaint had entered his list during their fight, one she'd never heard before. He'd implied that the grand love story she'd always believed he'd had with Tessa hadn't been as perfect after all.

Days later, she was still mulling the revelation over as she sat in the window seat of her room, looking out at the yard as her children and Cece played badminton on a hastily-constructed court. Malcolm was nowhere in sight, but just because Katya didn't see him didn't mean he wasn't there. She could hear the whiny voice of Gerald Campbell coming from somewhere nearby, and chances were, he wasn't talking to himself or a servant.

"They're both tasty little morsels," Gerry was saying. "Surely someone has taken a bite out of those apples."

Katya's gut clenched. She had half a mind to throw something out the window. The only thing that stopped her was the faintest hint of a growl. Malcolm was definitely down there somewhere.

"All right, all right," Gerry said. Katya could imagine his puffy face flapping in surprise that Malcolm had been offended by the comment. "My only point was that they've had a scandalous upbringing, or so my chum down in London tells me. Outspoken little chits they are." Gerry broke into a laugh. "You should have heard what old Boffo Lewis-Phipps said about the way the older one behaved at the theater last month. And she's not even out yet."

Katya pushed herself to stand, her hands shaking with rage. Insults against her were one thing, but anyone cowardly enough to insult her daughters for having the strength to display personality in public was beyond the pale. It was also the final sign that she'd spent too long licking her own wounds. There were more important things to do than mope about, counting her losses.

She dressed as quickly as she could without a maid's help, though she left her hair in a thick braid down her back instead of pinning it up. Once she was presentable enough, she marched down through the house and out onto the lawn where the badminton game was progressing.

"...and with the long-standing association between you and her mother, it wouldn't be unheard of for me to have a go." Gerry was still talking as Katya stormed toward him.

Gerry and Malcolm sat in folding chairs near the wall of the house, enjoying the scant warmth of a patch of sun. Malcolm had his arms crossed and an odd look that was a mixture of misery and resignation. His eyes were fixed on the badminton match, and by all outward appearances, he wasn't listening to Gerry at all. Gerry, on the other hand, had somehow managed to rest one ankle on his massive thigh. He leaned back in his chair with an oblivious smile. How the chair didn't splinter into matchsticks under his weight was a mystery.

The moment Katya stormed into view, however, both men sat up. Malcolm was so startled that he failed to hide a flash of hope in his eyes. Color splashed his cheeks, and for a heartbeat Katya thought he was going to smile.

The moment passed, and Malcolm hunched back into his chair.

"The Gorgon emerges at last," he muttered, focusing on the badminton game once more.

Katya tried her best not to be hurt by his words, but the usual sense of teasing and banter that had always existed between them was gone.

"I have been sitting up there in my window," she said, glaring at Gerry and ignoring Malcolm, "listening to everything you've been saying."

"Oh." Gerry's face took on a mottled blotch of color. "What did you hear?"

"How dare you insult my daughters with your disgusting innuendo," she charged on, in no mood for niceties. "Do you know how old they are? How dare you make such lascivious comments about mere girls."

"I…I wasn't saying anything…I didn't…." Gerry gulped like a fish on dry land in his feeble attempt to defend himself.

"And you should have defended them." Katya turned her frustration on Malcolm. He was the root of the anger and hopelessness writhing inside of her anyhow.

"Me?" Malcolm glanced incredulously at her. "You want me to defend them? When all you've ever done is gone on and one about how independent you are and how independent you want them to be? Are you certain you don't want them to defend themselves?"

The only thing that stopped Katya from stomping her foot—or smacking Malcolm into next week—was Gerry clumsily blurting, "He did defend them. I'll have those scorch marks for weeks."

Malcolm tightened his crossed arms and stared straight forward, blushing even harder—though whether from modesty or fury, it was hard to tell.

Katya pinched her mouth shut, balling her hands into fists at her sides. There were so many things she wanted to say to Malcolm, so many ways she wanted to yell at him and shake sense into him. He was behaving like a petulant child, and nothing she did could shake him out of it. If he would just talk to her, she was certain they could untangle the knot that had become of their hearts. At the same time, she was utterly unwilling to bow down to him and be the first to speak.

"Lady Stanhope, you look distressed," Gerry said, pushing himself to stand. The chair cracked ominously. "Allow me to escort you around the property so that I can make my apologies."

"I don't know if that will be necessary," Katya said, her narrowed eyes fixed on Malcolm.

"I insist," Gerry went on, crossing in front of Malcolm and stopping exactly at the point where he blocked Malcolm's view of the game. "I never meant to imply anything untoward about your lovely daughters," Gerry went on. "In fact, if truth be told, my tastes are more, shall we say, vintage." He wiggled his eyebrows at her.

Katya let out an impatient breath. "No thank you, Gerry. I'm not interested. At all."

She crossed in back of Malcolm, intent on determining if the chair Gerry had vacated was structurally sound enough for her to sit.

"Why not?" Malcolm asked, glowering as he leaned to one side to peer around Gerry at the game. "It must be days since you've had a man between your thighs. Aren't you afraid you'll get the delirium tremens from going without?"

If Katya had been close enough, she would have picked up Gerry's chair and smashed it over Malcolm's head. Instead, she used her recovered voice to shout, "Enough. I have had enough of your adolescent jealousy and your insults."

Malcolm flinched in surprise hard enough to nearly fall out of his chair. He blinked up at her, but Katya wasn't about to engage him in any more verbal jousts.

She marched away from him toward the badminton game —which had slowed down to a rate that hinted the children were aware of her presence and of her interaction with Malcolm.

"Mama, how nice of you to join us at last," Bianca said with a bright smile, immediately abandoning the game to approach her.

Katya was through with games and niceties. "Put those racquets away and go to your rooms to pack your things," she demanded. "We're going home. All of us," she finished, staring at Rupert in particular.

Immediately, the four young people burst into a flurry of protest.

"But Mama, we can't," Bianca insisted, on the edge of whining.

"I've only just gotten to know more of where I come from," Natalia argued.

"I'm concerned for your health, Mama," Rupert said, his

argument more rational on the surface, but equally as pleading as his sisters'.

"Surely whatever has been made wrong can be corrected," Cece said, perhaps the most distressed of all. "Isn't that true, Papa?"

Katya whirled around to find Malcolm marching toward her, his face like a thundercloud.

"No," he shouted. But before Katya could get her hopes up, he charged on with, "I won't have you children meddling in the affairs of grown-ups anymore. If Lady Stanhope wants to leave, then let her."

Instead of feeling justified by Malcolm's statement, Katya's heart ached as though he'd stabbed it. "I am finished with insults," she said, more for Malcolm than her children. "I didn't want to come here in the first place, and I certainly don't deserve to be called a gorgon and a harlot by you of all people."

"Papa, did you call Lady Stanhope those things?" Cece asked in shock.

"He did," Gerry said from the edges of the confrontation, a foolish grin on his face. "I heard him. Bloody impolite, if you ask me."

Katya ignored him. She ignored everyone but Malcolm. "You've built this image of me in your mind that is not only false, it's despicable. And then you cry in your pillow because I don't return your love the way you want me to, by lying at your feet and allowing you to walk all over me. I won't have it anymore."

She waited for Malcolm to say something, to contradict the picture she'd just painted of him, but he was silent. At least, he didn't speak. The bright red flush that painted his cheeks and the wounded fury in his eyes said far more than words could. He clenched his hands into fists at his sides, not out of anger, Katya guessed, but to stop himself from visibly shaking with pent-up emotion. Whatever sympathy she was inclined to feel for his emotional struggle was squashed by his failure to do the very least he could do and tell her that she was wrong.

When she'd waited long enough, she turned back to Rupert and said, "Pack your things. I'm sure we can take a train from Glasgow tonight."

"But the dance," Natalia protested.

"The tenants are having a dance," Bianca echoed. "We can't miss that."

"Surely you can work this out," Cece said, near tears.

"We can't travel now," Rupert added.

The four of them spoke over top of each other as they brought up every excuse they could think of.

"Fine," Katya barked at last, holding up her hands. "You lot can stay, but I am returning to London. Shayles's trial is at the end of the month anyhow, and I'm certain there's a mountain of work to prepare for that, with or without you," she added, glaring at Malcolm.

A prickling silence hung over the lawn as she finished. All eyes turned to Malcolm, waiting.

After what felt like an eternity, Malcolm finally whispered, "Fine. Do as you wish."

Fists still clenched, he turned and stormed off.

Tears stung at the back of Katya's eyes. How had things become so broken between them? As little as a fortnight ago, she had been happy with the assumption that they would be an intimate part of each other's lives until they both died. How had it all gone so horribly wrong in such a short time?

Blinking to fight back her tears, Katya turned to her children. "Come with me or not as you see fit," she said, praying they would take the hoarseness in her voice as a lingering symptom of her problems after the fire. "I can't stay here."

Her heart seemed to swell to the point of bursting with

her final words. She couldn't face her children anymore, couldn't face their sorrow or their innocence. She turned and walked away, unsure where she would go...in every way.

"Lady Stanhope, let me walk with you," Gerry said, jogging after her. "I promise I won't try anything. But you shouldn't be alone right now."

Katya didn't reply. She let Gerry walk beside her, but she didn't take his arm. She needed him there to stop her from bursting into tears. If she had nothing else, at least she still had her pride.

꽃

RUPERT WATCHED HIS MOTHER WALK AWAY WITH A CHURNING sensation in his stomach and a weight around his heart like nothing he'd ever experienced before. His mother was a goddess in his eyes and it was damnably upsetting to see her in so much pain. Part of him rebelled at the idea that she was human after all, but the truth of her humanity was staring him in the face. He'd never felt his age as keenly as he did at seeing his mother in obvious distress.

"We can't just stand here and do nothing," Cece said, putting words to all of the confusing emotion running through him.

"It's just so sad." Natalia burst into tears. "They love each other so much and they're being so horrible to each other."

"They *do* love each other," Bianca insisted. "Why can't they see it?"

"I don't think it's a matter of them not seeing it," Rupert said, speaking slowly at first as his inexperienced mind tried to grapple with reality. "But something happened between them. Something that's left both of them hurt."

"What is it?" Natalia sobbed, sniffing and wiping her nose on her sleeve. "Make it stop."

Rupert rubbed his chin, wracking his brain. "I'm not sure we can make it stop," he said. "Whatever it is, they need to be the ones to stop it."

"I agree," Cece said, turning her large, blue eyes on him. "But what can we do?"

"We can't know what to do unless we know what's wrong," Rupert said, frowning and twirling his badminton racquet in his hands. "I know for a fact that Mama and Lord Malcolm were on the very best of terms the night before Cece's presentation."

"How do you know that?" Natalia asked, batting her wet lashes innocently.

Heat rose up Rupert's neck. "Let's just say I'm certain and leave it at that."

A mysterious grin spread across Cece's face. "I have that same certainty," she admitted. "From about a week earlier."

Bianca suddenly caught on, her cheeks turning pink. "I see."

"What? What do you see?" Natalia asked, visibly impatient at being left out.

Rupert ignored her to ask, "What happened between then and now that has the two of them ready to either mount opposing armies or sail away and never see each other again."

"It's obvious, isn't it?" Cece asked. "Your mother failed to tell my father that Natalia was his daughter."

"Don't blame Mama for this." Bianca flashed to the defensive, glaring at Cece in a way that looked frighteningly like Katya.

"I'm not," Cece insisted. "I think I understand her reasons. What I don't understand is everything else. It's rather as though Natalia's paternity was the spark that set off a pile of kindling."

"I agree," Rupert said, feeling fonder of Cece than ever.

"Mama and Lord Malcolm have known each other since

before Natalia was born," Bianca said, crossing her arms and frowning in thought. "They've had a long, long time to build up grievances against each other."

"But if they hate each other so much, why are they in love?" Natalia asked.

Rupert couldn't help but grin at the way she phrased it.

"Why has your mother refused my father's proposal of marriage?" Cece asked. "I know he's asked her several times."

A thought hit Rupert that sent a shiver through him. "Can you imagine what might have happened—or not happened—between us if Mama had accepted him years ago?" he asked Cece.

Cece gasped, touching her fingers to her open mouth. "Do you suppose she knew we would...like each other as soon as we met and that she has refused Papa all these years to make things easier for us?"

"Perhaps," Rupert said, though he and Cece had only met a year and a half ago at Starcross Castle. He'd been drawn to her in an instant, though. Had his mother been surprised or had she predicted there would be a spark? "There's more going on than we know about," he concluded with a sigh.

"We need to know," Bianca said definitively.

"I'm not sure we *need* to know," Cece said. "But they certainly need to talk things through."

"But how are they going to talk when Mama is intent on going home and Lord Malcolm is being such a stick-in-the-mud?" Bianca asked, growing angry herself.

"We have to force them to talk," Natalia said, tilting her chin up. "Even if we have to kidnap them and tie them to chairs facing each other."

Rupert started to laugh at the image his sister painted, but stopped. He drew in a breath as an idea began to form. "You may be right," he said, running his free hand through his hair.

189

"What, about kidnapping and tying people to chairs?" Bianca snorted incredulously.

"About forcing them to talk somehow," Rupert said. "Which they would have to do if they were stuck somewhere for a length of time."

"Are you proposing we trap them alone together somehow?" Cece asked, her eyes flashing with excitement.

"That's exactly what I'm proposing," Rupert said. "I'm not sure how we would do it, though."

"We have to act fast," Bianca said. "Mama will try to leave tonight."

"Do you think the two of you can find a way to get her to delay until tomorrow morning?" Rupert asked his sisters.

Bianca and Natalia exchanged a look before answering in unison, "Yes."

"And I think I might have an idea of how we can not only get them alone, but trap them away from here so that they're without distractions," Cece added.

"Really?" Rupert glanced to her with a burst of pride. His mother was dead set against him marrying Cece while they were both so young, but he would have dropped to one knee right then and there if he hadn't had so many other things to deal with first.

Cece's whole face continued to shine with inspiration. "I think I know a way that we can lure both Papa and your mother away from Strathaven Glen and to a neutral location. I think we can get them to leave here with urgency and work together on something. And I might be able to call in a favor with my nanny, Mrs. Elkins, which will enable us to trap them in such a way that they'll be forced to talk."

"Your nanny?" Natalia shook her head in confusion. "What does she have to do with anything?"

Cece's grin broadened. "She has retired to a small cottage overlooking the River Esk, near Gretna Green."

"Gretna Green?" Bianca frowned in confusion. "Didn't people use to run away to get married there in our grandparents' time?"

Rupert burst into a laugh as the pieces came together in his mind. "That will certainly make them jump," he said. He would have kissed her cheek at least if his sisters hadn't been standing there. "What do you need to do to get in touch with your nanny?" he asked.

"I can send her a telegram," Cece said without hesitation. "I'm sure she'll help and that she can have her cottage prepared to be sealed by morning."

"Then we'd better get started," Rupert said, itching to put the plan into action.

"What are we doing?" Natalia asked with a huff. "I don't understand."

"You'll see," Cece said, practically giggling. "Once this machine is set into motion, Papa and your mother will fall into each other's arms again so fast there might be an earthquake."

CHAPTER 16

*K*atya didn't make it three hours before her plans for a speedy retreat were foiled. Malcolm's usually on point staff was maddeningly slow to respond to her request for a maid to help pack her things. She was tempted to think that Malcolm was behind the dereliction of duty, that he was intent on making her miserable, or that he was trying to keep her close, until she discovered the true source of the delay.

Somehow, after she'd stormed into the house, Natalia had managed to fall out of a tree.

"Why in Heaven's name were you climbing a tree?" Katya asked in exasperation as two maids helped Natalia into the afternoon drawing room. "You're not a child anymore."

"It was a dare," Natalia said with an overdramatic wince as the maids settled her on a sofa and rushed to bring her tea. "Bianca dared me."

"You didn't have to take my dare," Bianca insisted. The little hellion was having a hard time concealing a smile and mischief glittered in her eyes.

"Of course I did," Natalia answered. "I couldn't just stand

there and let you win, could I?" Natalia had an equal measure of mischief in her eyes.

Katya could only imagine what kind of trouble they'd been plotting before it was cut short by the fall. Or perhaps mischief was still in the works. Natalia looked surprisingly tidy for someone who had fallen out of a tree. Katya's suspicions were strengthened when she noticed the maids whispering to each other in a corner, their expressions full of mirth that was entirely inappropriate when a guest in their house had injured herself.

"Rest for a bit," Katya said at length with a sigh, "then go pack your things."

"Oh, but, Mama, I couldn't possibly travel in this state," Natalia protested.

"She's right," Bianca seconded her. "She would be such a bother with her ankle twisted as it is."

"I couldn't possibly run to catch trains like this," Natalia said, reaching to rub her left ankle.

Katya could have sworn she'd been favoring her right ankle when the maids had brought her in. She rolled her eyes and crossed her arms. "I'll give you until the morning to recuperate and pack. But we *will* leave first thing, injuries or not."

Bianca and Natalia seemed to pause for thought, exchanging a glance before Bianca said, "That would be sufficient time. All right, Mama, we'll leave tomorrow."

Katya took her supper in her room. She was still too stung by the things Malcolm had said and too aggravated by her life in general to be in company, even if that company was her family. Like it or not, Malcolm and Cece were like family to her. They had been for ages. It both galled Katya and saddened her beyond measure that it should all come to this after so much water under the bridge. She picked at her lamb, stirred circles in her soup, and sniffed at her pudding, but even in solitude, she didn't have much of an appetite.

What had gone wrong between Malcolm and Tessa? The question wouldn't leave her mind, not even after she sent her picked-at food back, undressed, and climbed into bed. She stayed awake, tossing and turning as possibilities rolled through her mind. Tessa had been perfect, for all she knew. She had been the love of Malcolm's life, no matter how badly Katya had wanted that spot herself. Malcolm had never had anything but glowing praise for the ghost of the woman. She was beautiful, refined, and tragic. He had rescued her from unbelievable hardship and given her a safe but short life.

Malcolm had been mourning Tessa when Katya met him, and had continued to mourn her ever since. Try as Katya had over the years, she'd never lived up to Tessa. She'd never been soft enough or sweet enough. God only knew how hard Malcolm had tried to make her as dependent and submissive as Tessa had been. That thought left her twice as restless, to the point where she crawled out of bed to pace in the moonlight instead of wrestling with the sheets. How different would her life be now if she had caved in to Malcolm's demands a decade ago and become the charming wife he'd always wanted? How different would it have been if she'd cut him loose the moment she realized that what he truly wanted from her was to take Tessa's place, to fit into the dead woman's shoes.

Both possible outcomes would have made her miserable. Not that the situation she found herself in currently was any better.

Sleep found her in the small hours of the morning, but it was a difficult, restless slumber. She awoke at dawn, bleary and depressed, but more than ready to flee Scotland and resume her life in London. She wasn't too old to take another lover or two or more. But as she packed her things—the maids still hadn't come to help her—that prospect left her feeling heavy and old. Lovers were too much trouble, when all was said and done. And no other man could hold a candle to Malcolm.

With her trunk packed at last and her heart miserable, Katya left her room and headed downstairs to find a footman to handle her things. She hadn't expected to find her children lined up and waiting to leave at the front door, but she didn't expect to find her girls in the state they were in either.

"What are you doing downstairs in your dressing gowns?" she demanded of Bianca and Natalia as they huddled in the morning parlor, whispering like thieves. "You should be dressed and ready to leave by now."

"Oh, Mama." Bianca straightened, blushing up a storm, and hiding something behind her back. "You're up early."

Katya sighed impatiently. "It's not early. What is that behind your back?"

"Have you eaten breakfast yet?" Natalia asked, her eyes bright with mischief as she rushed forward in an attempt to steer Katya out of the room. "You can't start a journey on an empty stomach."

"What the devil is going on here?" Katya asked as she was bustled into the hall.

Her puzzlement was cut short as she spotted Malcolm coming down the stairs. He'd dressed without care and hadn't bothered to shave. Katya's heart skipped a beat at the hints of ginger stubble in his mostly grey facial hair and the sad set of his shoulders. She wanted to run to him and embrace him and tell him everything would be all right, that they would be all right.

His pace slowed as soon as he caught her staring at him, and he descended the last few steps with heaviness. "You're ready to go, I see."

Katya swallowed and straightened, trying to be regal and

not betray her grief as she crossed to meet him at the bottom of the stairs. "You know this is for the best, Malcolm."

To her surprise, he nodded sadly. "I don't know what we were thinking," he said in an uncharacteristically defeated voice. "We're all wrong for each other."

"I have too much fire in my blood for you," Katya agreed, resisting the urge to break into a sob.

"And I'm too much of an ass for you," he said.

In spite of herself, Katya broke into a weak grin. "I would say something about your ass, but there are young ears nearby."

Malcolm managed a grin as well and glanced past Katya to where Bianca and Natalia were hovering in the doorway. The two of them looked eager to hear what they'd say next.

"I'm only sorry that I kept you from finding someone who would truly make you happy," Katya went on, her smile fading.

Malcolm looked stricken by the comment. "I was happy with you. What makes you think I wasn't?"

Katya shook her head. "We both know that I wasn't Tessa. I could never fill those shoes."

Malcolm scowled. "Of course, you could never be Tessa. Tessa was—"

"Malcolm," she cut him off, raising a hand. "Let's just leave it there. Too much has happened to bring it all out now. I'm leaving, and you'll never have to put up with me again."

Malcolm's mouth hung open for a few more seconds before he snapped it shut and tensed. "Fine. If that's what you want. Goodbye."

He pushed forward, heading toward the breakfast room. Katya started for the front door, where Mr. Mackay stood, observing the whole scene like a statue.

But before Katya could ask him to have a footman bring

her trunk down, Bianca and Natalia burst out from their observation post.

"Wait," Bianca called, producing a small letter from behind her back. "You can't go."

"And you can't walk away, Lord Malcolm," Natalia called out, stopping Malcolm in his tracks.

When both Katya and Malcolm stared questioningly at the girls, Bianca went on with, "Rupert and Cece are gone. They left this note." She scurried forward to hand the letter to Katya.

"They've run off to elope," Natalia burst as Katya opened the letter, far too much glee in her voice.

"What?" Malcolm bellowed, striding toward Katya with renewed energy.

He reached Katya's side and glanced over her shoulder as she read the letter.

"Dear Mama and Papa," it read. *"We know that your plans are to break for good, for Mama to return to London, parting the two of us as surely as you are parting yourselves. We cannot stand for it, though. We are in love, and we intend to act upon that. We are leaving immediately for Gretna Green, where we will be married by the local blacksmith. By the time you read this, we may already be man and wife. Be happy for us and for our love."* It was sighed, *"Your loving children, Rupert and Cecelia."*

"What in the name of all that is sacred," Malcolm began, plucking the letter out of Katya's hands. "They can't do this."

"You're right," Katya said, full of renewed energy and anger. "Don't those two idiots realize that marriages at Gretna Green were outlawed decades ago?"

"I've let Cece read too many romantic novels," Malcolm growled. He folded the letter and handed it back to Katya. "The fools."

"I told Cece not to do this," Katya sighed, rubbing her forehead and beginning to pace.

"You told her what?" Malcolm stood still, following her with his eyes.

"I told her not to marry so young. It was a disaster for me, and I don't want her to face the same fate as I did." She shook her head, incredulity building inside of her. "They'll ruin themselves."

"But marriages are no longer performed in Gretna Green," Malcolm said.

"Of course they aren't," Katya snapped. "But what do you suppose they'll do once they reach there? They'll get a room together. Even if they don't physically do anything, rumors will fly."

"From a dozy old place like Gretna Green?" Malcolm stopped her when she paced near him.

"Rumors can start anywhere," Katya said, facing him squarely. "And be honest. Those two have been in love since the moment they met. Blacksmith marriage or not, do you think they'll contain themselves once they realize they're alone without prying eyes?" Malcolm didn't look convinced until Katya added, "Would we have contained ourselves?"

A new understanding lit his eyes. "Mackay," he snapped at his butler. "Have a carriage prepared at once." He turned to Katya. "If we leave immediately, we should be able to make it to Gretna Green in a matter of hours."

Katya nodded in agreement.

"Wait for us," Bianca said as she and Natalia rushed for the stairs. "It won't take but a moment for us to dress."

"Did the two of you have anything to do with this?" Malcolm asked, catching Natalia by the arm as she rushed past.

"No, Papa," Natalia said, blinking innocently at him. She was a terrible actress.

"We would never interfere with anything," Bianca attempted to support her.

Katya laughed humorlessly. "You're a terrible liar, my dear, and if anything untoward happens between your brother and Cece, I'll pack the two of you up and send you off to Peru."

"We didn't do anything, Mama," Natalia insisted, still doing a poor job of feigning innocence.

"Get dressed," Malcolm snapped. "You're coming with us."

Katya turned to him. "Are you certain that's wise?"

"Would you rather leave the two of them alone here, to get into who knows what kind of mischief?" he asked.

"You have a good point," Katya said, then turned to her girls. "Go. And hurry." As soon as the girls had scurried up the stairs and slammed the door to their room, Katya turned back to Malcolm. "You realize this is most likely a plot to stop the two of us from parting ways."

"Naturally," Malcolm growled, marching to the door and opening it to peer outside, as if anxious for his carriage to appear. "They can plot all they like, but it won't work."

TRY AS HE DID TO KEEP HIS WITS ABOUT HIM, MALCOLM'S heart pounded the whole way to Gretna Green. Not out of anxiety for Cece—although if she had found a way to marry Rupert, he would throttle both of them—but because the wild goose chase meant he had a few more hours before Katya walked out of his life for good. He sat silently in the rear-facing seat of his rattling carriage, Natalia by his side, staring at Katya for most of the journey.

She looked tired, and looking tired made her appear older. At some point in the previous years, she'd developed faint lines around her eyes and across her brow. He'd never noticed them before. Her skin was still fresh, and he knew full well her body was still lithe and limber. It came as a shock to think that he would never again feel the heat of her flesh against his, taste the sweet salt of her skin, or hear the tantalizing sounds she made as she came. Losing those things felt like a monumental loss, but more than that, he wasn't sure how he would survive without her laughter when he made a joke—or did something foolish—or without her wise counsel when he needed advice.

He wasn't going to survive without her. The truth hit him squarely in the heart as the carriage lurched to a stop in front of the old blacksmith's shop in Gretna Green. He wouldn't die, not physically, but without her, he could never truly be alive.

"Are they here?" Natalia asked, sliding toward the door as soon as the driver opened it for her. "They must be here." Her eager tone hinted that, even if Katya's girls had known about Cece and Rupert's mad plan, they didn't know all of it.

Malcolm exchanged a knowing glance with Katya before stepping down from the carriage so that he could help her. She took his hand, and once her feet were on the ground, she seemed reluctant to let it go. Perhaps she didn't truly want to leave him after all. Perhaps there was still a measure of hope.

"I don't see them anywhere," Bianca said, making a quick circle around the carriage and searching in all directions.

"They should be here somewhere," Natalia said.

"They're still hiding something," Katya told Malcolm as they started toward the blacksmith's shop.

"They're absolutely hiding something," Malcolm said. "I'm more convinced than ever this is a plot against us."

"Our children? Plotting against us?" Katya said, her voice full of sarcasm.

Malcolm grinned. He was tempted to find the situation amusing, and would have, if the underlying mood weren't so dismal. He steered Katya toward the blacksmith, who was hammering away at the open forge, making a horseshoe.

"Excuse me," Malcolm called out. "We're looking for a

foolish young couple who seem to have gotten it into their minds that illicit marriages are still performed here."

The blacksmith glanced up and laughed. "We see at least a dozen couples a year laboring under the same false assumption."

"This couple would have come by last night," Katya said. "Rupert Marlowe and Cecelia Campbell. He's about yay high." She held her hand six inches over her height, then lowered it to the level of her chin. "And she's about this tall. She's blonde with blue eyes and he has brown hair and eyes."

"Aye." The blacksmith nodded, breaking into a grin that resembled Natalia and Bianca's horrible acting a little too closely. "I know exactly who you're talking about."

Natalia and Bianca stopped scanning the area and leapt over to see what would happen next, their faces shining with excitement. Malcolm arched an eyebrow at Katya. He couldn't shake the feeling they'd played exactly into Cece's and Rupert's hands.

The blacksmith confirmed as much by saying, "They told me you'd be by. Right on schedule, by their reckoning."

"Where are they?" Malcolm growled. His hands itched to wring Rupert's neck. Although it was just as likely that Cece was the mastermind behind whatever plot they'd hatched.

"The girl told me to tell you to visit her old nanny," the blacksmith said.

Malcolm frowned. "Did they say that Mrs. Elkins would know where they are?"

The blacksmith shrugged. "All they said was to make sure you knew to go to the nanny's house." He chuckled. "That boy paid me a pretty penny to send you there."

"Where does this nanny live?" Katya asked, gripping Malcolm's arm as though he were responsible for the mess instead of the children.

"Down by the river, I think," Malcolm said. "Her people

are from here. She retired to the area when Cece outgrew having a nanny."

"She lives in Esk Cottage," the blacksmith interrupted. "Head that way—" He pointed off across the green. "—then turn right when you reach the grocer's. Keep going for a bit, then take the road where the fallen tree is. The cottage is the third house down on the right."

"Thanks," Malcolm said, reaching into his pocket to find a coin for the man.

As soon as the blacksmith was paid, Malcolm took Katya's hand and marched off to find the cottage. Bianca and Natalia followed.

"Are you certain you two don't want to wait in the carriage?" Katya asked them.

"No," they answered in unison, far too suspicious for Malcolm's liking.

The cottage was farther outside of town than Malcolm anticipated. Katya started to cough from exertion before they reached the fallen tree. Deep concern bubbled up in him and he slowed down, but Katya didn't seem to be in the mood to pause for a rest. She soldiered on valiantly, filling Malcolm with a sense of pride that he was no longer sure he had a right to.

"There it is," Bianca called out, running ahead when they spotted the quaint cottage near a bend in the river.

"We're here, we're here," Natalia ran after her, disappearing around the corner of the house.

"Do you get the sense we're walking into a trap?" Katya asked as they approached.

"Yes," Malcolm answered. He squared his shoulders and marched on, determined not to be bested. "Cece, if you and Rupert are there, come out at once," he shouted.

There was a brief silence before a clatter and thumping.

Malcolm led Katya to the cottage door and knocked. More rattling followed.

"We're inside." Cece's voice sounded distant.

"Are you there as well, Mama?" Rupert called, sounding distant as well.

"I'm here," Katya shouted. "And you're about to wish you weren't."

"Come in, then," Cece said.

Malcolm tried the doorknob, finding it unlocked. He pushed the door open and stormed in, Katya right behind him. "The two of you had better be decent," he said, squinting in the cottage's dark front room. The windows were shuttered and the only light came from the cheerfully crackling fire and the open front door.

"And you'd better not be married," Katya said, turning in a circle to get her bearings.

All at once, the front door smacked shut, and there was a thump and clatter outside. Malcolm whipped around and marched over to open the door, but the handle wouldn't turn and the door was stuck tight.

"What the devil is going on here?" he bellowed, pounding on the door.

"You're sealed in," Rupert announced from the other side of the door. "All of the doors and windows are fastened shut. You won't be able to open them from the inside."

"So help me, Rupert," Katya roared, marching toward the door. "Earl or not, I will tan your backside as soon as I get out of here."

"Behave yourself, Mama," Bianca answered. "It's time you and Lord Malcolm sat down and talked things through."

"Yes," Cece agreed. "We're not letting the two of you out until you've said all the things that you haven't been saying to each other, starting with admitting that you're in love and you can't live without each other. Do I make myself clear?"

Malcolm wasn't sure whether he was more surprised or angry at the children's plot. It galled his pride to no end that he'd fallen for their trick so handily. "Let us out of here at once," he growled, banging on the door for good measure.

"No," all four of them shouted.

"The little shits," Katya hissed, turning and walking away.

Malcolm turned to watch as she searched for and found lamps and matches to light them. A lump formed in his stomach that pulsed its way up to his chest. He had a horrible feeling he might have to do what the children wanted him to do.

CHAPTER 17

"*L*et us out of here," Malcolm shouted, continuing to bang on the door.

Katya rolled her eyes and searched for more lamps. If she was going to be stuck in a tiny, two-room cottage with Malcolm in a rage for an indeterminate amount of time, the least she could have was light. As soon as the lamp on the counter in the kitchen area was blazing, she carried the matches she'd found around the room to light all the candles she could find.

"I don't hear you talking to Lacy Stanhope, Papa," Cece scolded Malcolm from the other side of the door.

"If you don't let me out of here this instant, young lady, I'll—"

"Let it be, Malcolm," Katya snapped from the other side of the room as she peered into the cottage's small bedroom. "They nabbed us fair and square."

As Malcolm pounded on the door one last time—more out of frustration, by the sound of it, than any real conviction —Katya stepped into the bedroom to search for a lamp. Her tired face dropped into an irritated frown at the sight of the room. The bed was freshly made with flower petals strewn across the pillows. A vase of flowers sat on the bedside table, along with a lamp. Did the children really think a few words would end with her and Malcolm in bed?

She huffed and snatched the lamp off the table, beginning to believe everyone who had told her she was far too liberal with her girls' education had been right.

"This is insufferable," Malcolm growled when she returned to the main room. He was pacing, running his hand through his hair as he did. Tension rippled off him.

Katya lit the lamp and set it on a tiny table near one of the windows that she supposed was the nanny's dining room table. "Stop acting like a caged animal," she said, sitting in one of the dining room chairs and crossing her legs. "You'll only wear yourself out."

"What am I supposed to do?" Malcolm bellowed, marching toward her.

"You're supposed to talk to Mama," Natalia's voice came from the other side of the window, a mere foot from where Katya sat.

Katya clenched her jaw and narrowed her eyes at the window. "I won't say a word if I know the lot of you are listening."

Her threat was followed by a squeak and a rustle that Katya assumed was Natalia moving away from the window.

"They'll just creep back up to the windows again," Malcolm groused, returning to his pacing.

"Not if they know what's good for them," Katya said, directing the comment over her shoulder.

All the same, she got up and moved to the lumpy, old sofa closer to the fireplace, in the middle of the room. She was determined not to let a passel of young people get the better of her. As she sat, she crossed her arms, ready to wait as long as it took to prove to them her will was stronger than theirs.

"Sit down, Malcolm," she ordered after a few minutes silence.

"I don't want to sit down," he grumbled. "I want to get out of here and wring their necks."

"They're not going to let us out unless they think we've talked things through," Katya argued. "And they're not going to believe we've talked things through unless some time has passed. So quit fussing like an old hen and *sit down*."

Malcolm turned to her, the glare he sent her fading fast into a look of bitter resignation. He strode to the sofa and sat at the far end, crossing his legs and twisting away from Katya.

"That's a fine posture," she said, full of sarcasm. "Shut me out and behave like a child. You're very good at it."

"*I'm* good at shutting people out?" He shifted to face her, incredulity widening his eyes. "This from the queen of secrets."

"There's a vast difference between secrets and discretion and you know it," Katya snapped, settling into her corner of the sofa. She knew Malcolm well enough to know the children were about to get exactly what they'd hoped for. Malcolm was less than ten seconds away from exploding like an overheated jar of jam.

"So it was discretion that kept you from telling me I had a child all these years?" he demanded.

Katya would have grinned over her ability to predict his actions if she hadn't been so exhausted by his rage.

"As I told you," she said, "Natalia is my daughter. I could no more have told you the truth of her paternity when she was born than I could have run to the moon and back."

"Balderdash. You could have sent me a letter or sought me out in person to tell me," he argued. "I had a right to know."

"Your memory is appalling, Malcolm. Don't you

remember what things were like in those days?" Katya leaned slightly toward him.

"It shouldn't have made a difference," Malcolm said, but he couldn't hold her gaze.

Katya laughed and shook her head. "Robert was still alive when Natalia was born, but just barely. Or do you not remember how his health declined over that last year before his heart failed?" When Malcolm didn't answer, she went on with, "Of course, you must remember. The entire reason you abandoned me was because you suddenly decided you couldn't carry on with a sick man's wife behind his back."

"I didn't abandon you," Malcolm insisted, pink flooding his cheeks. "I had business to take care of and Cece to raise."

"You ran faster than a thoroughbred the moment your conscience pricked you," she said bitterly. "You left me with an indifferent, ailing husband, two toddlers, and a baby on the way."

"Well you didn't waste any time finding someone else to warm your bed," Malcolm said with renewed anger.

Katya tutted and shook her head. "You always have had an overblown idea of my promiscuity."

"Are you denying the fact that you've had a whole stable of lovers?"

Katya paused, glancing toward the fireplace. "No," she answered at last.

Malcolm made a victorious sound and leaned back, crossing his arms.

Katya turned her head to glare at him. "You don't know what it was like back then."

"It must have been a true hardship to have so many men between your legs, servicing you every night," he snorted.

If she'd been close enough, Katya would have slapped him. "I was forced to marry Robert when I was barely eighteen," she said, her voice raised, instead. "I was younger than Cece is now. My parents arranged the whole thing without my knowledge. I was informed less than a fortnight before the wedding that not only would I not get a season or two, like every one of my friends and other girls my age, but I was condemned to marry a man fifteen years older than me whom I'd never met."

"So you took revenge on them all by becoming a tart," Malcolm grumbled, though Katya could see uncertainty beginning to form in his expression.

"I was no such thing," she told him, the pain of that time in her life returning. "I was a child myself, but I tried to be the best wife I could be to Robert. He wasn't a bad man, just indifferent. The only reason he wanted me was because of my family's connection to the Romanovs. He wanted his heir to have royal blood. I did my duty and gave him an heir within a year of our marriage."

"Good for you," Malcolm said. "And once you'd done your duty, you opened shop for every other man who wanted a taste of something royal?"

Katya bit her lip, the young, lost woman she'd been crying through the hard layers life and age had built up within her. "It was Robert's idea," she said at last.

Malcolm's brow knit in confusion, but he remained silent.

"It was Robert's idea," she repeated, as if justifying everything that happened next in her life. "After Bianca was born, he had what he wanted. It was clear Rupert was healthy and would live, so he didn't feel the need to keep trying for another boy. He had a mistress at that point who he cared about far more than me. He styled himself a man of modern attitudes, and during one of the numerous house parties he threw in the summers, he encouraged me to bed whoever I wanted."

"He didn't," Malcolm said, more an exclamation than a contradiction.

"He didn't just encourage it, he made suggestions, introductions." Katya glanced down to her hands in her lap. "I was terrified at first. I didn't want to be an adulteress, but I was only twenty at that point and too terrified to contradict my husband's wishes to say no. I shook like a leaf the first time a man who wasn't my husband took me to bed." Her mouth pulled into an ironic twist, but she continued to stare at her hands. "Robert was beyond clever, though. I think he made sure that first lover was young, attractive, and highly skilled. I felt things Robert himself had never made me feel."

"Who was it?" Malcolm snapped, his tone thick with jealousy.

Katya sent him a flat stare. "Under no circumstances will I ever tell you, so don't even try. The point is, Robert set me on a path that I felt helpless to resist, particularly as it provided me with so much pleasure. But as delightful as my nights were, my days were bitter with regret. I could barely meet my own eyes in the mirror, and I couldn't look at Robert at all. Until you came along."

Malcolm blinked in confusion. "Me?"

There didn't seem to be any point in holding back anymore. Too much water had passed under the bridge. "I'd been had by half a dozen men by the time we met, Malcolm, but I never loved anyone until I met you."

He opened his mouth, but no sound came out.

"You were fiery," Katya pushed on, unwilling to let silence fall between them. "And grieving. You touched my heart along with my body. You were the first man to talk with me as though my opinion mattered, to tell me ribald jokes and laugh along with me instead of at me. I knew you were mourning Tessa, and I wanted to be the one to heal your heart."

"You were," he said, though the words came out with stilted reluctance, making Katya question whether he meant them or whether he was humoring her.

"My young heart thought it had found its match at last," she said with a sigh, remembering how beautiful and innocent the feeling had been. "I knew that you were the father as soon as I fell pregnant again. I hadn't been with anyone else for months before you, not even Robert."

"So Robert knew he wasn't Natalia's father either?" Malcolm asked.

"He knew," Katya said, more emotions she thought were long dead pinching her insides. "He didn't care. He told me he'd claim the child as his, but he knew it wasn't. I think he suspected that his illness was more than a lingering pain by that point anyhow. He died less than a month after Natalia was born."

"You should have told me," Malcolm said, though this time the words held an entirely different kind of regret. "I would have been by your side in a heartbeat."

Katya swallowed, pressing a hand to her stomach at the memories of the worst days of her life. "Everyone and their brother was by my side, and every one of them wanted a piece of the pie that had fallen into my lap. Robert's brother Henry tried to sail in and take over control of the title and the estate, saying he would act as a sort of regent until Rupert came of age. My father tried to use me as a way to drain the Stanhope wealth as well. I had solicitors at the house every day, Robert's seedier friends stepping forward with offers to 'comfort' me in my time of trial. I had at least ten proposals of marriage, including one from a man who went so far as to corner me in a sitting room in an attempt to rape his way into marriage."

"I'll kill him," Malcolm growled. "Whoever he was, I'll kill him."

Katya sighed and rubbed her forehead. "He's been dead eight years now, so be my guest."

"You should have sent for me, I would have—"

"Joined the legion of men offering to protect me and organize my affairs for me?" Katya asked, then huffed a laugh. "No thank you. I beat the man who tried to rape me off with a candelabra, and in the process, I realized a hard truth. If I was going to be anything other than a pawn in some man's game, I had to learn to fight for myself, to fight for my children. I had to be smarter than every man in the room. I had to know more about running an estate and about politics and about the world than anyone I came across. I had to claim what was mine and hold onto it with an iron fist. I had to take lovers the way that men did to stop them from seeing me as a fragile flower who could be plucked and controlled."

Malcolm gaped at her. "Don't tell me that you didn't want to take all those lovers. That would be a bald-faced lie."

"I took the men I wanted as lovers and rejected the ones I didn't want, which is far, far more than most women have the luxury of saying. I made friends with people I trusted, which, as you will recall, is how our paths crossed again."

"Was it Basil?" Malcolm asked, his jaw tight. "Was he your lover?"

Katya kept her lips pressed tightly shut.

"Were any of the others your lovers too?"

She met his eyes and held them tight. "You know I would never betray the confidences of my true friends."

"It was—" Malcolm stopped, then sighed and rubbed a hand over his face, sinking back into the sofa. "So what was I, then? Another way to prove you had power over men?"

"You were my reward," she admitted, lowering her eyes.

Malcolm snorted. "Fantastic. I was a prize in your game."

"Not a prize." She met his eyes. "My reward. For establishing myself as I wanted to be."

He frowned. "I don't understand."

"I had gained control of the Stanhope title and estate. Every man who had tried to take what rightfully belonged to my children had been set in his place. My reputation as a powerful woman was established. I had nothing left to prove to anyone."

"So you celebrated by inviting me to your flat in St. John's Woods for supper and sin?" he asked, trying to sound tough but clearly confused.

"Yes," Katya answered with a shrug. "For me, that night was a way to mark the end of the war I'd been waging and the beginning of the rest of my life."

He studied her with narrowed eyes, clearly delving into his memories to recapture that night. "All I remember was that I was so happy to be back in your arms again that, well, I outdid myself."

"You certainly did," Katya agreed, a wicked grin playing at her lips.

"But that was just one night," Malcolm went on, shaking his head. "You were still the catch of London in those days. You had men lining up for the chance to be seen with you."

"Of course," she said with a coquettish shrug. "I was a wealthy, powerful widow who had entered politics. Escorting me to the opera instantly raised a man's status in the eyes of other men. I can name half a dozen men whose political careers advanced because they danced with me more times than was proper at a ball."

"I bet you can," Malcolm muttered, jealousy hot in his expression once more.

Katya tsked and shook her head. "You don't understand. After all this time, you still don't understand."

"I understand that you take far too much pleasure in what you can do for eager young bucks," Malcolm snapped.

"Being *seen* with me made their reputations. My endorsement helped them politically." She paused, meeting his eyes and holding them. "I never went to bed with any of them."

"Of course you did," Malcolm said, looking confused again. "You just said—"

"I said that, after Robert died, in order to protect myself and build the reputation I needed in order to control my own destiny and my children's fortune, I carefully chose a series of lovers. And then I said that once I'd achieved my goal, I chose you as my reward."

Malcolm started to speak but stopped himself. Slowly, like bricks falling into place, understanding began to dawn in Malcolm's eyes. Katya watched as the truth took hold, as he fought against it, rejecting the possibility that he'd been wrong for so many years, and then as startled acceptance left him reeling. It was time for the full truth to be told.

"Malcolm, you're the only lover I've had for the past twelve years. You're the only man I've ever loved at all," she said, surprised at how easy the words were to speak after all this time.

"You can't...you don't mean that, do you?" he asked in a hoarse voice.

"I am telling the gospel truth," she said, staring straight at him so that there was no way he could doubt her veracity.

"They why didn't you marry me?" he burst, full of emotion. "I've asked and asked and asked, but you've always turned me down. Why would you be so cruel if you love me?"

"Because if I'd married you, everything I spent all those years working for would be ruined," she said, meeting the intensity of his emotion. "I love you, Malcolm, but given half the chance, you would have marched into my life, taken control of the earldom, barred me from my own finances, and forbidden me from living a political life, just like every other man in my life has tried to do."

He gaped at her. "No I wouldn't have," he nearly shouted. "How dare you even think that?"

For the first time since sitting down, Katya felt uneasy. "Of course you would have," she said. "You're always arguing with me and contradicting me and trying to get me to do whatever you tell me to do."

"Because I like arguing with you, you madwoman," he shouted. "I *like* fighting with you. It arouses me in ridiculous ways. No one challenges me the way you do. I've spent my whole life with people kowtowing to me because I'm a stupid, bloody marquess, but not you. You're strong. You're fierce. Do you know how many pale, fussy, insufferably dull women have tried to throw themselves or their daughters at me so they can reap the benefits of the Campbell fortune? They're all idiots compared to you."

"Don't be ridiculous, Malcolm. You're not that twisted," she said, in spite of the fact that her body reacted to his confession in entirely inconvenient ways.

"I am," he argued, leaning toward her. "You're the only woman who has ever been able to boil my blood at a moment's notice in every possible way."

"That's a flat lie," Katya said, shifting to face him more fully. "You loved Tessa far more than you ever loved me."

He jerked back, staring incredulously at her. "Is that what you think?"

"I think it because it's true," she said. "You risked your life to save Tessa, and everything you've done since her death, the way you've pursued Shayles with single-minded focus, is because of her."

"Yes," Malcolm admitted with a nod. "I've dedicated my life to bringing Shayles down because of what he did to

Tessa, what he's done to too many women since then. But you don't know the whole story."

"Then tell me," Katya pleaded. "The whole point of the children locking us in here is so we share the secrets we've been keeping from each other. You know all my secrets now —yes, you do, so don't give me that look." She pointed at him before he could protest. "It's your turn to bare your soul to me, Malcolm Campbell."

"Fine," he snapped, the old fire back in his eyes. "You want to know all my secrets?"

"Yes, I do."

"Then how's this for a secret—Tessa never loved me." His voice faltered with a sudden burst of pain that went far deeper than Katya would have expected. Silence hung between them for a moment. "She never loved me," he repeated.

"I'm certain she did," Katya said, but her conviction was slipping by the second.

Malcolm shook his head and fell back against the sofa, rubbing his face. "I met her after I came back from the war," he said, his tone haunted. "The war was terrible. Too many young men, cut down in the prime of their lives. And for what? It was a stupid cause. We never should have gotten involved in the Crimea. I came home sick, wounded, and angry at the world."

"And you found Tessa," Katya suggested when it looked like he might not go on.

Malcolm shook his head, his face contorted in bitterness. "I found Shayles. I'd known him at university, but we met again by chance. He told me he'd recently started a club for gentlemen, one where frustrations like the kind he could see in me could be soothed. Damnable idiot that I was, I took him up on his offer to be let into the inner circle."

A long silence followed that Katya didn't feel she could

break. Malcolm was clearly reliving things that went back further than she did.

"I'm not proud of the things I did," he said at last in a shaky voice. "Though back then, the club didn't hold a candle to what it became. It wasn't much different than a regular brothel. One woman in particular calmed my anger over everything the way I needed it to be calmed. Only later did I find out she was Shayles's own wife, that she was a dubious participant in the activities of the club, and that Shayles got off on humiliating her."

"I always knew he was a bastard," Katya said, shaking her head.

"Tessa begged me to rescue her from Shayles one night," Malcolm went on. "That's when I turned a corner. My life was no longer about the horror of the war, it was about justice, redemption. I nearly ruined my fortune and my reputation getting Tessa away from Shayles. We escaped from the club one night. I hid her in my townhouse for months and helped her initiate divorce proceedings. She couldn't initiate them herself, of course. Shayles had to be the one to set things in motion. I was close enough to Shayles to pay him off and blackmail him into letting her go."

He paused, shaking his head and lowering it. "I should have known."

"Known what?" Katya asked gently.

Malcolm sighed and sat straight, still not looking at her. "Shayles must have contacted her behind my back. I don't know what they said or how often they communicated, but he let her go far too easily. Or rather, he let her go for the gigantic sum I had to mortgage my townhouse to pay him. As soon as the divorce was final, I married Tessa. She was pregnant in no time. Honestly, I think she was already pregnant before we were officially married. She was happy, but there was also a wistfulness about her. I explained it away because she was with child."

He stopped. Katya respected his silence. She knew what happened next at any rate. Tessa had died in a difficult childbirth. Cece had almost died as well. Malcolm had told her everything when they'd met six months later at one of Robert's house parties.

As if to confirm that his thoughts had gone to the same place hers had, he said, "The birth was a nightmare. The midwife tried to keep me out, but I refused to be anywhere but by Tessa's side. The screaming, the blood." He swallowed and shook his head. "It was a miracle Cece survived."

Katya scooted closer to him, reaching out to take his hand as it rested on the cushion, but he pulled away.

"The last words Tessa spoke," he said in a harsh whisper. "The last thing she spoke as she lay there, bleeding to death because of me, was to call for Shayles."

Katya gasped, the pain she could see in Malcolm's face echoing in her heart.

"After everything I'd done for her, everything she meant to me, she called out his name as she died," he said, staring hollowly at the fire. "And I never got answers," he went on. "I never found out if she loved him or was cursing his name, or if she ever loved me, or why she begged me to take her away from him. I never found out what she and Shayles said to each other behind my back. I never found out for certain if she was a willing participant in his club or if she'd been forced into it, as she told me. I'll never know."

A tear slipped from Katya's eye and tickled her cheek, startling her. She wiped it away and sniffled. "You could have told me, you know," she said. "I would have listened."

He turned to stare at her. "You could have told me about Natalia, even if it meant telling me to stay away as well."

She glanced down at the expanse of sofa between them.

He was right, though there was no way she could have known it until now. "It seems we've spent so much time being lovers and rivals that we've failed to simply be friends."

He huffed a humorless laugh in agreement and stretched his hand toward her. Katya took it, simply holding it.

"I feel so old," Malcolm said at last with a sigh. He rubbed his free hand over his face. "I've failed at so many things for so long, and I don't have the energy to keep pretending I'm young."

"You haven't failed at everything, Malcolm," Katya said, rubbing her thumb over his knuckles. "You've beaten Shayles more times than you realize. It was you who did the work that led to his arrest, regardless of Christopher's help."

Malcolm snorted. "I knew all along he wasn't your lover. I just despise the young pup for being by your side when I wanted to be."

"In all fairness," Katya said with a weak smirk, "I believe he's in his thirties. And he asked me to help him find a suitable young bride, because he's had no luck catching a girl's eye on his own."

"Are you everyone's matchmaker now?" Malcolm turned to her with an exhausted smile.

Katya huffed. "I've never felt so ancient as I did when he asked me to find him a *young* woman. Men like that used to ask for *me*."

"His estate is in Cornwall, isn't it?" Malcolm asked, the question a peaceful signal that the storm of their past was over. When Katya nodded, he said, "What about Victoria Travers?"

"That's exactly who I was thinking."

He smiled and squeezed her hand. They continued to sit at arm's length, hands joined, the weight of the world still pressing down.

Time seemed to drag, so Katya had no idea how much of

it had passed before Malcolm said, "I withdraw all previous offers of marriage."

Katya blinked and turned to him. "You do?"

He nodded heavily, staring at the fire, not her. "They were made without a full grasp of the situation. You deserve better than that."

The corner of Katya's mouth twitched, but she wasn't sure if it was a smile. Her heart felt oddly empty. "And you deserve better than to live in the shadow of self-doubt."

He turned to her, a questioning eyebrow raised.

"I don't know whether Tessa was true or false with her affections," Katya went on. "I never knew her. But I know that your intentions toward her, your efforts to save her, were as pure and genuine as could be. You did the right thing, Malcolm. I knew it from the first moment I met you. It's why I fell in love with you. And either way, Tessa gave you Cecelia."

"I didn't know love like that was possible until I held Cece in my arms and thanked God she survived," Malcolm said, dissolving into tears. "I'm so proud of the woman she's become."

Katya blinked into tears with him. She slid across the sofa, closing the gap between them, and tucked her arms around him in a quiet embrace. There was nothing suggestive or lascivious about the way their bodies fit together, only deep respect and a love that ran far closer to the bone than either of them had realized.

"I haven't just been fighting against Shayles, you know," Malcolm said a minute later, sniffing and clearing his throat as he sat straight and resumed his gruff demeanor. "I've been fighting for the bill we want to pass, for the rights of all women. That's the true battle of my life, and I'm fighting it for Cece, and for you."

"And you'll win, I'm sure," Katya said, wiping away her

tears. "You're the most experienced fighter in Parliament. It's only a shame that silly title of yours prevents you from running for a seat in Commons."

"Maybe I should give it up," he said with a lop-sided grin. "I don't need a title anyhow."

"Oh no." Katya shook her head. "If you gave it up, that sniveling nephew of yours would become marquess, and nobody wants that."

"It's a shame women can't inherit. Cece would make a brilliant marchioness." He paused, tilting his head to the side. "Maybe I'll fight for equal inheritance laws once we win this first battle for women."

Katya laughed at the idea, not because it was foolish, but because it was so far beyond progressive that even she had never thought of it. "I would stand behind you all the way," she said.

"Good," he answered.

He brushed a hand over her face, cradling her cheek and leaning in for a kiss. Katya closed her eyes and parted her lips, finally ready to give in to him as part of her had longed to do for ages.

But before Malcolm's lips met hers, there was a horrendous crash and the front door flew open, revealing Rupert. Katya and Malcolm jumped apart, but the expression on Rupert's face was not one of excitement or joy that his plan had worked. Instead, he looked far more alarmed than Katya had ever seen him.

"Mama, Lord Malcolm, you have to come now," he said, all seriousness. "Shayles's trial has been moved to tomorrow."

CHAPTER 18

*I*n an instant, the sticky swirl of emotion that had made Malcolm feel as though he were drowning was replaced by familiar fury. He leapt up from the sofa with the energy of a man half his age and marched to Rupert.

"How do you know?" he demanded, more out of frustration for Shayles's capacity to worm his way out of any situation than because he doubted Rupert.

"Because I told him."

Shock lodged like a shard of iron in Malcolm's gut as Mark Gatwick stepped into the cottage. The man was dressed for a London soiree rather than the wilds of Scotland, but where Malcolm expected him to sneer at his surroundings, Gatwick barely seemed to notice them. He wore an expression of uncharacteristic focus as he nodded a greeting to Malcolm and to Katya as she stood and walked to Malcolm's side.

"What are you doing here?" Katya asked, suspicion warring with surprise on her face. "I thought you were in Paris."

"I was," Gatwick answered. "I returned as soon as I heard Shayles was in custody."

"Returned to help the bastard go free, no doubt," Malcolm growled. "You're responsible for having his trial miraculously moved up, aren't you?"

"No," Gatwick replied, absolutely straight. "You may find it difficult to believe, but I want Shayles taken care of as much as you do."

"I'm sure you do," Malcolm said, enough sarcasm in his voice to hint that he meant exactly the opposite.

But there was nothing in Gatwick's demeanor that suggested he was anything other than honest in all he said. He studied Malcolm with an unreadable expression before saying, "My reasons for wanting Shayles brought to justice go back much farther than yours."

Malcolm wanted to challenge that statement, to remind Gatwick that he'd been Shayles's closest friend and toady for decades. Why would a man who wanted justice cling so closely to a devil like Shayles unless they were, in fact, friends?

But before Malcolm could say anything, Katya narrowed her eyes and asked, "How did you know we were here?"

"Lady Lavinia informed me the two of you had retreated to Scotland," Gatwick answered. "Your butler informed me you'd come here specifically."

"I'll wring Mackay's neck," Malcolm said, starting for the door.

"He had good reason to be open with me," Gatwick said, following him.

Katya and Rupert brought up the rear. The girls were waiting outside, along with Cecelia's old nanny, Mrs. Elkins. All four women looked anxious, and the girls seemed ready to charge off into whatever battle waited for them. Malcolm nodded to Mrs. Elkins, wishing he had more time to either thank her or berate her for enabling his daughter to get into mischief, he wasn't sure which.

"How did Shayles manage to get his trial moved to tomorrow?" he asked as their entire group started back toward the center of town, where Malcolm's carriage—and presumably whatever conveyance Gatwick had taken to reach them—waited.

"He has powerful friends," Gatwick answered. "Friends who will be present at the Palace of Westminster tomorrow, even if others aren't."

Malcolm huffed a humorless laugh. It was exactly as he thought, even without elaboration. "Shayles is trying to pack the House of Lords full of his allies and push the trial through while his opponents are away."

"Peter is still in Cornwall, awaiting the birth of his second child, isn't he?" Katya asked.

"He is. And Basil is languishing in Cumbria, ignoring it all." Malcolm swore under his breath. "At least Armand is in town. And we may be up here, but we can make it to London by tomorrow morning if we head straight to the train station," he said, thinking aloud. "Rupert, I'll need you to linger behind to make arrangements with Mackay to send my things and your mother's things after us. And somebody needs to send telegrams to Peter and Basil advising them to get their arses back to London immediately."

"Yes, sir," Rupert agreed with a nod.

"I want to come with you," Cece insisted, rushing to Malcolm's side.

Malcolm paused to take her hand. "There are many things I've allowed you to do over the years that I shouldn't have, my darling, but this will not be one of them."

"But it's just a trial, Papa," she argued, looking far more

grown up than Malcolm wanted her too. "What harm could come to me by sitting in the gallery to watch?"

"With Shayles involved, far more harm than I care to contemplate." He started walking forward again, still holding Cece's hand. "There's no telling what sort of muck and mire will be dredged up as part of the proceedings."

"We should come too," Bianca insisted as she and Natalia surged forward to flank Katya. "We're as involved as anyone else."

"I need you to oversee the packing of our things," Katya said diplomatically. "You can come back to London with Rupert in a day or two." She sent a sly look to Rupert, who nodded with maturity beyond his years.

Malcolm indulged in a momentary smile. Katya had raised a fine man. Cece had excellent judgment in setting her cap for him. Malcolm was confident that the young man would delay the girls in Scotland as long as he could to keep them out of trouble. That meant that he and Katya could focus on the trial without distraction.

Gatwick had a carriage waiting once they returned to Gretna Green. There was ample space for the seven of them to pile in for the ride back to Strathaven Glen. Malcolm reminded himself to find out how Rupert and Cece had traveled to Gretna Green without stealing any of his carriages later. For the time being, he had bigger fish to fry.

The journey back to Strathaven Glen wasn't a silent one, however.

"So?" Bianca asked as the carriage sped on. She and Natalia sat facing Malcolm and Katya in Malcolm's carriage. Rupert and Cece had chosen to drive with Gatwick.

"Would you care to elaborate on that brief syllable?" Katya raised an eyebrow at her daughter.

Bianca huffed and exchanged an eye-roll with Natalia.

"Was our plan a success?" she asked, sounding irritated that asking was necessary.

"Yes, are you madly in love and engaged to be married now, as you should be?" Natalia followed, her eyes dancing with excitement.

Katya glanced to Malcolm, her expression flat. At least, it likely appeared flat to anyone who hadn't known her and loved her for nearly two decades. What her silence said to Malcolm was that she intended to make the children suffer for the trick they'd played. Even if the outcome had been a positive one. Although if he were honest, Malcolm wasn't entirely sure what the outcome was.

Katya glanced back to her daughters. "My discussion in the cottage with Lord Malcolm is none of your business," she said, her brow knitting into a slight frown.

"But, Mama—"

"That's not fair—"

Both girls spoke at once, going on to claim to have a right to know and to call Katya cruel for not telling them everything.

Malcolm would have liked an answer himself. He wasn't sure where he stood anymore, with Katya or with himself. Her revelations had struck him deeply. He'd had no idea what her life was like before they'd met, no idea that Robert had been so cruel to her. Of course, he'd known Robert somewhat. The man would never have dreamed his treatment of Katya could be deemed cruelty. He would have thought his attitude of permissiveness was generous. Which shed a whole new light on the way he'd turned a blind eye to Malcolm's original affair with Katya. Malcolm had assumed the man was an ignorant cuckold, which had been the source of his own, crushing guilt. Chances were that Robert had known all along.

But it was everything else Katya had said, everything

about her conquests—or the lack thereof—that had turned his world upside down. He'd never dreamed a woman could ruin her reputation in order to make a new one. He'd always assumed Katya simply enjoyed sex. She'd always enjoyed it with him, to a creative degree that made him blush to think about. It changed everything to know that, after the first few years as a widow, she'd been secretly faithful to him. That revelation was a seismic shift to his world.

"Something must have happened," Natalia said, interrupting his thoughts. "You're far too quiet for it to be otherwise."

"Yes," Bianca agreed. "You have an odd look on your face, Lord Malcolm."

"My digestion is upset," Malcolm grumbled, snapping himself out of his difficult thoughts. "You might want to open the window, just in case."

"Lord Malcolm," Bianca scolded him, crossing her arms and slumping in her seat.

"He's teasing us," Natalia concluded. "They both are. Just look at Mama."

Malcolm shifted to peek at her. Katya was struggling to hide a laugh. But what caused a hitch in his chest and made him want to take her hand in spite of the meddling young women sitting across from them was the sparkle in her eyes. That was the Katya he knew and loved. He hadn't realized how much he'd missed the vivacious, sometimes wicked, always clever woman he'd fallen in love with over the last few weeks. With that woman back and by his side, he was confident they could find a way to bring Shayles to justice.

THE JOURNEY BACK TO LONDON WAS A WHIRLWIND THAT LEFT Katya feeling as though she didn't know which way was up. They spent less than an hour at Strathaven Glen after the trip from Gretna Green. Lord Gatwick didn't even get out of his carriage. He let Rupert and Cece out, then continued on without a word.

"I don't think that man is on our side," Malcolm said as he and Katya paused to watch Gatwick's carriage roll away.

"I don't think he's on Shayles's side either," Katya said. She never would have believed she'd hear herself say those words, but she stood by them.

"Did he say anything on the way here?" Malcolm asked Rupert as the lot of them hurried inside the house.

"No," Rupert said with a frown. "He didn't say a word."

"Not a single word," Cece confirmed. "It was odd." She rubbed her arms as if the time she'd spent cloistered with Gatwick had left her with a chill.

"Still," Katya argued, "he alerted us to the change in the trial."

"Could he be lying?" Cece asked.

Katya wondered the same thing, but the question was answered moments later as Mackay came forward with a telegram he had received from Alex Croydon mere minutes after Gatwick had arrived on Strathaven Glen's doorstep. There was no time to waste.

They were fortunate to catch a train heading south shortly after arriving at the station in Glasgow. Katya said a prayer of thanks for the rail service, then spent the next several hours cursing it in every way as she writhed and squirmed through the night, trying to find a comfortable way to sleep. Even first-class cabins left much to be desired when it came to journeys as long and as sudden as the one she and Malcolm took.

By the time they arrived in London early in the morning, Katya was sore, the clothes she had worn for nearly twenty-four hours were wrinkled and uncomfortable, and her head pulsed with a dull throb from lack of sleep. But to her and Malcolm's surprise, Alex was waiting for them at the station.

"Rupert telegraphed that you were on your way," he said, gathering Katya and Malcolm up and ushering them out to his waiting carriage. "We've no time to lose."

"How the devil did Shayles manage to get his trial moved up so drastically?" Malcolm asked as they dodged their way through dozy morning passengers, on their way to or from work.

"Gatwick says he has friends in the courts," Katya added.

Alex nearly skidded to a stop. "Gatwick?"

"He was the one who informed us of the change in the trial," Katya said. "He showed up on Malcolm's doorstep to tell us before your telegram arrived." She left out the complicated bit about Gretna Green in the middle. There would be plenty of time to recount that story to their friends later. Katya herself wasn't certain what the effect of the children's prank would be herself. It was easier to focus on Shayles.

"Gatwick went all the way to Scotland to warn you the trial was today?" Alex asked, his tone incredulous.

"I don't trust him," Malcolm said as they continued on, out of the station and to Alex's waiting carriage. "But I'm beginning to believe he's not as staunch an ally to Shayles as we've previously believed."

"Lavinia swears he's turned over a new leaf," Alex said, pausing to tell his driver to move on once they were all settled. "She insists he's good."

"I wouldn't go that far," Katya said. "But there's definitely more to him than any of us suspected."

"Forget about Gatwick for a moment," Malcolm said, leaning toward Alex, who sat opposite him and Katya. "Is the case against Shayles strong enough as it is? Has Craig gathered enough proof of his villainy for a court to convict him?

And for God's sake, have Peter and Basil arrived in town yet?"

"Peter arrived after midnight. Basil is having a harder time getting here. I don't know about the rest, though," Alex answered honestly and gravely. "All I know is that Craig wasn't able to get even half of the evidence he wanted, as the club burned too quickly."

"He wanted photographs, documents from the club, testimonies from patrons," Malcolm said, sitting back and rubbing his face. He hadn't shaved the day before, and was close to sporting a beard now.

"He obtained a few documents," Alex said, "but there was no time for photographs. And as I understand it, there hasn't been enough time to coerce significant witnesses to testify under oath."

"That must be why Shayles has pushed for a quick trial," Malcolm said, fury radiating from him. "He must believe that if he can stand before the House of Lords and challenge the scant evidence Craig has gathered, and if Craig hasn't had a chance to instill fear in Shayles's patrons, he'll get away with it." He paused, then hissed, "Dammit, half the men in Lords are Shayles's patrons. They won't convict him unless Craig's case is rock-solid."

"We won't let him get away with it," Katya said, reaching for Malcolm's hand.

He took it, but didn't smile. The look he wore was closer to one a man might wear before charging into battle. She felt rather like she was about to enter the decisive battle of a long war herself, which meant that she would need reinforcements.

"Can you take me home?" she asked Alex as they turned a corner into Mayfair.

"Are you sure?" Alex asked. "The trial could begin within an hour."

APRIL SEDUCTION

"Which is why it's even more important that I go home first," Katya said.

Malcolm turned to her with a frown. "What are you plotting?" he asked.

"The same thing I've been plotting for the past ten years," she answered. "To bring Shayles down by means he would never expect and has taken for granted all these years."

CHAPTER 19

here was no point in going anywhere but the Palace of Westminster after dropping Katya at her townhouse. Alex offered to take Malcolm home or to his house so that he could bathe and shave, but Malcolm wasn't interested. Knowing Shayles, he could be up to any number of dirty tricks in an attempt to finish what should have been a days-long trial before any of them had a chance to show up.

Malcolm wasn't far off the mark. By the time he and Alex arrived at the chamber for House of Lords, pushed their way through the milling crowd of clerks and press who were curious about the case, and slipped into the chamber itself, the trial was already underway. The benches were sparsely populated, confirming Malcolm's suspicion that the whole purpose of speeding the trial was so that Shayles could stack the deck. Aside from Peter—who looked as though he hadn't slept in a month—most of the peers in attendance were friendly with Shayles at the very least and long-time patrons of the Black Strap Club at the worse.

Shayles himself stood at the front of the room, looking as elegant as a fashion plate, as though he were there to debate a bill instead of pleading for his freedom. When Malcolm burst into the room, he turned to smile at him, as smug as a badger.

"Well, well. If it isn't Lord Malcolm Campbell," he said with a sly grin. His eyes held a measure of anxiety, though. It was a small victory for Malcolm.

Jack Craig was seated on a front bench, but he jumped up and strode to meet Malcolm, bringing the trial to a pause.

"It's about time you got here," Craig murmured, making no attempt to hide his common accent. "Where've you been?"

"I'm here now," Malcolm ignored the question. They had better things to talk about. "How do things stand?"

"We've just begun," Craig said, gesturing for Malcolm to follow him to the front bench.

Several of the lords in attendance balked as Malcolm wove his way through the rows of benches to take a seat well out of the area his title's precedence entitled him to. Now was not the time to quibble about rank and place, though.

"Shayles is painting himself as a victim," Craig whispered as he and Malcolm sat. He darted a look around at the half-empty chamber. "He's loaded the place with men who will see things his way."

"I can see that," Malcolm said, glaring at a few of the men who he knew were in Shayles's pocket. "Alex is working to round up as many voting members as he can."

"They'd better get here soon," Craig said. "Otherwise this whole thing will be over before it's begun."

The words burned hot in Malcolm's gut. He couldn't let Shayles get away with everything, not now, not after so many years and so much effort. As long as there were people working against the bastard, there was hope. Katya still had a card up her sleeve. He just wished he knew what it was.

He leaned closer to Craig. "Lady Stanhope is planning—"

"Did we all come here for social hour?" Shayles interrupted, glaring at Malcolm and Craig as though they were heckling his grand performance. "Or did we come here for a trial?"

"I'm surprised you're so eager to expose your villainy to the world, Shayles," Malcolm said, refusing to be put in his place. His place was standing before Shayles, challenging him until the man got what he deserved.

"I'm here to defend myself against the gross and baseless accusations being made against me," Shayles insisted, feigning innocence. "For as I was saying," he turned back to the pack of his cronies, sitting together on a bench across the chamber from Malcolm, "what has the aristocracy come to when one of its members can be accused of all manner of false and vile dealings by common street trash?" He gestured toward Craig.

Craig sucked in a frustrated breath, tension rippling from him, but to his credit, he didn't rise to Shayles's bait. "I have yet to hear a reasonable explanation for the evidence presented to the House, my lord," he said, standing. "You admit to being the owner of the property in question. Numerous witnesses place you there on the night of the fire and hundreds of nights before. Documentation of the activities of your club, including depositions from notable members of this chamber, have been presented. How do you answer these charges?"

"Again," Shayles said with an overdramatic, impatient sigh, "I tell you I am innocent. Yes, I was the owner of a gentlemen's club located at the address in question in Kensington, but I deny all charges of illegal or improper activity at that location."

Malcolm snorted loud enough to draw Shayles's attention.

"Do you contest my claims, Lord Malcolm?" Shayles stared pointedly at him.

"I absolutely do," Malcolm answered, standing and glaring at Shayles. "You and I, and half the members in this chamber, know exactly what kind of establishment you were running."

"Is that so?" Shayles's mouth twitched as though he'd won a point instead of being in danger of losing it. "How would you know, Lord Malcolm?"

Heat shot through Malcolm, pushing its way onto his face. "The Black Strap Club is well known in certain circles."

"Certain circles that you are a part of?" Shayles continued to needle him. It was clear the man was trying to get Malcolm to indict himself, possibly to destroy his credibility.

Malcolm was saved from having to defend himself without forethought by a commotion at the chamber door. Sir Christopher Dowland burst into the room, tripping over one of the back benches and sending a cushion flying. A few of the lords near him chuckled at his clumsiness. Malcolm was surprisingly glad to see the man.

Dowland spotted Malcolm and Craig and hurried down to them. "I'm sorry I'm late," he said, out of breath. "I only just heard the trial had started twenty minutes ago. I got here as soon as I could. What can I do?"

Malcolm studied the man with narrowed eyes. He didn't know how he had mistaken the man for Katya's lover. Dowland wasn't remotely Katya's type. He had no finesse, even if he was as intelligent as everyone claimed he was. But he was a key witness in the proceedings, and far more valuable than anyone expected.

"I brought this," he said, presenting Craig with a large envelope.

"What is that?" Malcolm asked, frowning as Craig opened the envelope to take out several smaller letters.

"It's correspondence between my father and Lord Shayles dating back several years," Dowland said, his face stony. "You were right about the connection," he said to Craig.

Shayles's expression had lost some of its smugness at Dowland's arrival. He, along with most of the men in the room, looked on eagerly to see what new piece had just been added to the puzzle.

Craig laughed as he scanned a few of the letters, a renewed fire in his eyes. "My Lord." He turned to Lord Watson, the Senior Law Lord presiding over the case. "I wish to submit new evidence."

"It isn't more hearsay and gossip, is it?" Lord Watson asked, looking bored. He directed a clerk to bring him the letters.

"No, my lord," Craig said, waiting until Lord Watson had the letters in hand. Lord Watson's expression shifted from dullness to interest as he read the first letter. He sat straight. Craig went on. "These are letters in Shayles's own hand, sent to the previous Baronet of Penrose. As you can see, they detail activities at the Black Strap Club on several occasions. These letters prove that the club was not merely a brothel, but was, in fact, a den of torture that relied upon young women who were illegally coerced into prostitution."

"I demand to see them," Shayles said, his voice tight and his posture tense.

"I'd like to see them too," one of the lords who was presumably on Shayles's side called out. He was seconded by several others, but all of the men had a gossipy glint in their eyes, as if they wanted to see the letters to relive the good old days instead of as a way to incriminate Shayles.

"The letters will be made available for those who wish to read them," Lord Watson said. He turned to Shayles. "You, my lord, have some explaining to do."

"And I am perfectly willing to answer any questions you

may have." Shayles returned to playing the part of the suave gentleman.

A knot burned in Malcolm's gut. Even with the revelation of the letters, things weren't going the way they needed to go. Shayles had more or less chosen a jury of his peers to try him in more ways than one. A few more, haggard-looking gentlemen had staggered into the chamber, whispering to their neighbors to get caught up.

Shayles seemed to sense the same thing Malcolm was realizing, that time was not on his side. "My lord," he said, turning to Lord Watson with an obsequious smile. "Aside from a few fictitious imaginings that the late Sir Richard and I had engaged in years ago, those letters prove nothing."

"I'm not so certain about that," Lord Watson muttered.

Shayles nodded in a brief show of respect, but went on to say, "I fail to see the need to take up more of the House's valuable time. Prostitution, whether I had any connection to it or not—and I do not—is not illegal. Why don't we put the issue of my innocence to a vote and get on with regular business?"

"Prostitution is not illegal, but coercing women into it is. Profiting from prostitution is also illegal, as is blatant abuse and torture," Craig objected immediately. "My lord, the purpose of this trial is to bring to justice a man who has destroyed the lives of countless innocent women over the years through systematic, illegal assault and torture."

"I would hardly say they were innocent," Shayles muttered.

A burst of energy surged through Malcolm like a lightning bolt. "So you admit that you were responsible for the corruption of hundreds of women over the years?" he called out.

A rush of color filled Shayles's face as he looked to be scrambling to recover what he'd just said. "I didn't say I had anything to do with them, just that they were probably strumpets. And either way, nothing I've done is illegal."

"You seem to be speaking with authority," Malcolm pushed on. "How do you know so much about criminal morality laws if you weren't so deeply engaged in breaking them?"

"I misspoke," Shayles snapped. "I have no association with any such women at all."

"That's not what you said on New Year's Eve," one of the lords on Shayles's side shouted, then burst into laughter.

Shayles turned to glare at the man. A few of the lords sitting around him squirmed uneasily on their benches. One man sitting next to the heckler whispered in his ear. The heckler turned white.

"I...I didn't mean that at all," he stammered. "I was just having a laugh."

Frustration roiled through Malcolm, making it hard for him to sit still. It was painfully obvious that every man in the room knew Shayles was as guilty as sin, but it was equally obvious that very few of them were willing to speak out against him. Shayles must have had a means of blackmailing each and every one of them. The only way to convince them to convict Shayles was to make their reasons for speaking out bigger than their reasons for staying quiet.

"Enough of this," he said, slamming his hand on the rail in front of him. "This farce has gone on long enough. Every man here knows that Shayles is the devil himself."

"Why, Lord Malcolm, I'm flattered that you find me so important," Shayles said, provoking a laugh from his cronies.

"You aren't important," Malcolm said, a strange chill passing through him as the truth blossomed in his chest. His shoulders relaxed, and a tightness that had had a grip on him for years loosened. "You were never important. You're just a criminally abusive pimp who thinks too highly of himself."

The observing lords gasped, but Malcolm went on, his voice softer. "Tessa was important, no matter what was going on in her heart and mind. Maybe she never loved me, maybe she did and those last words of hers meant something other than the meaning I've been carrying around for the last twenty years. I've been wrong about so many things, so why not that too?"

"Lord Campbell, do you have a point to this self-examination?" Lord Watson asked.

"I do, my lord," Malcolm went on. "And the point is this." He turned to address the lords, both those who were Shayles's friends and those who opposed him. "I've dedicated the last twenty years of my life to bringing Lord Shayles to justice for his crimes. But this whole time, I've been wrong."

"Is this a declaration of my innocence?" Shayles asked, still attempting to play to the room and treat the whole situation with far less seriousness than it deserved.

"Absolutely not." Malcolm faced Shayles once more. "You're a criminal, plain and simple. You should be brought to justice. But not for your sake. You should be brought to justice for the sake of every woman whose life you ruined. Those women deserve justice for the loss of their innocence and their self-respect. What man among you—" Malcolm turned to address the room, "—would not move heaven and earth to seek justice if your wife was wounded? What one of you would not dedicate your life to righteousness if your daughter had her innocence stolen from her? Which of you wouldn't tear down any man who insulted your mistress or caused her ruin? And yet, you sit here today, treating this matter as if it were a joke."

Several of the men who had been sitting idly aside, watching the proceedings as though they were a play, began to squirm. Shayles's core group continued to scoff and make faces, but they were a growing minority.

Malcolm turned back to Shayles. "I haven't pursued you for so long because I want to seek revenge on you," he said, meeting and holding Shayles's eyes. "I've worked so hard for so long because Tessa deserved better. She might never have loved me, but I loved her." His voice cracked, but he ignored it. "I loved her. I love her daughter. In their names and in the names of every young woman you have tainted with your selfish filth, I will seek justice. If you walk out of this room today a free man, I will continue to seek justice for them, and for every woman, by doing my duty to them and seeing that their persons and their rights are protected by law. You will fade and die, but the women we have loved and taken for granted for so long will rise, mark my words."

Malcolm expected to hear the usual round of scoffing and indignation that followed every speech made extoling the rights of women in either House of Parliament. He expected a flurry of shouts about how women were weak, how they didn't have the mental capacity for anything other than home life, how protection should come from their husbands, in their homes. Instead, he was met with silence.

At least until Katya called from the back of the room, "He won't walk out of here a free man."

KATYA'S HEART FLUTTERED IN HER CHEST, BUT NOT BECAUSE OF the bold and outrageous act she was about to put on. She'd never been so proud of Malcolm in all the years she'd known him. He was temperamental, peevish, and selfish more often than he would ever admit, but he'd just proven to her and to the assembly of lords that he was also noble, dedicated, and progressive. She could only pray that her gambit worked so that he would also be vindicated.

"Good lord," Lord Watson exclaimed, sitting up in his chair and gaping as Katya marched down to the floor of the chamber, a dozen of the women who had worked for her at the Black Strap Club over the years marching with her. They all carried suitcases and boxes filled with documents and photographs, which they deposited on the table in the center of the floor. "Get those women out of here," Lord Watson went on. "Women are not allowed in this chamber."

"Not even if they are witnesses in the current trial?" Katya asked. She sent a sideways look to Malcolm as she took up a place by his and Inspector Craig's sides.

"You beautiful, blessed woman," Malcolm murmured, swaying closer to her. "What have you done?"

"It wasn't me," she said, loud enough for Inspector Craig to hear as well. "It was them."

She nodded to the women as they finished presenting their bags and boxes and moved to stand together at the far end of the floor.

"What is all this?" Shayles demanded, glaring at the women. He'd gone pale, though, and began to shift nervously when his glares failed to have any visible effect of intimidation. "I demand these women be expelled from the room immediately and their...whatever this mess is be tossed out with them." He waved a dismissive hand at the table.

"My lord," Inspector Craig spoke up, "I think we should at least see what the young ladies have brought." He sent a questioning look to Katya.

Katya's estimation of the young inspector rose. He hadn't caused a fuss or demanded to speak with her in private. He must have trusted her enough to let whatever plan she had devised play out. Men like that were few and far between.

Lord Watson sighed and rubbed his chin. "I don't want this to become a circus," he said. "But we might as well open Pandora's boxes to see what's inside."

Inspector Craig approached the table, sending another glance over his shoulder to Katya before opening the suitcase closest to him. Immediately, his eyes went wide. He started pulling out piles of loose-leaf documents detailing contracts with clients, prices for particular services, and even a coroner's report that was filed after the death of a young woman at the hands of Shayles himself. Along with the papers were photographs that the girls had secretly taken over the years. Katya had sifted through enough of it at the flat where Lottie now lived to know what her girls had, even if she hadn't had time to look at every piece herself before getting them all to Westminster.

"My lord," Inspector Craig said, bursting into a victorious grin as he moved on to open the second suitcase, "I think every man in this room needs to get a look at this."

"It's all lies," Shayles said, white as a sheet. "They've made all of it up. They're women, after all. They're prone to jealousy and flights of fancy. I've never seen half of those women before." He flung an arm out to the cluster of defiant women.

"So you do know half of them?" Malcolm asked as the room slowly began to descend into chaos. "Where do you know them from?

"I don't…I never said…I don't know."

Shayles's words were drowned out as lords on both sides of the case rushed to the table to get a look at the new evidence. More than a few of them blanched at what they saw. Some tried to stuff papers into their pockets or began ripping them to shreds, presumably because they were implicated.

Katya's heart beat into her throat as she watched the clever plan tipping into potential disaster. "Unhand those papers," she shouted, rushing forward. "Put that down. My lord," she appealed to Lord Watson. "These men are destroying evidence."

"Cease this behavior at once," Lord Watson shouted, though it was unclear whether his anger was directed at

Katya or the lords. "This is preposterously irregular. All of you, get back to your seats. You women, leave this chamber at once."

"They are witnesses, my lord," Inspector Craig shouted in their defense over the chaos of lords rushing either back to their seats or out of the room entirely.

"Stop them," Katya said, hurrying toward the door in an attempt to catch half a dozen lords who were fleeing with their pockets stuffed. "They're getting away."

Malcolm caught her by the wrist and held her back. "Those men would have voted to acquit Shayles," he whispered. "For God's sake, let them go."

The truth of the situation hit Katya, gluing her feet to the spot. The chamber was still in disarray, but Lord Watson had ordered bailiffs to close the doors and restore order.

"Enough of this," he shouted, rising from his seat. "This is not how we conduct ourselves. We are the House of Lords, for Christ's sake. Be seated, all of you." As the remaining lords did as they were ordered, the noise in the room began to subside. "Inspector Craig," Lord Watson went on. "You say these women are witnesses. Women are not allowed in this chamber. Choose one to speak for them and send the others away."

Katya bristled with indignation, but there was nothing she could do.

Inspector Craig moved to her side. "Would you like to speak, my lady?"

"Gracious, no," Katya exclaimed. She glanced around, catching Lottie's eye. "Lottie should speak. She's been on the inside, and she was the one who coordinated the evidence."

"Very well." Inspector Craig nodded. He gestured to Lottie, who stepped forward.

Katya turned to shepherd the rest of the young women out of the room.

"Lord Watson, Lady Stanhope should be allowed to stay," Malcolm called out before she could take two steps.

"Of course not," Lord Watson snapped back with a frown. "But she may watch from the gallery."

Katya clenched her jaw in frustration, but she would take what she could get. "I'll be right up there," she told Malcolm, nodding to the gallery above.

Malcolm didn't look any happier about the situation than she did, but he was equally helpless. Katya left him to sort things out with Inspector Craig and led the young women who had sacrificed so much for her and for each other to follow her out of the chamber.

In the hall, she nearly ran headlong into Basil.

"Am I too late?" he asked, out of breath. "My train just got in."

"You're not too late," Katya told him, beyond relieved to have another friend in the chamber. "Get in there and help Malcolm," she said before continuing on to the gallery stairs.

By the time she was seated with the other curious onlookers—most of whom were male members of the press—Lottie had already begun speaking.

"I worked at the Black Strap Club for three years, my lord," she addressed Lord Watson in an extraordinarily brave voice.

"My lord," Shayles sneered. "How can anyone here be expected to believe the word of a self-proclaimed whore?"

"Are you admitting that your club employed prostitutes?" Malcolm all but shouted as soon as the words were out of Shayles's mouth.

"I...I'm not...You can't assume...." Shayles writhed on the spot like a bug about to have a pin stuck through it.

"I'm warning you, Lord Campbell," Lord Watson said. "This is a trial, not a circus, and it will remain as such."

"It is a trial," Inspector Craig said, moving to stand by

Lottie's side. "So let's discuss the evidence. Miss Hart, what have you and your friends brought to us today?"

All eyes turned to Lottie. Lottie glanced to Lord Watson, who had shifted from tolerating her presence to curiosity that matched the rest of the room.

"Me lord," she dropped a quick curtsy. "I'll make this quick, because I don't want to be here any more 'n you want me here."

"I won't have impertinence, young lady," Lord Watson growled.

"And I won't give you none," Lottie said, curtsying again. "The Black Strap Club burned down on purpose," she went on. "We all knew Lord Shayles had the place piped with gas so that he could burn it in a flash if the coppers moved in on him, which they did."

"Slander, my lord," Shayles barked. "I refuse to be slandered like this."

Lord Watson held up his hand to silence him. Katya noticed a slight quiver in Lottie's stance before she went on.

"We all knew, me lord," she said. "We knew the point was to destroy anything that would show how wicked Lord Shayles was and the kinds of things he'd make us do. He hurt us, me lord. Girls died because of him. That's what this trial should be about, me lord, murder, pure 'n simple. But I was working for Lady Stanhope, not him, my lord. I did the things Lord Shayles paid me for, but Lady Stanhope paid me more to keep the other girls safe, to get them out when I could, and to keep an eye on Lord Shayles."

"Lady Stanhope is not at issue in this trial," Lord Watson said, though he scanned the gallery until he spotted Katya. He frowned, then looked to Lottie. "Go on."

"We knew Lord Shayles would burn it all, me lord, so we made sure we got all the important stuff out long before anything could happen. Stuff that proves he kidnapped girls off the street, underage ones 'n all, and that he abused us," Lottie revealed, her voice wavering. "Kept it all at Janie's mum's house, we did, all the bills, reports, notices, and photographs, me lord. It's all right here." She nodded to the table. "And it speaks for us more 'n I can."

"No doubt you're right," Lord Watson said, his tone unimpressed.

His disapproving attitude toward Lottie frustrated Katya beyond measure, but he wouldn't be able to deny the story that the evidence told. Shayles seemed to know that as well. He stared at the piles of paper and photographs on the table as though he wanted to torch the whole thing. He was just as restrained and helpless as Katya in the gallery, though. At last, they had finally trapped him in a noose he couldn't escape from.

"Miss Hart, you may go," Lord Watson told Lottie, then immediately ignored her as though she was never there. "The evidence before us needs to be taken into consideration. I will give the members of the House until three this afternoon to peruse these things at their leisure. Not a piece of it is to be removed from this room," he added, raising his voice. "Guards will be posted to ensure as much. At three o'clock, the House will vote on the matter of Lord Shayles's guilt or innocence."

CHAPTER 20

The hours passed with agonizing slowness. Malcolm had no idea whether Lord Watson believed the story he'd told or if he would take Sir Christopher's testimony into consideration. He especially wondered if the man would give weight to the evidence Katya's girls had laid before the lords. It grated on Malcolm's last nerve to know that, if the evidence had been presented by a man, there would have been no doubt about the veracity of the story. His word and Sir Christopher's might have to be enough on their own.

"We'll prevail," Craig assured him as Malcolm paced by the door to the chamber, watching lords of every leaning return for the vote, even some who he'd hoped had fled and wouldn't return. "Even I have faith in the conscience of the aristocracy in the face of so much damning evidence."

Malcolm managed a wry grin for Craig. Whatever the man's background, he wasn't dazzled by the rich and lofty, which meant he would either have a viciously short career or a long and fruitful one, depending on how he played his cards with the titled class.

"The evidence is overwhelming," Peter said. He still looked thoroughly exhausted as he stood by, watching Malcolm pace.

"And we all know Shayles is guilty," Basil added. "We've all known for years."

Armand, who had recently arrived himself, nodded in agreement.

Malcolm agreed with both of his friends, but it was Katya who he glanced to for support.

Katya stood with the Peter, Basil, and Armand, looking every bit as though she had as much of a right to be there as the men did. And so she did. Katya had done more work than anyone to prove Shayles's villainy. It was a crime that she wouldn't be able to vote in the proceedings.

"Whether the House of Lords finds him guilty or not," she said, "his reputation is shattered and his fortune is gone. He'll pay a price, rest assured on that score."

Malcolm would have said that no price short of lifelong imprisonment or death was good enough, but a commotion turned his attention farther down the hall. Rupert was rushing toward their group, looking as though he'd just arrived from Scotland. Thankfully, neither Cece nor Katya's daughters were with him. But Gatwick was. At least, Gatwick strolled down the hall just behind Rupert, his face a mask of indifference as usual.

"Am I too late to vote?" Rupert asked, out of breath, as he reached their group.

"You're just in time," Malcolm said, greeting him with a slap on the back. He still had an issue with the way Rupert and the girls had manipulated him into spilling his soul to Katya, but that score could be settled later.

Gatwick reached their group, but he didn't slow down or break stride as he sailed past into the chamber. He didn't look at the rest of them or give so much as a hint that he saw them at all. Burning suspicion turned in Malcolm's gut. Was the man an ally or still Shayles's staunchest supporter? The only way to find out was to watch him.

"Come on," he said, starting toward the door. "Let's bring this to an end."

"Inspector Craig and I will be in the gallery," Katya said, reaching out for Craig's arm so that he could escort her to the gallery stairs.

Malcolm sent her one last, long look. So much water had flooded out the bridge between them. He still wanted her with every fiber of his being, but he understood now why she didn't want him. At least not the way he had wanted to be wanted. As soon as Shayles was done and dusted, it would be time for the much more arduous work of untangling the knot they'd made of their lives. At least he still felt as though they were knotted together.

The Lords chamber was buzzing with conversations and alive with energy as Malcolm marched to his usual seat, Peter and Basil with him, Armand sitting farther back, as his title was newer. Far more lords were present now than had been there when the trial started. The whole thing had happened in such a whirlwind, sensationalism overriding usual procedure, that Malcolm's skin prickled with uncertainty. There was no telling which way the vote would go.

More worrying still, Gatwick had resumed his usual place by Shayles's side as Shayles stood near the center of the room. The two had their heads together. Gatwick remained all but expressionless, but it was clear that Shayles was furious with him. Malcolm was too far away to hear the substance of their conversation, but he imagined it had something to do with Shayles demanding to know where Gatwick had been in the hour of his need. Malcolm itched to know the answer to the question himself.

The puzzle of Gatwick was momentarily forgotten as

Malcolm caught a swish of movement from the gallery and glanced up to see Katya taking her seat at the very front. She looked more anxious than Malcolm had seen her in ages, though she managed to look strong and determined in spite of that hint of worry. She caught him studying her and smiled. The look went straight to Malcolm's heart. No matter what happened with the verdict, he could be happy if the two of them were able to work out their differences and reunite.

No, that was a lie, he thought to himself as he turned toward Lord Watson. Nothing would make him happier than to see Shayles defeated at last.

All eyes in the room turned toward Lord Watson and all conversations hushed as he took his seat. As if eager to find out Shayles's fate, every man hurried to his seat and settled, ready to vote.

"The chamber will come to order," the steward declared in a booming voice, then turned to Lord Watson.

"It's time we put an end to this matter once and for all," Lord Watson said. "For one, it's an embarrassment to this body and to the crown. For another, as Shayles implied, we have much more pressing matters to attend to."

Malcolm's heart sank at the mention of Shayles being right.

"The charges before Lord Theodore Shayles are those of criminal abuse of the women employed by him over the course of two decades and profiting off the practice of pros-titution. How do you find the defendant?" Lord Watson glanced to the most junior lord in attendance, who sat farthest away from him.

Before the young baron could rise from his seat to say, "Guilty, my lord," Malcolm's heart sank further and his stomach tied in knots. Lord Watson had made no mention of the murders of the women who had died working for him.

He'd said nothing about kidnapping or coercion, or any number of more serious crimes Shayles could have been convicted of.

The lords rose one by one to announce their vote, starting with the newest and youngest titles and working their way up to the loftiest, most senior noblemen present. For every guilty vote there was at least one not guilty, mostly from men Malcolm knew full well had visited the club or were under Shayles's thumb.

Worse still, Shayles stood at the front of the room, a sickening grin on his face, as though he knew how the vote would go.

The vote came around to Malcolm and his friends. Basil and Peter both stood and said, "Guilty, my lord," before taking their seats.

Malcolm stood, staring daggers at Shayles, and declared, "Guilty as hell, my lord."

Shayles merely sneered at him, then pretended Malcolm didn't exist. He studied the lords who had yet to vote, seeming to mentally count them. Malcolm did the same. It was clear as day how each of the remaining men would vote. A simple majority was needed to convict Shayles, and it appeared as though they would fall one vote short.

One vote. It all came down to one bloody vote. Shayles would walk free, getting away with the misery he'd caused so many women over the years. All because he'd manipulated things behind the scenes to push up the trial, preventing Craig from speaking to men who might have otherwise been swayed to vote against him. It was a bloody crime within itself.

Malcolm was on the verge of giving up and leaving the room when Gatwick stood to vote. No one seemed to be paying much attention to him, as his vote was a foregone conclusion. But when Gatwick cleared his throat and said,

"Guilty, my lord," it was as though the air had been sucked out of the room.

No one moved. All eyes were fixed on Gatwick as he nodded to Lord Watson, then resumed his seat as though intermission at the opera was over. The room crackled with incredulity. Several men gaped openly. Shayles lost his smile slowly, his eyes widening as though he were just comprehending what Gatwick had said. All color drained from his face.

A swirl of whispers shattered the silence, growing louder by the second. Malcolm's heart thundered through it all as the storm broke. The lord seated beside Gatwick—one Malcolm was absolutely positive would declare Shayles not guilty—rose and declared, "Guilty, my lord." He was followed by another and another and another, all declaring Shayles guilty, all looking at Gatwick as they did. They must have concluded what everyone else seemed to be concluding—that if Shayles's closest friend and companion for the past two decades was declaring him guilty, he must be guilty.

Malcolm's heart was so light that he thought he might fly up out of his chair when Lord Watson finally declared. "As per the vote, Lord Theodore Shayles, you have been found guilty of the crimes brought before this chamber. You will be taken from this place and incarcerated in the appropriate facility until such a time as your sentence can be determined. Guards, please escort Lord Shayles out."

"I'll kill you," Shayles roared, not at Malcolm or his friends, for a change, but at Gatwick.

Gatwick stared at Shayles from his bench, his only emotion that of slight bafflement over Shayles's reaction. He picked at the hem of his sleeve, looking bored.

"I'll murder you in your sleep, you filthy, back-stabbing bastard," Shayles railed on as two guards leapt forward to grab his arms. "I'll kill you for this."

Gatwick continued to fuss over his clothes, not acknowledging Shayles, but Malcolm could have sworn he saw the man's lips form the words, "Not if I kill you first."

Malcolm slumped back in his bench, watching, absolutely stunned, as Shayles was dragged out of the chamber, kicking and screaming. A lightness filled Malcolm's heart the likes of which he'd never felt before. It was over. After years of anguish and battle, it was finally over. Shayles would be carted off to prison for a long, long time, if there was any justice in the world. Even if he managed to get out, he would forever be a broken man, shunned by society and penniless to boot.

"It's done, Tessa," Malcolm said, glancing up to the painted ceiling of the chamber. "Whether it was what you wanted or not, it's done."

A second weight lifted from Malcolm's shoulders. As Shayles's shouts faded in the hall outside the chamber, the echo of Tessa's final words faded as well. Malcolm had avenged her as best he could. He lowered his head, letting go of the ache of all those years ago with a solemn sigh. It was over at last.

"Don't just sit there, man." Peter roused Malcolm from his moment of reverie. "We have a victory celebration to plan." The exhaustion had disappeared from Peter's face, leaving him as lively as a man half his age.

Joy filled Malcolm's heart and he stood, turning to embrace his friends. Armand rushed from his bench to join them. They weren't the only ones he wanted to embrace, though. He made his way toward the chamber door, Peter and Basil flanking him, Armand at his back. They were stopped a dozen times along the way to be congratulated by their peers.

"I imagine this will have a dazzling effect on your efforts

to pass that bill protecting the rights of women," one young viscount said, thumping him on the back.

"Mr. Croydon will be ecstatic," another said as they neared the chamber door.

In fact, Alex was waiting for them, Marigold and Lavinia in tears of joy by his side, when they finally made it out into the hall.

"I can't believe they voted against him," Alex said, embracing Malcolm and the others, regardless of who was there to witness the informality. "They actually voted against him."

"I knew they would," Marigold said, happier than Malcolm had ever seen her.

"Where's Katya?" Malcolm asked, scanning the hall and squinting at the gallery stairs.

His question went unanswered as Gatwick emerged from the chamber and walked past him. Malcolm and the others stared at him in silence, as though they didn't quite know what to make of him. Rather than marching past as though he were the only one in the entire Palace of Westminster, however, Gatwick stopped suddenly, eyes fixed on Lavinia, and changed direction to approach her.

"Dear cousin Lavinia," he said, taking her offered hand and bowing over it. "How pleasant it is to see you."

"The pleasure is all mine," Lavinia said, brimming with joy. She squeezed Gatwick's hand as though he were an old friend. "I hear we have you to thank for this, and I cannot thank you enough."

"It was nothing, my lady," Gatwick said with self-effacing calm.

Malcolm exchanged a glance with Peter as the rest of them held back, neither offering thanks nor rushing into accusations. Malcolm suspected that, like him, not one of his friends had the first clue what to make of Gatwick on any level anymore.

"I'm sure we will have some sort of celebration tonight," Lavinia went on, glancing to a frowning Armand. "I would so love it if you would attend."

Everyone in their group tensed at the invitation, but not one of them opened their mouths to contradict Lavinia.

Fortunately, Gatwick shook his head in polite refusal. "I am deeply sorry that I won't be able to attend, my lady. I have business elsewhere that will keep me occupied."

"Business?" Alex asked, eyes narrowed in suspicion.

Gatwick studied him for a moment before saying, "Speaking the truth carries consequences. No doubt there will be others who fear what I might say against them, having said just one word against Shayles."

"The word 'guilty' speaks volumes," Armand said, crossing his arms. "If it is said once, it could be said again."

"Precisely," Gatwick said with a bow. "I believe it would be in my best interest to retire to my country estate as soon as possible."

"Stay safe," Lavinia said, genuine concern for him lighting her eyes.

"For you, dear cousin, anything," Gatwick said, bowed to her one final time, then turned to march away with slightly more speed than was usual for him.

"Do you think people will target him for what he did today?" Marigold asked, biting her lip as she watched Gatwick go.

"I don't think Shayles's threat to kill him was an idle one," Malcolm said.

"But he'll be in prison," Marigold argued.

"Prison walls do nothing to stop a man hell-bent on revenge," Basil said in an ominous voice.

They were all silent for a moment. Malcolm contem-

plated whether he wanted to extend himself to protect
Gatwick or whether the man who had spent so long by
Shayles's side was on his own.

The question only plagued him for a few seconds before
his greater concern returned. "What happened to Katya?" he
asked, glancing around again. "And Craig, for that matter."

"Craig followed when they brought Shayles out," Alex
said, reaching into his jacket pocket. "And as for Katya, she
gave me this."

Alex handed Malcolm a small, tightly folded note.
Malcolm's heart and groin thrummed with excitement
before he even opened the folded paper. He knew exactly
what the note was. It was a vote of confidence, a declaration
of intent, and the beginning of the rest of his life.

CHAPTER 21

*B*y the time Katya heard Malcolm's knock on the door of her St. John's Woods flat, she had everything arranged perfectly. The water in the huge copper tub was steaming, tea was laid out on the table, the bedsheets were turned down and scented with lavender, and she was completely naked under her Japanese robe. She couldn't repress her wicked grin as she practically skipped to the door, brimming with excitement that was already having a decidedly physical effect on her.

She peeked through the peephole to make certain it really was Malcolm and not, God forbid, one of her children, then threw open the door and posed seductively against the doorframe.

"Hello, Lord Campbell," she said in a low purr, giving him her most seductive look through lowered lashes.

Malcolm gaped at her for half a second, visibly stunned, then launched toward her. He slammed the door behind him and pulled her into his arms as though he'd circumnavigated the globe, fought fifty wars, and had finally come home to her. Katya couldn't help but laugh as his mouth crashed down over hers, then sighed as his hand circled her backside and his kiss set her on fire.

"We won," he gasped as he backed her deeper into the room, clearly headed for the bedroom. He managed to shed his jacket while groping her curves and stealing kisses. "We finally beat him."

"I know." Katya planted her feet when they were near the bathtub, leaning into him to deepen their kiss.

A large part of her wanted to push him to the floor and ride him then and there, but as soon as she raked her fingers through his matted hair and felt the scratch of three days' beard growth against her cheek, she opted to stick to her original plan.

"Get your clothes off and get in the bath," she ordered him, working at the buttons of his waistcoat. "I'm not taking a dirty vagrant into my bed."

"I thought you liked me dirty," he growled, the light in his eyes positively carnal.

Katya tugged his shirt up out of the waist of his trousers and over his head. When it was tossed aside, she raked her fingernails down his chest to the line of hair disappearing below his belt. She swayed close and whispered, "Not this kind of dirty."

Malcolm had the good sense to laugh. The sound was as pure and free as anything Katya had ever heard, and it made her heart light. He kissed her again with more fondness than lust, then tugged at the sash of her robe. "If I'm getting in that bath, you're getting in with me."

"You know that neither of us are limber enough anymore for carnal gymnastics in a tub," she said with a raised eyebrow.

"Who said anything about gymnastics?" he asked, unbuttoning his trousers. "I'm not limber enough to scrub my own back anymore. I need you to do it."

Katya laughed, so happy that it brought her near tears. She shrugged out of her robe, tossed it aside, then helped Malcolm remove the rest of his clothes. He stepped into the tub, sitting with a long, gratifying sigh as she fetched the tea tray and carried it to a chair placed beside the tub.

"What's that for?" Malcolm asked as she poured two cups, then left them on the tray to sink into the water with him. She'd filled the tub purposely so that it wouldn't overflow with both of them in it.

"I figured that we could accomplish two things at once," she said, handing him the soap with one hand and reaching for a scone with the other. "Since neither of us are quite up to that third thing in the confines of a tub."

"This is luxury enough," he said, dipping the soap into the water to bring it to a lather.

Katya sat back against her side of the tub, where she'd draped a towel to serve as a cushion, and indulged in the sight of Malcolm scrubbing off days' worth of soil and cares while she sipped tea. She knew his body so well that she could practically feel what the suds were feeling as they slipped across his skin. He was clearly eager to get clean above all else and scrubbed his limbs and torso, even his back, in spite of his claims not to be able to reach it, and washed his hair while she observed, feeling hotter by the second.

"You know, you're very well-preserved for a man past the half-century mark," she said, nibbling seductively on the corner of a scone.

Malcolm let out a wry laugh, then reached for the pitcher beside the tub to rinse his hair. "The thirst for vengeance has kept me young all these years," he said as he rubbed his eyes and slicked his hand back through his hair. "Now that Shayles is in jail, I'm going to let it all go and turn into a flabby, decrepit old man."

Katya nudged his thigh with her toes and set her scone aside. "No, you're not." She surged forward risking bruises on her knees to kneel between his spread legs. She smoothed her hands up his now clean chest. "You're going to get younger by the years because you finally have what you've always wanted."

"And what have I always wanted?" he asked, his tone dropping to a seductive growl as he raked his fingers across her sides and up to toy with her breasts. "Shayles's defeat?"

"Perhaps," she said, kissing him lightly as steam curled around them.

"My daughter grown into a fine young woman?" he went on, teasing her nipples into hard points.

"That, of course." He was teasing her in more ways than one, which fanned the inferno forming within her. She sought to provoke equal desire in him by sliding her hands down toward what she knew would be waiting for her under the water.

"Basil back among his friends where he belongs?" he asked on, his lips twitching into a grin.

"Now you're just being silly," she said, one eyebrow arched as she closed her hand around his stiffening cock and stroked him from balls to tip.

"What else could I possibly have that I've wanted all this time?" he asked, a hitch in his voice as she pleasured him.

She cupped her hands around his balls, holding them firmly enough to make him gasp. "Are you sure you want to keep toying with me this way?"

He surprised her by swaying forward and tipping her off balance. Her back thumped against the wet towel on her side of the tub as his hand slipped deftly between her legs. "I want to spend the rest of my life toying with you," he growled as he did just that.

Katya caught her breath as he circled her clitoris. She was

already aroused and ready, but she lifted her legs to rest her ankles on the sides of the tub so that he could stroke her more fully. She knew he'd enjoy the sight of her lost in pleasure that way and treated him to a vivid expression of erotic satisfaction as he drove her into orgasm.

She arched forward as waves of pleasure throbbed through her, bringing the tips of her breasts above the water. Malcolm groaned in satisfaction and thrust a finger inside of her to feel her body's contractions. His thumb continued to tease her clit, drawing her climax on and on.

"My God, woman," he growled at last, as her tremors subsided. "You come so hard and so easily that I nearly spent here in the water."

"You make me feel this way," she panted, languishing in her exposed and satisfied pose, even though her ankles would be hopelessly bruised by the lip of the tub. It clearly aroused him to look at her that way. "You're the only one who can make me feel this decadent."

"You're a shameless hussy, you know," he told her with a sly grin, shifting as though he was ready to stand.

"You like me this way," she replied as wickedly as she could. "You like me a lot of other ways too."

As she predicted, he stood. His cock leapt up in magnificent splendor, a sure sign that the evening had just begun. "We'd better explore as many of those ways as possible before we shrivel up into prunes on the tree."

The moment of erotic teasing dissolved into the utterly graceless act of Katya moving her aching legs from the side of the tub and Malcolm helping her to stand. As soon as they were both on dry, relatively stable ground, she couldn't resist plastering her body against his while they were both still wet. He accepted her at once, kissing her with reckless passion and tracing her curves with his hands.

"This is all the motivation I need to keep myself fit well

into my twilight years," he told her in a low voice, brushing his fingers deep into the cleft between her legs before lifting one of them over his hip. "I have to keep up with you."

"Yes, you do," she hummed, reaching between them to close her hand around his cock. It didn't matter that they had the rest of their lives to indulge in each other as much as they wanted, she needed to have him inside her as quickly as possible and to keep him there as long as she could.

He must have sensed her urgency. With a deep sound of pleasure, he broke their kiss and hurried her into the bedroom. As soon as she turned her back to him, he smacked her backside, causing her to gasp and shiver.

"Are you ever going to tire of spanking me like a disobedient child?" Katya asked as she reached the bed and lay her still-dripping body across the coverlet.

"No," Malcolm answered, stretching atop her with a devilish gleam in his eyes. "Because I doubt you're ever going to stop behaving like you need a good spanking."

She laughed deep in her throat. "You wouldn't want me to anyhow," she said, opening herself to him and wrapping her arms and legs around him as he covered her.

"No, I wouldn't," he said with a sudden strain of seriousness. "I love you just as you are, brazen, impossible, clever, and oh-so-desirable."

He kissed her between each word, saving his longest and slowest kiss for last. Their tongues met in a dance that was as familiar as the beating of her heart and as necessary as the blood that pumped wildly through her veins. She nibbled at his lips, arching into him and abandoning all inhibition to meld with him. Malcolm's body was as much a part of hers as the organs that kept her alive. His spirit and his love were as essential to her as water and air. They could bicker and snap, they could even bare their teeth and claws now and then, but she couldn't live without him.

"I need you, Malcolm," she whispered as his kisses trailed from her lips to her neck and lower. "I need you now and forever."

"Then you'll have me," he purred, repositioning himself so that he could drive into her.

His entry was so fast that she gasped in surprise, then let out a long sigh of victory as he continued to plunder her. She'd had him in every way imaginable, but she still craved him. His thrusts told her that he felt the same way, that the new and novel from ages ago couldn't hold a candle to the sheer pleasure of seasoned love, of knowing someone so well one could feel what the other felt as their bodies joined.

"I love you, Katya," he said with passionate intensity as his thrusts grew harder. Heat poured off of him. She had no idea how he managed such delicious stamina at his age, but his determination had her spiraling closer and closer to another orgasm in no time. "I love you so much it drives me mad."

She moaned in approval, clasping his backside and digging her nails in hard. It was just the thing to send him over the edge. With a loud curse that would have shocked the sunshine out of half of the sweet society ladies of London, his body tensed with a powerful orgasm. The joy of feeling him let loose was enough to launch her into bliss for a second time, and her body throbbed with his, milking him as he used the last of his energy on a few, final, weaker thrusts.

Once spent, he collapsed by her side. She rolled with him, a tangle of damp arms and legs, her heart soaring.

"Making love with you will never get old," she panted, twining her body with his, even though they were both blazing hot, and threading her fingers through his hair.

"Let's do it much more often," he agreed, working to catch his breath. "At least until my heart seizes up *in flagrante* and I die in your arms."

"I humbly request that you wait at least another twenty

years to expire in the throes of passion," she said, giggling and kissing his shoulder.

"If you command it, I'll obey," he said.

Whether it was the pleasure of the moment of the joy of achieving victory over Shayles at last, Katya couldn't stop herself from laughing once the giggles started. Her whole body shook as she clung to Malcolm, which made him laugh with her. The two of them lay there, in a pile of rumbled, damp bedcovers, trying to kiss each other between giggles. As far as Katya was concerned, they deserved every ridiculous moment, every hysterical fit of silliness they could manage.

When their bodies cooled to the point of being uncomfortable, they got up to finish drying off, then quickly tumbled under the bedcovers, resting their heads on the pillows.

"You're a brilliant woman to think of making love while sopping wet on top of the bed so that this part remained dry," Malcolm said, a distinct note of exhaustion in his voice.

Katya hummed in agreement, too tired for the moment to think of a clever enough reply. They both needed a nap. They needed more than that. Five years at least to do nothing but curl in each other's arms, alternating between athletic love-making and sleeping like the dead ought to do the trick. But before they gave in and slept—at least until they would be forced to get up, dress, and make an appearance at whatever party their friends were bound to throw to celebrate Shayles's defeat—there were other matters to be settled.

"Malcolm?" she asked, brushing her fingers across his still-bearded cheek as he appeared to be drifting off.

"Hmm?" he hummed, confirming that he was all but lost to slumber.

"Will you marry me?"

His eyes popped wide open. He stared at her, blinking,

then pushed himself up to one arm so that he could gaze down at her with incredulous surprise. "*Now* you want to get married?" he asked, his tone outraged even though pure elation shone in his eyes.

Katya shrugged. "Well, yes. It seems like as good a time as any."

He gaped down at her, then launched into motion, attempting to roll her to her stomach. "Where is that luscious backside of yours. It definitely needs a spanking right now."

Katya laughed and put up very little struggle as he rolled her onto his knees and began paddling her bottom. She would be ready for a whole new round of lovemaking long before she knew he'd be capable of it if he wasn't careful.

"Stop, Malcolm, stop," she laughed, gasping when he smacked her particularly hard. "I mean it. I want to marry you."

"You were just waiting for me to stop asking so that you could ask yourself," he said, smacking her one more time before sinking into the bed with her and rolling her into his arms atop him. "Weren't you?" he asked again, far more tender and filled with love.

"Of course," she teased him, stretching to cover him completely. "Well, and I was waiting for a few other obstacles between us to be cleared. Our meddling children, for example," she said, glancing to the side with feigned innocence. "The specter of Shayles, the secrets of our past, the miserable failure to properly communicated."

"So just a few minor things," he said with equally faked casualness.

"Just a few." She glanced at him with a smile, then leaned in for a long, slow kiss. "Now that those things are all out of the way, however...."

He laughed low in his throat, then rolled her to her back, kissing her with renewed passion. "So does this mean I get to be the next Mr. Lady Stanhope?" he asked, sliding a hand between them to cup her breast and tease her nipple.

"Absolutely," she replied. "I wouldn't have it any other way."

"Then let me see if I can't coax these old bones to perform a small miracle of aged stamina," he said, stealing a kiss, then going on with, "I'm going to have to work hard to keep my younger wife satisfied."

"You are indeed," Katya answered with a wicked flicker of her eyebrow. Though she was certain they were both up to the challenge.

*T*he wedding was a small, summer affair with only friends and family present. Peter offered to host it at Starcross Castle, mostly because at the beginning of May, Mariah gave birth to a beautiful, healthy baby girl—whom they named Annalisa in what Katya thought was a touching tribute to Peter's tragic first wife—and neither of them wanted to be far from home.

Starcross Castle was perfect, as far as Katya was concerned. She and Malcolm were able to have a quiet ceremony at the local chapel, and then a loud and raucous celebration at the castle itself.

"I knew the two of you would marry eventually," Natalia declared, unable to stop giggling after Katya allowed her to have a single glass of punch. "I knew it."

"To be honest, we all knew it," Peter told her, then plucked the half-empty crystal punch glass from her hands. He handed the glass to Marigold, who stood nearby with Alex and young Master James beside her. James hugged her skirts, shy of the celebrating adults around him.

"Did you really?" Lavinia asked, blinking innocently as

she leaned heavily on Armand's arm, looking pleasantly round and in the family way. "All the two of you used to do was fight."

"We enjoy fighting," Katya said, turning a saucy grin on Malcolm, whose hand she hadn't let go of since she joined him at the front of the chapel.

"Fighting means making up is that much more exciting," Malcolm agreed with a wink.

"Oh," Natalia exclaimed, then hiccupped loudly. Her cheeks went bright pink.

"Perhaps you would like to come see the baby?" Peter asked, resting a hand on the small of her back and steering her to the other end of the lawn, where Mariah and Annalisa were surrounded by a ring of admirers, including Basil and Elaine—who had made the long trip from Brynthwaite for the occasion—and Victoria, who held baby Peter, and Sir Christopher Dowland.

"Have there been any sparks between the two of them yet?" Armand asked, nodding to Victoria and Christopher.

"Christopher let slip to me last night that he's impressed with Vicky," Katya revealed as their group all turned to watch the interaction. "But Victoria is keeping her emotions veiled these days."

"Poor thing," Lavinia sighed. "Do you suppose she's still traumatized by the things William deVere did to her?"

Katya sent a wry grin Lavinia's way. The young woman must have had a bit too much to drink to speak so openly about something so terrible and personal for Victoria.

"I think that's it exactly," Katya said. "But time heals all wounds." She turned her smile to Malcolm, and when that wasn't enough to express her joy and relief, she leaned in to kiss his lips.

"Mama," Rupert scolded her, striding forward with Cece

on his arm. "There's no need to engage in shocking displays of affection in public."

He was teasing her, but all the same, Katya replied, "Just wait until you find yourself in a similar position, young man."

Katya glanced to Cece, intending to wink at the woman she was certain would end up as her daughter-in-law as well as her step-daughter, but Cece lowered her eyes with a hint of wistfulness.

"I don't think that will be happening any time soon, Lady Stanhope." Cece glanced up. "Or are you Lady Campbell now?"

"I'm Mama to you, thank you very much," Katya said. Her expression filled with concern. "Is there something we need to talk about?" she asked, peeking at Rupert.

Rupert cleared his throat. "I've decided to enlist in the army, at least for a time."

Katya opened her mouth to express her shock and worry and to tell him off, but Rupert rushed on.

"I inherited the earldom at such a young age, Mama, and the last year has shown me that a university education is not enough to make effective decisions, either at home or in the House of Lords. I need more experience of the world, and a commission in the army is the way to accomplish that."

"Rupert, how could you—"

"A wise decision," Malcolm said, cutting Katya off and slapping Rupert's back. "A stint abroad, fighting for queen and country, is just the thing a young man needs."

Katya gaped at Malcolm, ready to slap him. "He could be hurt or killed," she argued. "That would break more hearts than just mine."

"A man cannot make all his decisions based on the softness of a woman's heart," Malcolm replied with a frown.

"I assure you, my heart can be as hard as steel when it needs to be," Katya snapped.

"As I well know," Malcolm grumbled.

"Don't you go picking a fight with me, Malcolm. I'll best you every time."

"Is that so?"

"Yes."

Katya planted her fists on her hips and was about to go on when Cece burst into laughter.

"Some things will never change," she said. "No matter who marries or doesn't marry." She sent a sly, sideways look to Rupert.

Rupert flushed, looking tense and embarrassed. "It wouldn't do to make any decisions in haste," he said. "And it will only be a few years."

"Will it?" Cece asked, indignant. "How many is a few?"

"Not very many," Rupert told her, growing defensive. "You'll see."

"Oh, will I?" Cece stared hard at him.

In spite of her fear on Rupert's behalf, Katya's lips twitched into a grin and glanced to Malcolm. "Isn't there a saying about apples and trees and the distance from one to the other?" she asked.

"There is," he replied with mock gravity. "We have no one to blame but ourselves."

"At least we agree on that score."

The further questions Katya wanted to ask Rupert about his potentially mad endeavor were prevented by the sight of Inspector Craig marching across the lawn.

"Craig," Malcolm greeted him, a note of surprise in his voice. "I didn't expect you to accept the invitation." He escorted Katya across the lawn to meet him.

"I haven't accepted the invitation," Inspector Craig

replied. "Not exactly. I just arrived by train to let you know—"

A flash of skirts and a high-pitched squeal interrupted him as Bianca tore across the lawn as fast as a thoroughbred. "Good heavens! Inspector Craig. I didn't inspect you to be here." Bianca followed her words with a mad giggle, proving she'd had as much punch as Natalia had or more. "I mean, expect," she added, turning pink from her forehead to the exposed expanse of her décolletage.

"Lady Bianca," Inspector Craig greeted her with a broad, knowing grin and a polite bow. "Lovely to see you."

"Likewise, I'm sure," Bianca said, her eyes full of stars.

"I've just come to tell your mother and Lord Malcolm that Lord Shayles has finally been sentenced," he said, his smile fading into a look of gravity.

The silence that followed his statement was like that of the world holding still after a rumble of thunder. The others noticed as well and left Mariah and Victoria with the babies to hurry over to hear what Inspector Craig had to say.

"Tell me it's the noose," Malcolm said, eyes narrowed, old enmity on display.

Inspector Craig let out a breath and ran a hand through his hair. "Hardly. He's been fined fifty-thousand pounds and sentenced to six months in prison, including the month he's already served."

Katya gasped in horror and indignation. Malcolm radiated fury. Their friends expressed a broad range of shock and frustration.

"That's preposterous," Peter said. "After all the evidence that was presented?"

"Did they not take the deaths of the women who were trapped in that hellhole into consideration?" Rupert asked.

"No," Inspector Craig said with a simple shrug. "In the end, he was convicted of profiting off prostitution and a few counts of temporarily holding women against their will. All the other charges were ignored or dismissed."

"That's an outrage," Malcolm seethed.

"We'll do something about it," Alex reassured him. "In Parliament if not elsewhere."

"You might not have to do much," Inspector Craig went on. "The man is penniless and friendless, if I'm reading things right. And he seems to have forgotten you lot."

"Forgotten us?" Katya blinked.

Inspector Craig nodded. "His guards say that all he can talk about is Lord Gatwick and how he'll make sure the man gets what he deserves in October."

"October?" Lavinia asked. She, more than anyone else, looked desperately worried for Gatwick.

"When Lord Shayles gets out," Inspector Craig confirmed. "Come this autumn, Lord Gatwick had better watch his back."

"We have to help him," Lavinia said, pleading with Armand.

Armand raised her hand and kissed it. "We will," he said, though Katya could tell he was at war with himself.

None of the rest of them seemed excited about jumping to Mark Gatwick's defense.

"Enough of this bad news," Katya said, putting on a smile. "We're here to celebrate. Inspector Craig, you're more than welcome to stay and celebrate with us."

Inspector Craig glanced to Bianca, who hadn't taken her eyes off him. "Thanks, m'lady. I think I will."

"We've all got our eyes on you, Craig," Malcolm warned him in a fatherly tone.

Inspector Craig seemed amused by the threat. "I know where the lines are, my lord, and I won't cross them."

"Oh," Bianca said with a disappointed sigh.

Natalia burst into a giggle behind her, and within

seconds, the group had broken up and gone their own ways, to seek refreshments, to coo over baby Annalisa, or to stroll through the garden.

Katya stayed with Malcolm, surveying the whole scene. "I think we've done rather well in the end," she said, looping her arm through his and hugging him.

"Not bad," Malcolm grumbled in his usual dour tone.

Katya laughed at him. "Are you upset about Shayles?"

Malcolm considered her question, then shrugged. "Yes and no. The man is ruined, one way or another. If he truly is intent on seeking revenge against Gatwick, then that proves his guilt further."

"Does it?" Katya asked.

"Shayles wouldn't be so hell-bent on revenge if he thought the game was over for him. Gatwick must still know things that would destroy Shayles even more."

"I suppose you're right." Katya paused. "Should we offer help to Gatwick?"

"Gatwick can take care of himself," Malcolm said with an air of menace. He turned to Katya, and that menace melted into a smile. "I'm through with throwing my life away on Shayles," he declared. "He's had enough of my time. I want to give the rest of it to you, unreservedly."

Katya's heart fluttered as though she were a girl receiving her first compliment at a ball. She swayed into Malcolm, sliding her arms over his shoulders and leaning in to kiss him.

"I love you, Malcolm Campbell. I always have and I always will," she said, then kissed him again.

"Good," Malcolm nodded, tugging her close. "Because you're stuck with me now."

Katya laughed deep in her throat, feeling wicked and wonderful. She'd never been so happy to be a part of something as she was to be part of the couple they'd always been.

§.

I HOPE YOU'VE ENJOYED KATYA AND MALCOLM'S STORY! BUT what about Lord Mark Gatwick? Is he a good guy or a bad guy, and what made him the way he is? How is he going to handle Shayle's release from prison? What if love made that even more complicated? Find out in March with the release of *October Revenge*, Book 6 in *The Silver Foxes of Westminster*!

AND WHILE WE'RE THINKING AHEAD, WHAT WILL BECOME OF Cece Campbell and Rupert Marlowe? Will true love endure or will time and distance drive a wedge between the two of them? You'll find out next summer with *A Lady's First Lie*, the first book in an all new series, *The May Flowers*.

BE SURE TO SIGN UP FOR MY NEWSLETTER SO THAT YOU CAN BE alerted when all of these exciting books are released!

Click here for a complete list of other works by Merry Farmer.

ABOUT THE AUTHOR

I hope you have enjoyed *April Seduction*. If you'd like to be the first to learn about when new books in the series come out and more, please sign up for my newsletter here: http://eepurl.com/cbaVMH And remember, Read it, Review it, Share it! For a complete list of works by Merry Farmer with links, please visit http://wp.me/P5ttjb-14F.

Merry Farmer is an award-winning novelist who lives in suburban Philadelphia with her cats, Torpedo, her grumpy old man, and Justine, her hyperactive new baby. She has been writing since she was ten years old and realized one day that she didn't have to wait for the teacher to assign a creative writing project to write something. It was the best day of her life. She then went on to earn not one but two degrees in History so that she would always have something to write about. Her books have reached the Top 100 at Amazon, iBooks, and Barnes & Noble, and have been named finalists in the prestigious RONE and Rom Com Reader's Crown awards.

ACKNOWLEDGMENTS

I owe a huge debt of gratitude to my awesome beta-readers, Caroline Lee and Jolene Stewart, for their suggestions and advice. And double thanks to Julie Tague, for being a truly excellent editor and assistant!

Click here for a complete list of other works by Merry Farmer.